Secrets

A collection of fifteen adult short stories

Gary Baxter

Printed in Australia
First Printing 2023

Paperback ISBN - 978-0-6454790-5-8
E-Book ISBN - 978-0-6454790-6-5

Welcome

Thank you!

Not only for purchasing this book, but for allowing yourself the time to indulge in these little anecdotes. Some are based on real-life encounters, with a little fantasy thrown in. I hope you find them entertaining.

A few others have helped in the creation of this book; weaving their own touch of magic to bring it to life. So, I extend my deepest thanks to:

Cecily Potter for her editing and internal formatting.

Amanda Croy for creating the perfect cover design (and help during the publishing phase!).

Josephine and Kathleen for their final eye's proofing.

Kate for continuing to encourage and promote my writing and assist in the publishing journey.

Mostly, to those special people whom I've had to the pleasure to encounter, being so willing to share their fantasies, pleasures and personal experience, that inspired these stores.

Gary

Contents

Love at First Sight

A wave of excitement tremored through Troy's body as he hung up the phone. He had, at the last minute, upgraded to the 20th floor penthouse suite in the prestigious Gold Coast hotel. He would be there as a test driver for a new passenger tyre release for Japan's biggest manufacturer. It was uncharacteristically indulgent, despite this new international client sparing no expense to engage his services. But the penthouse choice had nothing to do with his work or tyres. It was for a far more pleasurable reason than driving fast cars around a racetrack. He was to spend a weekend with a beautiful woman who he'd only met once. He wanted everything to be perfect.

A month earlier, Troy was in Melbourne, where he had organised a stall at a big motoring event. He was there to promote his precision and stunt driving business to car companies and the like. Event Designs was the company who ran the exhibition, so one of his first jobs on arrival in Melbourne was to call into their office to pay the balance for his site.

Then the most unexpected happened. Over the counter as he casually handed over his credit card to the account manager, their eyes had met, and time had stopped. Troy was suspended in her gaze as he struggled to find his usual cool racing driver composure.

He couldn't even remember what happened next. For all he knew, he may well have just been standing there with his mouth open, dribbling down his shirt. Her deep brown eyes had breached his shell and cupped his heart, tenderly caressing it, as every emotion of lust flooded through him. It was intoxicating.

He knew she'd said something, but he didn't hear it; the volume of her beauty was deafening. Her eyes were burning through him.

She broke the gaze and looked down to process the payment; a slightly embarrassed smile on her face. He finally had the much needed few seconds to recover. She held out her hand to return his card. He reached to receive it, taking in her name from the badge that was pinned to her shirt.

'Thank you, Jane,' he said softly, only just recovering enough to speak. Then her fingers touched his, gently and slowly as she handed back his card.

He took the card, resisting the temptation to entwine his fingers around hers and draw her toward him. They both smiled, their eyes locking and lingering for a moment longer than needed. He thanked her again, slowly, as if he didn't want to leave. He then turned and walked toward the door of the office.

My God, what just happened? he thought as he walked away, desperate to look back. He dared not, but he was fully aware he simply had to see her again. He'd been so overwhelmed by the connection that his heart thumped, and he was sure she felt it too.

Jane Coles had arrived at work on that Tuesday morning in the same way she did any other day. As usual, arriving in the carpark behind the offices, she sat for a couple of minutes, sipping her tea from her travel mug. She took a deep breath. This space in time was the transition that allowed her to regroup from the unbearable, bellowing tension at home. A moment to find the Jane who could relax enough to allow her natural responsive self to come forward once again and deal with work and her customers. No one knew how much pain she swallowed before each day began.

She checked her to-do list for the day before she ventured inside. Meeting the man of her dreams wasn't on the list. It was yet another mundane day, the same as the hundreds before.

But on this Tuesday, when Troy Courtney appeared at her desk, her whole world changed. It had happened silently and in seconds.

The intensity of his presence was resounding, without fanfare or demand. His voice was strong and confident, yet each word was spoken casually with a gentle, seductive tone that had made her melt.

Troy sat in his Porsche but hadn't started the engine. He sat there, revisiting the image of her piercing eyes, her smile as it broke gently across her face like the first of the sun's rays on a beautiful summers' morning. Then the fleeting touch, the sensation of her fingers on his. He didn't want to move, not wanting anything to blur the image of her.

He eventually shook away the vision and left the car park. He drove the black sportscar in a trance, desperately trying to put the experience in perspective and carry on with his busy life. Reaching his hotel, he pulled into his reserved park, turned off the ignition and just sat there, again, replaying in his mind her smile, her eyes, and her beauty. He eventually walked inside and caught the elevator to his room. He flopped into the chair at the dark timber desk. Despite his efforts to get cracking into emails and the scheduling for the next event, he couldn't find his usual rhythm or focus. An hour had passed, and she was still all he could think about. *I'm going back, I'll think of a reason on the way.*

He stood up, grabbed his keys, and headed out of the hotel and to his car. He drove at speed, still not sure of a good reason to be back there yet.

On his arrival back at the Exhibit Designs office, he glanced through the glass doors to the entrance, checking to see if she was still seated at the reception desk. She was. The sight of her made his heart pound again; he felt like a teenager. He entered from the side car park entrance, so it looked like he hadn't left. He gripped the door handle, took a breath, and walked inside and up to the counter. Despite wanting to appear controlled and matter of fact, his voice betrayed him, such was his slightly nervous tone.

'Hi Jane, I just wanted to check if you could send me a receipt, please?' he said, at the same time handing her his business card. She accepted the card, glanced at it briefly, and then looked up at him and smiled.

'Certainly Mr Courtney, I'd be happy to do that,' she replied, offering the card back to him. 'I already have your details on file.'

'Great, thank you.' As he took back his card from her outstretched hand he noticed her ring. It was nearly identical to the engagement ring he'd had made for his fiancée five years ago.

'That's a beautiful ring... Do you mind?' he asked.

She placed her hand in his, almost encouraging him to take it. He cupped his fingers around hers as if he was holding a baby sparrow that had fallen from its nest.

Her hand held there in his, without moving. He could sense that she enjoyed his delicate touch.

'I have a ring very similar to this,' he said, flinching as a slight pain that he hadn't felt for a long time hit him. 'I know what a ring like this costs. You're very lucky,' he said.

'It's not real, I certainly couldn't afford a real one,' she said as she slowly removed her hand, now a little embarrassed. 'A bit out of my budget unfortunately. Is your ring for someone special?' she asked.

Troy looked down and drew a deep breath. 'It's not a happy story I'm afraid.'

He could see Jane wished she could take back the question.

'I see.'

There was a slight awkward silence as Jane looked away, swallowing the question she really wanted to ask.

Sensing he owed her some explanation, he said, 'Well, it was a tough time in my life.'

Troy then proceeded to tell her briefly about how the love of his life was taken from him just before their wedding day in a horrible car crash. She'd been killed on the day she bought her wedding dress. He explained how he had designed the ring especially for her and now it was only a bittersweet reminder of her. The vision of Johanna, lying motionless at the morgue with only her hand and the ring visible as he approached to identify her, flashed through his mind.

Jane could see the tears starting to well in his eyes as he spoke. She had to fight hard to overcome tears herself and the urge to reach out and hug him.

'I'm so sorry,' was all she could say.

'It's okay. It probably does me good to talk about it now and then. So, thank you for listening.'

Not sure exactly what to say, Jane merely smiled back, a look of deep admiration on her face.

Troy checked his watch. 'I really should get going. It was such a pleasure meeting you, Jane. You've put a smile in my heart.'

Jane blushed and said, 'I have enjoyed meeting you as well, Mr Courtney.'

Troy caught the very sincere meaning in her reply and offered a warm smile as he turned to leave.

After two small steps he stopped, looked back to her and said, 'You have my details, Jane, I would love to hear from you some time.'

'Thank you for your business, Mr Courtney,' Jane said with a smile and no idea of how to professionally respond to that comment.

A few weeks had passed when he noticed an email from a Jane Coles. He opened it without thought and started to read it.

From: Jane Coles <Jane.coles@exhibitdesigns.com>
To: Troy Courtney <troy.courtney@gcb.net>

Dear Troy,

It's Jane from Exhibit Designs. I'm not sure if you remember me. It has taken me a while to send this. I am very aware that this is completely inappropriate, and I could lose my job, but I found you so interesting and I would love to hear a little more of your amazing life. I felt like something I can't really explain happened. I don't know what it was, but I would love the chance to chat more.

If you feel it is inappropriate, please just delete and forgive me.

Jane.

Troy's heart was smiling as he read the email again. He desperately wanted to reply straight away but thought better of it. *I don't want to leave her hanging, but I need to think about this. How best do I respond?*

He walked around his apartment for an hour drafting what to say, then, he sat down and typed.

From: Troy Courtney <troy.courtney@gcb.net>
To: Jane Coles <Jane.coles@exhibitdesigns.com>

Dear Jane,

It is lovely to hear from you and of course I remember you. I, too, have been thinking about you and our meeting. Well, seeing that we're being honest here, I want to say that I thought you were the most beautiful woman I have ever seen and I would certainly love to see you again.

Troy.

Jane replied immediately.

From: Jane Coles <Jane.coles@exhibitdesigns.com>
To: Troy Courtney <troy.courtney@gcb.net>

Hi Troy,

I'm not sure that you can see me blushing from where you are, but I certainly am. Thank you. Please know I have never done this before or ever been close to being so forward, it's just... I actually don't know why, but sometimes something special happens and I believe one would be foolish to just sit back and let it cruise by.

Jane.

Troy just knew that any opportunity to be with this gorgeous creature was not something to be missed. But how? He wasn't planning to travel to Melbourne for some time and his calendar was brimming with work.

Then he had an idea. He was to be in the Gold Coast this week, as he was scheduled to test tyres and speak at a conference. It was simple! He would invite her to stay with him for the weekend.

He emailed her again.

From: Troy Courtney <troy.courtney@gcb.net>
To: Jane Coles <Jane.coles@exhibitdesigns.com>

Jane, I know we don't know each other at all, but I will be working in Queensland this week and would love for you to join me for the weekend. No agenda, just a chance to get to know each other. I know it's crazy but sometimes you need to step out of your comfort zone and go for it.

Troy.

For Jane, the reality of what she had started had now snowballed. Her thoughts went into overdrive.

If I say no now, the man that brought life to my dead heart will be gone forever. If I say yes, what does that mean? If I fly to Queensland, which is something I really can't afford, I'll probably fall head over heels when he makes love to me, and then be heartbroken when he tells me, 'Thanks, it was fun,' and disappears again out of my life.

From: Jane Coles <Jane.coles@exhibitdesigns.com>
To: Troy Courtney <troy.courtney@gcb.net>

Oh Troy, that does sound very romantic but let's be honest, we don't really know each other at all. I've never done anything like this before. I can't just run off with a stranger for the weekend.
Regards Jane.

From: Troy Courtney <troy.courtney@gcb.net>
To: Jane Coles <Jane.coles@exhibitdesigns.com>

Jane, I realise this is a crazy spontaneous thing to do. But there would be no agenda or expectation, we only do what feels right and nothing more. I will pay for everything including your flights. Jane, please let me spoil you and simply enjoy your company.
Troy x

Jane was torn. This is exactly what she needed. Her life was so boring. No, in real terms, it was just horrible. Her kids were in their late teens and never home and her husband could only be described as a pig. She had become his slave, to be worked and abused. But how could she possibly do this? A man doesn't invite you on a weekend away in the sun and not expect something in return. What was she thinking would happen when she first emailed him?

She knew he was attracted to her, that's why he came back to ask for a receipt that could easily have been emailed. But she did like him. A real man, a gentleman, who thought she was beautiful. What did he say? 'The most beautiful woman he had ever seen.' A warmth burst from her heart and, just for a moment, she found it hard to breathe. She closed her eyes and pictured him saying it to her as he held her in his arms. Jane opened her eyes to see her boss standing in front of her.

'Are you okay, Janie dear?' he asked.

'Yes, well, err, no... Bill, is there any chance I can have tomorrow off?'

'I guess so, organise someone to cover for you and that will be fine. Are you sure you're okay?'

'I am now, thank you Bill.' As a smile started to form on her face, her heart was racing. She would fly up tomorrow afternoon, make it look like a work trip. She was starting to shiver with excitement. She decided that if she had to repay the handsome man who thinks she is so beautiful with her body, then that was a price she was prepared to pay.

Then the realisation hit—in not much more than twenty-four hours, she could well be naked and making love to a man she doesn't even know past his name and occupation. What will he think of her? Will he be disappointed in her lack of sexual experience?

A dark cloud of apprehension surrounded her. What was she doing? Her husband wouldn't let her go, even if it was for work. He will find every excuse as to why she was irresponsible and inconsiderate to leave him alone. She wanted to scream as loud as she could. Her face was now buried tight in her hands, but then, suddenly as if by divine intervention, she looked up and typed her response.

From: Jane Coles <Jane.coles@exhibitdesigns.com>
To: Troy Courtney <troy.courtney@gcb.net>

Dear Troy,

I would love nothing more than to spend the weekend with you in Queensland. If you are still happy to cover my costs, I have arranged the day off for tomorrow. I wish I could afford to pay my way, but I just can't at the moment. I'm sorry, but I will save and pay you back every cent. I am extremely nervous and the sensible side of me has been clashing ferociously with the new me that you have awakened. And you can now see which side won the battle.

Jane x

Troy's reply was almost immediate.

From: Troy Courtney <troy.courtney@gcb.net>
To: Jane Coles <Jane.coles@exhibitdesigns.com>

Jane, you have no idea how happy you have just made me. As for the money, please don't worry about it! I would spend thousands more to spend just one minute with you. I will be working till 5 p.m. tomorrow at the conference and will arrange a flight for you to be there around that time, if that's okay. I will send through the details. Tomorrow could just be the best day of my life.

Love Troy xx

Jane's heart was bursting as she read his email; already just this message alone was a dream come true. A man that thinks she is beautiful and would pay any amount to have her with him. She wanted to clutch her chest and spin around. She was starting to feel faint, but quickly steadied herself. She had to tell Wayne about her 'trip,' and that wasn't going to be fun.

Her flight details appeared on her computer only minutes after her last email from Troy. It was really going to happen. The wheels were in motion.

Jane arrived home to a cold, dark, empty house. She knew Wayne would be at the pub and wouldn't be home until he was sure Jane would be home, and more importantly-that dinner was ready.

She made pasta, enough for five people. She was already preparing for the battle about her going away, anticipating the usual retorts from the 'Master of the House.' 'What will I eat?' would be the first.

She then prepared a pasta dish, so she was armed with meals for the two nights she'd be away.

At 7.30 p.m. the back door burst open, and his first words were, 'Is dinner ready? I'm starving.'

'It's nearly ready,' she replied, not bothering to turn towards him. He continued pacing through the kitchen to the toilet to drain away some of the five beers he'd drunk at the Royal Hotel's front bar. Jane served out two meals for herself and Wayne, knowing the kids wouldn't be home. She also packed the extra servings into second-hand takeaway containers that substituted for the lack of Tupperware.

By this time, Wayne had grabbed a beer from the fridge and pulled out a seat to sit in front of the steaming meal Jane had placed in front of him. He picked up his fork, and without another word started eating.

Jane played with her meal, preparing for her next statement. She forked a strand of fettuccine and said, 'Bill is sending me to the Gold Coast for a conference tomorrow.'

'Pigs fucking arse he is,' Wayne replied with creamy mushroom sauce all over his mouth.

'It's to learn the new software that we've had installed, remember I told you?'

'When the fuck would you be back?'

'Sunday afternoon.'

'No fucking way! Tell that fucking loser to fuck himself. Who the fuck will feed me while you are up there spending money we don't have?'

'I have food already prepared, easy just to microwave. Besides, all expenses are paid; it won't cost us anything.'

'It's the fucking weekend, you have work to do here around the house,' he said, shovelling another fork load of pasta into his mouth.

'I have the washing on, and you know I'll have everything clean and sorted for you like I always do.'

'Are you getting paid double time? I bet that fucking tightarse is only paying time and a half.'

With his mouth still full he continued his rant, 'If it's not double time tell him to go fuck himself!'

That was something she hadn't thought about, now realising she may have to borrow some money from her mother to look like she was actually being paid extra for that week. With a burp, Wayne flicked his plate to the centre of the table and stood up, the chair squawking heavily on the old lino floor. He walked into the lounge room, beer in hand, and switched on the television. Jane fell back into her chair, her appetite completely lost. She let out a breath. That signalled the end of round one.

Wayne was asleep on the couch by the time she'd hung out the last of the washing. A little flicker of warmth burned softly in her heart knowing a man waited for her in Queensland, who thought she was beautiful, and he was only one sleep away. She hardly slept that night.

Jane awoke with a start. She hadn't set her alarm as her flight wasn't till lunchtime. Wayne had long gone to work, and she doubted he would even remember the conversation from the night before. She would leave him a note on the kitchen table, reminding him of the details and that there were meals in the fridge for him.

A very nervous and excited Jane boarded the plane to Coolangatta on the Gold Coast. She sat back in her business class seat, staring out the window of the Boeing 737 as it climbed away from the cold Melbourne winter, through the clouds, and into the sun. She smiled as she thought about how the first twenty minutes of the flight almost mirrored her feelings.

Then she thought about her husband, Wayne. *Sure, he wasn't a great example of the perfect man, but he was hers, and yet, she was about to spend the weekend with another, who, unlike Wayne, filled her with happiness.*

A stab hit her as she imagined Wayne finding out. *What if he called Bill, demanding he pay her double time and Bill not knowing what the hell he was talking about?* She doubted Wayne would actually do that, because in most cases he was all booze, bullshit talk, and definitely no action.

Her thoughts turned to Troy, the rich, charming racing car driver that she was about to spend the weekend with. She was joining the club, of which many of her girlfriends were members, the club of adultery. A smile started to form on her face as she imagined telling her friends that she was flying off to make love to a man she'd met for just one minute. They wouldn't believe her. She tried to imagine she was in a movie and she was the leading lady, able to flaunt the risks and be consumed with lust and hot sex. This wasn't a movie, but she was the leading lady, and would direct the scene as she wanted, the male star at her beck and call.

She again closed her eyes, the hum of the jet background noise in her ears. The flight attendant brought her the meal that she had selected from the menu along with a glass of chardonnay. She relished in the little delight that she'd never had a drink at this time of day. She imagined for a moment that this was her life; rich, with business class flights and being served wine in the middle of the day, or any time she desired. But it wasn't her life, and she knew that her real life awaited her, back in the dank and cold of her Melbourne home on Sunday afternoon.

As the plane descended, she felt she was being lowered into a new world, and a sense of calm swept her body. She was to grab these two days with both hands, doubting this would ever happen again.

The tremors of excitement surged as she alighted the cab in front of a huge hotel.

My God, look at this place, she thought as she entered, glancing around the marble foyer.

She approached the reception desk. 'Good afternoon. I am here to collect a room key left for me by Mr Troy Courtney.'

'Certainly, Mrs Courtney, we've been expecting you. Welcome to our hotel. It is such a pleasure to have you join us. The concierge will escort you to your suite. We certainly hope you enjoy your stay with us and please don't hesitate to call if there is anything you need.'

On hearing 'Mrs Courtney' and 'suite' Jane's knees nearly buckled as she offered a barely audible, 'Thank you very much.'

Jane drew in a breath as she entered the room. It took all her resolve to retain her outward calm while listening to the concierge as he pointed out the basic details of the suite.

'We will return shortly with your bag madam.'

Jane stood, motionless in the middle of the suite, turning around slowly, taking in every feature of this amazing place. It was as big as her whole house. The deep blue Pacific Ocean filled the panoramic view of almost half of the room.

A little knock on the door startled her back into reality. She opened the door to find a bellboy and a waiter.

'Your luggage, madam. Shall I put this in the bedroom for you? Mr Courtney has arranged some refreshments for you. It's such a lovely day, would you like me to set these on the balcony?'

'Thank you,' Jane said, still completely overwhelmed.

'Please call us if there is anything else you require. We are here at your service, especially for our special guests, Mrs. Courtney.'

Jane simply nodded and smiled as they deposited her bag and set the table on the balcony. Once the two men disappeared, she walked through the huge sliding door and onto the balcony to find a grazing platter, champagne, and an assortment of magazines. An envelope with her name was strategically leaning against the stem of the glass.

She opened it.

Welcome Jane
I can't wait to see you. I hope to be there before 5.00 p.m.
Troy x

She was completely overcome. Such an exquisitely appointed room, the total elegance and indulgence of this place, and the fact that Troy had clearly paid attention to every detail—this was something she had never experienced in her whole life. Her body tremors were now electrified. This was so much more than she could have ever imagined.

During his meeting, Jane was all Troy could think about. *She should be here by now.* His thoughts drifted, mostly to counting down the minutes until they were face to face once more. *Will those eyes still mesmerise me?*

The meeting finished and he was quickly in his car and on his way from Brisbane to the coast. He thought about calling her but decided against it.

Arriving at the door of the suite, he stopped, took a deep breath, and opened it. He looked inside. She was sitting on the balcony reading a magazine. He was consumed by an inner warmth, the same as the first time he saw her sitting behind her desk at the exhibition centre. She looked comfortable and relaxed, dressed casually in an almost see-through white linen top. He could just see the white lacy bra that her perfect breasts filled. It was certainly the vision of an angel.

As he walked toward her, she looked up and smiled, a look that almost made his legs turn to jelly. She stood as he reached her.

He placed a hand on each cheek and gave her a gentle, lingering kiss on her soft lips. He pulled back and looked at her. 'You are even more beautiful than I remembered.'

She looked down shyly and said softly, 'Thank you.'

'Did you get in okay, no hassles at reception?'

'No, I was treated like a VIP.'

'As you should be,' Troy said, smiling at her. He could tell this was all completely foreign to her.

Troy poured himself a glass of champagne.

'I cannot believe this place, thank you so much for inviting me.'

'It's my absolute pleasure. How was your trip?'

'It was fine. It's just so lovely to be here in the warmth. It's been a long time since I have been on a plane to anywhere. Did your conference go okay?'

'It was alright, but I just wanted it to be over so I could get back here to see you.'

Troy took a seat next to her and asked about her work, which he listened too with interest, but it wasn't until he told her about his jet set lifestyle that Jane was blown away. She started to wonder, *is he really so into her, or is this just his way to lure women to his bed before quickly discarding them once he had his way with them?* But she dismissed the thought, reminding herself again that it was just a special weekend away and her real life was sitting, waiting for her in the cold Melbourne house, just two days in the future.

Troy finished his glass of champagne and said, 'Let me have a quick shower and then what's say we find a nice place for dinner?'

'Sounds perfect,' Jane replied, relaxing a little for the first time since she'd left.

As Troy walked back inside the apartment, he noticed her bag still packed and in the main room. He smiled at the innocence and non-assumption that she would be sleeping with him.

After about fifteen minutes, Troy emerged from the bathroom and found Jane again on the balcony, singing along to an Eagles cover that a live band was playing at a restaurant in the mall twenty floors below.

'I'm ready, let's go eat,' he said, as he reached for her hand and led her towards the door.

Troy hadn't felt this way for a long time. He was really looking forward to tonight, to watch her relax in his company, smile, laugh, and maybe after, to hold her, taste her, and make love to her. The thought sent a shiver through him. She was somehow forbidden fruit that he was desperate to consume.

Once in the elevator, he pushed the ground floor button, her hand still in his. He turned to her and touched her cheek.

'Are you feeling comfortable with all of this?'

'Yes, scarily so,' she replied with a nervous smile.

Hand in hand, they strolled through the hotel lobby and into the mall. It was busy with a combination of workers returning home and casually dressed people going out for dinner. Jane slowed as they reach the band playing outside the restaurant opposite. It was the same music she'd been listening to from the balcony.

'How about here?' Jane said softly.

'Italian, that's fine with me.'

They were ushered to a table and they sat facing toward the band and their music. It was perfect, not too loud but not background either. Troy ordered a wine and a creamy pasta dish. An image of Wayne demolishing a similar dish the night before, sent a stabbing pain through her. Jane ordered a Saltimbocca.

Troy watched her as she took in the surroundings. This was his life, but he could tell it was a long way from hers. She looked so happy and so eager to take in the whole experience. The wine was doing its job, and he could see her relax as she now gently swayed to the music. Whatever was at home, she had clearly left it behind her now.

Troy studied her for a moment and said, 'What a perfect night, it really couldn't be better.'

'It is,' she replied, as she turned her head back towards him from the band. 'This is the best day of my life.'

'Surely not?' he said, truly surprised.

Jane just nodded. Troy was completely intoxicated by this amazing woman. It was like he had found a precious relic that had been buried for years and the more he cleaned away the dust, the more beautiful it became.

Their meals soon arrived, and they continued to talk about their jobs and the amazing Gold Coast environment. Jane's home life wasn't brought up, and Troy wasn't going to introduce any demons he suspected may be hovering below the surface. He didn't want anything to sour their evening. It wasn't long before their plates were gone, the wine bottle empty, and the check delivered.

Troy fixed the bill, and they walked slowly back to the hotel hand in hand. The wine had certainly had an effect on Jane as she giggled and touched him with a complete sense of familiarity by the time they strolled through the lobby to the elevator.

As the elevator climbed, the anticipation of what was to happen next had Troy's heart racing. It might only be seconds before he might be kissing the delicious lips of this breathtaking lady. Troy sobered as his mind raced, trying to decide how he should proceed once the door of the penthouse suite closed behind them.

He opened the door and held it open for her. As she stepped into the room, Troy let the door close softly and the click of the catch somehow signalled the start of something beautiful. Jane walked towards the open door to the balcony; the breeze had the white sheer curtains dancing to the music below. She stepped out, placing her hands on the chrome rail. A moment of realisation swept over her. The soft, warm, balmy breeze that teased the curtains was now caressing her face. Her hair felt so light, as if a million fingers were massaging each strand. Her eyes were closed when she felt his hands on her shoulders and run down her arms to rest on her fingers that still grasped the railing. She could now feel his body against hers and his lips kissed her ear. She let her head fall back to his shoulder, and in that moment, she knew that tonight she would be giving herself to him.

Jane's eyes were still closed as she turned to face him. As her back found the railing she opened them and looked up into his deep brown seductive eyes. Her look was not of happiness or excitement, it was of total surrender. A look that she'd never had before and may never have again. She wanted him to devour her in whatever way he chose. She was no longer Jane Coles from Melbourne, but a woman to be sacrificed to the wolves of passion and lust. To be consumed and exploited at her captor's wishes and desires.

She stared into his eyes that had cast a magical spell on her. His lips touched hers and her eyes closed. The kiss was so soft and gentle. Her heart was pounding, and her body was reacting immediately to his tender kisses. The warmth that radiated from deep in her stomach filled her. She put her arms around him, finding his bare skin warm under his shirt; she could feel each muscle as she ran her fingers up his back. He moved back slowly, allowing her to remove his shirt. She pulled it over his head and let it fall to the floor. Their lips joined again, and she felt his hands on her soft, bare skin beneath the white linen top she wore. The touch that travelled up her back was slow and soft, the pressure perfectly consistent. Her skin seemed to meld into his fingertips.

The linen top rose with his hands and was soon shed to lay over the back of a balcony chair. Their lips reunited, the kisses now deepening and becoming more passionate. She felt the slight tightness as he pulled the clip of her bra together, and without any noticeable movement, she felt the firmness of the restraint slowly release. It happened so slowly she barely felt the transition. He lifted the straps from her shoulders and let them glide down her arms. She dropped her arms, letting her bra fall away. She could feel that her nipples were puckered and hoped he could feel them against his chest as she hugged him tight. *Was it the night air cooling or the gentle touch of his fingers caressing her back that covered her body in goosebumps? It didn't matter.*

Troy stepped back, his naked chest filling her vision. She noticed his look at her semi-nakedness and his smile of approval. He took her hand and led her to the bedroom. She couldn't believe how natural it felt being naked with him as she walked through the moonlit apartment. When they reached the end of the king size bed, he turned to her again pressing his lips to hers, soft and gentle like the first kiss on the balcony. She loved that he was savouring the moment making her think that just maybe, she may not be just another woman to him.

His hands ran down her back and she felt him easily release the clip at the top of her skirt. The zip was next, and she felt it slide down, revealing her bare legs. His hands ran the circumference of the band of her panties before his fingers slipped inside. Within seconds, they soon joined the skirt on the floor. His fingers were now exploring their way from her neck to as far as he could reach down her back and between her legs. She was so wet and her nipples so hard they almost hurt. She reached for the button and zip of his shorts, and without any of the delicate precision he showed her, removed them down to his ankles. He was biting her neck when she reached inside his briefs and ran her fingers along him. He was so big and hard. She heard him gasp as her hand closed firmly around the part of him that she now wanted most. Her body was screaming for the full, throbbing flesh she held in her hand. She released him and lowered his underwear to the floor, following down to kneel in front of him, her vision now filled with his hard erection, firm and at full attention.

She placed her right hand around him, and without any thought or consideration, placed her mouth over his knob. His moan of pleasure was clearly heard as she ran her tongue around and over his resplendent penis. She hadn't done this to a man in over twenty years, but somehow it felt as if she'd been practicing all her life. She took him fully then drew back slowly, her lips clinging tight, as he slipped from her mouth. She stood, and for just a fleeting moment, they again looked into each other's eyes. Troy placed an arm around her shoulders and the other under her legs, lifting her up easily. Jane couldn't even start to explain how that felt. The weightlessness was as if she was suspended on a cloud, it was heavenly.

Their eyes were locked as he carried her and lowered her naked body gently onto the bed. She looked up at the man that in only a few seconds time would make her an adulterer, a cheater, an unfaithful wife.

In that second, a coldness enveloped her. Her horrible husband had entered her thoughts. He was somehow robbing her of this special moment. Her legs came together, and she bent them toward her, feeling that somehow it covered her nudity. Jane placed her hands over her face and started cry. She knew Troy would be confused or even frustrated with her, but she couldn't control it. Wayne had somehow managed to ruin the best day of her life. With her face covered and eyes closed, she felt Troy sit on the bed next to her, his hand stroking her arms. He didn't say anything, just comforted her with his touch.

Eventually she let her hands slide away from her face. She could only imagine what she looked like. Her eyes, still filled with tears, focused on his. He ran his finger down each of her cheeks, wiping away the tears.

'I'm a married woman, Troy,' she said, her eyes fixed on his.

'I figured you were,' he said without judgement. She felt a little shocked at his casual response.

'That doesn't worry you?' she asked, though immediately wishing she hadn't.

'Jane, you are the most beautiful thing I have ever seen in my life and my selfish desire to touch you, feel you, kiss you, and love you, far exceeds any guilt that your personal circumstance presents.'

Jane again burst into tears. She rolled over, turning her back to him. He lay down beside her, again not offering any comments, just a soft caress of her back. He put his arm around her and pulled her close. Immediately, the closeness softened her pain. She figured the tears and hurt were punishment for what she was doing, and then, an amazing feeling came over her that somehow made her recognise her debt had been paid.

She couldn't believe how her horrible husband had nearly ruined this for her. She didn't understand how or why, but for some reason she felt free, as if the cloak of darkness was being lifted from her. She turned to Troy, placed her hands on his cheeks, and pulled him towards her. She kissed him with a passion that she was sure confused the hell out of him. But this was her weekend, her day, her night, her moment, and she was going to have what she desperately wanted.

She pulled him on top of her, his left leg falling between hers. Her legs fell apart, inviting as much of him as he wanted to give her. She could feel he had softened slightly during her moment of self-reproach, but was already starting to press firmly against her thigh. His skin against her bare chest alone was almost more than she could stand. His thigh pushed up hard between her legs and she could feel her wetness lubricating his skin as it rubbed her. His muscular thigh, tight into her groin and rubbing her firmly, had her tingling all over. A feeling she had never felt before. Troy lifted his body and placed himself between her now spread legs. his lips never leaving hers. She was in a dream, or somehow transported to another world. She felt him touch her, her swollen folds parting to accept what she wanted. He held the pressure against her and lifted his face away from her, looking into her eyes as she opened them.

'Are you sure you want this?' he asked, entering her slightly, as if giving some encouragement to the reply he wanted. Her eyes gave him the answer—no words were needed. She felt him slowly penetrate her, their eyes burning a beam of lust between them. Her body arched as he entered her further, every millimetre draining her resolve. He continued slowly filling her till their groins touched. He was so deep inside her that she knew that their two bodies were now one. He pulled back and again entered her deep and hard. The heat rose quickly in her body. His thrusts were still slow but hard, and she could feel that whatever it was that was about to happen to her, it was very welcome. She'd never had an orgasm in all her life. She now knew that was about to change. He quickened the pace and she felt as if he was even deeper inside her now. The heat continued to build, every nerve in her body tingled; she was starting to shake, and she couldn't control it. She felt like her body might explode. Troy was pounding her hard now as every muscle in her body pushed, pushed towards her vagina, with the pressure building to an unimaginable level.

Then she exploded, the built-up tension flushed from her body. She screamed—not a high-pitched scream, but a scream all the same—it was loud and deep from her diaphragm. The feeling was like nothing she had ever felt before; her body pulsed, shook, and throbbed as the released heat rushed through her.

She didn't realise that he had come as well, but she felt him pulsing deep inside her as he filled her with his orgasmic fluid.

Her fall back to earth was heavenly, as if she was falling in a weightless world. Every nerve tingled from her soul to her fingertips. The hard flesh that was still deep inside her body burned, but it was a massive part of this incredible feeling, and she held him tight so he couldn't leave her.

She opened her eyes to see him propped above her, a smile on his face; his eyes wore a look of contentment and comfort. A smile started to form as she looked at her lover. He lowered himself and kissed her, her smile now gone as she took in what had just happened. She realised, for the first time in her life, she'd truly made love to a man. A stranger that had swept her from her feet and made a real woman of her. A woman she now wanted to be.

Troy's smile had also disappeared as he also took in the enormity of the moment. He kissed her again and she knew in that second that this couldn't be just a fling. Troy slowly removed himself from her to lay beside her, and she rolled to her side, placing her head on his shoulder. She pressed her body against his, placing her left arm across his chest to hold him tight against her.

Jane's life flashed before her eyes; she had never felt adored or pleasured like this before, not even close. Her body tingled with a delicious soreness where he had been inside her. She squeezed him tight, kissing the side of his face. His smell was delicious. But then a moment of concern filled her as he lay silent beside her. No reaction to her kiss; he was deep in thought. *Would this be it—the thanks, but no thanks?* she wondered.

He turned to her, a serious look on his face, and finally, he spoke.

'Jane, would you leave your husband for me, I don't want to live another second without you in my life?' Troy asked softly, his hand caressing the side of her face. She now knew why he'd been quiet. Jane was shocked as the option she had never imagined possible was presented.

She squeezed him as tight as she could.

'Yes,' she replied.

Same Room

Ed and Sara lay side by side, still panting after the alcohol-induced passion. Ed's arm lay across her body, giving him the feeling that they were still intimately connected. He didn't know why, but the feeling of removing himself completely from her after such passionate sex just didn't seem right. He loved to feel the rise and fall of her chest as her breathing slowly returned to its rested state, while he remained connected—inside and out.

After a moment or two in which they lay breathless and spent, he was the first to completely recover and rolled onto his side to face her. He caressed her exquisite body, running the softest touch around her breast, tummy, and bikini line. Just her breasts, ribs, and mound penetrated the horizontal. She was certainly a sleek, trim woman. She occasionally jumped as a tickle or arousal tingled through her.

Sara was in paradise, her body still cooling from the heat of her orgasm, and the feathered touch of Ed's fingers was just heavenly. He lifted his hand to run a finger down her cheek and she slowly turned towards him. Her eyes opened and a smile formed on her face.

'Babe, you went off when I made out that I was someone else,' Ed offered softly.

'I know; there's something about that naughtiness, don't you think?'

'Do you often think of other men when we make love?' Ed asked, not really sure if he wanted to hear the answer. Sara turned to him and placed her hand on his concerned face.

'Do you want the honest answer or the one you want to hear?' Sara said, with a smile of reassurance.

'Well, I don't have a lot of choice when you put it like that,' he said indignantly.

'Okay. Yes, I do think of other guys, but not very often. Just when I need a little extra naughty to get me there, to that heightened place. It's never anyone we know, it might just be someone I saw that day or a movie star, but I always imagine you there as well somehow, holding my hand or kissing me, never just on my own.'

Ed rolled over onto his back and Sara's heart jolted, panicked that she had upset him. She turned to him, reaching out her hand to tentatively stroke his arm.

'Does that upset you, babe? I'm so sorry, but we're always so honest with each other.'

'Not at all, my sweetheart, but it has got me thinking,' Ed said, still staring at the ceiling.

Sara drew in a breath, then exhaled. She simply had to ask. 'Do you sometimes think of another woman while you make love to me?'

'Not very often, but I'd be lying if I said no, same as you. Never anyone we know.'

'Ed, would you like to fuck someone else? Honestly?'

Ed turned onto his side to face her. He looked straight into her eyes. 'Honestly?'

'Yes,' Sara said softly.

'Well, I guess everyone would like to take his neighbour's Ferrari for a spin every now and then, but it doesn't mean he wants to own one.'

Sara laughed at the analogy.

'What about you, babe, would you like to test drive a different model occasionally?' Ed was happy he didn't have to say the exact words.

'I really don't know. It's all good in theory, but I think I would get into it and be looking for you; I don't really think I could do it,' Sara replied.

Ed ran his fingers along her forehead, pulling back her blonde hair that was now covering half her face.

'Do you mean like a threesome?' he asked.

'Babe, I don't know what I mean. I just know, if I'm going to have sex, you need to be there.'

Ed rolled onto his back and again stared at the ceiling ornament that surrounded the light. This was a lot to take in. *Could he possibly share his wife with another man, watch as he filled her, watch him remove himself, and see his cum running from between her legs?* He shivered at the thought. He turned back to her.

'My darling, this has been a great conversation and might just give us a chance to move our perfect sex life to the next level, but I really need to think about it some more. What about we chat about it tomorrow?'

Sara leant over and kissed him. 'Deal.' she said and reached to turn out the dimmed light. Ed spooned in behind her, but sleep was not going to come quickly for him. Not so for Sara, who was now thinking about the man who she'd imagined, just thirty minutes ago was between her legs and brought her the blissful delight she desired.

Sara was awake before the alarm and Ed woke to find she'd already risen from bed. He lay there, again staring at the ceiling as he ran through his mind last night's conversation about expanding their sexual experience. He knew today would include a bit of time on the internet exploring options. He jumped out of bed and hopped into the shower.

As the warm water covered his body, he tried to imagine a room of people all showering together; that thought appealed to him. Or a spa full of naked bodies, hands wandering around below the bubbling surface. That scene excited him even more. So much so, he started to stroke himself in the warm shower. He turned off the water and left the bathroom, still with sexy images lingering in his mind. Downstairs he found Sara dressed and having a piece of toast while at the same time typing something with one hand into her computer.

'Good morning, babe, you look busy!' Ed said, kissing her on the cheek.

'I've found a site with people looking for almost every possible sexual combination.'

'Really?' Ed said, stepping back to look at the screen.

'Yes, there's threesomes, foursomes, orgies, and anything else your heart desires. Do you know what soft swing is?' Sara asked, looking at him.

'Not sure, maybe swinging on a soft bed,' he said with a smile.

'Well, whatever it is, I like the sound of it.'

She's caught a dose of the same arousal, thought Ed, as he turned to get his much needed first coffee. He heard her still typing furiously.

'Okay, it's also known as "same room sex" where two couples have sex with their own partners while another couple is doing the same in the room or on the same bed. Apparently sometimes a little touching is accepted or encouraged,' Sara said, reading from the screen.

'I could do that,' Ed replied with enthusiasm.

'I could as well, as long as they're a nice couple,' Sara said, closing her laptop.

Ed finished making his coffee and placed two pieces of bread in the toaster. Sara kissed him on the cheek as she packed her work bag and headed out the door.

'Find us a nice couple to play with,' she called out as she closed the door behind her.

Ed was delighted with her enthusiasm, but still somewhat taken aback at how she had jumped way past apprehension, into asking him to search for others to potentially play with.

Ed's first job when he sat down at his desk was to get onto the site and see who was out there in swing land. He found that soft swing was popular, especially amongst first timers. He replied to three advertisements that sounded genuine and a good match for them.

By the end of the day, all three had replied and a few photos were swapped. He discounted one couple, but the other two looked promising. By day's end, he had arranged to meet each of the couples separately at their local hotel later that week. He hadn't told Sara yet but was busting to share the news as he walked in the door that night.

Sara was swaying to some music as she stood at the stove, stirring a tomato-based pasta sauce that was simmering away. Ed walked up behind her and gave her a hug.

'Smells delicious,' he said, as he walked off to get a glass to share the red wine Sara had already opened. 'I found a couple of potential soft swing couples today,' Ed offered as he poured the wine.

'Really?' Sara said, turning from the stove to look at him.

'I chatted to three couples; one was not our type, but I've arranged for us to meet with the other two, I'll show you a photo.'

Sara placed the wooden spoon in the sauce and turned down the flame slightly, leaving the pasta still bubbling away in the saucepan next to it. Ed opened his phone and showed her a picture of a couple somewhere on a beach, probably Asia. They were about their age, and both wore friendly warm smiles.

'They look nice,' Sara said, still studying the picture.

'These are my favorites though,' Ed said, flicking to the next picture. This was a young couple at dinner, both holding a glass of wine. It was probably taken by one of those professionals that sometimes haunt the more expensive restaurants.

'They're nice too,' Sara said.

'Yeah, we messaged most of the day, they are first timers as well and still very unsure, but like us just looking to spice things up a little.'

Sara turned back to the now overflowing saucepan that was boiling the pasta.

'What did you arrange? Sara said, stirring the pasta sauce.

Ed started to set the table as he explained that he had arranged to meet at their local hotel at 7.00 p.m. tomorrow night and then meet the other couple the night after.

'Wow, no mucking around then,' Sara said, turning to him with a smile. 'What would I wear?' she added, draining the water from the pasta.

'A smile,' Ed replied.

Sara turned to him with a look that answered his sarcasm.

That night their lovemaking included talk of another couple with them, watching them, touching them, and that quickly brought each to their climax.

The next evening when Ed arrived home there was excitement in the air. They had decided to go earlier and have dinner at the hotel, which gave Sara time to dress instead of cooking.

'I'm ready,' Sara called out from upstairs.

'You look amazing, babe, but our new friends are only interested in seeing you without clothes on.'

'I suppose you're right, but a nice present should have equally nice wrapping,' Sara said, taking his hand.

They arrived at the hotel's restaurant an hour before the agreed meet time. Ed ordered a drink for them both and collected two menus from the bar.

'What will we talk about?' Sara asked in a way that seemed like she didn't want anyone to hear.

'I don't know, maybe what we have done before or what each of us might expect, not sure.'

'Well, I guess we just see how it goes,' Sara said.

They ordered their meals, which arrived quickly. Neither of them noticed the couple arrive and sit at the far end of the bar. Ed checked his watch; it was nearly time. His phone rang and he answered it almost on the first ring.

'This is Ed.'

'Hi Ed, Adam. We are here.'

'Hi Adam, we are at the southern end of the lounge bar. I have on a white work shirt and Sara a blue dress.'

Ed stood and saw the couple walking towards them, each with a drink in hand. Adam was tall, with thinning dark hair that was probably premature for his age. Julie was quite short, well, appeared to be next to her tall husband. She had shoulder-length, mousy-coloured hair. They could see she had just brushed it as it sat perfectly around her face. She was attractive in a sexy way and her green eyes were mesmerising. She wore a white cotton top and a black pencil skirt, suggesting she'd probably come straight from work. Sara also stood as the pair arrived.

'Welcome, it's nice to meet you both,' Ed offered, holding out his hand to shake Adam's. The four of them instantly qualifying each other.

After the cheek kisses to the girls, they all sat back down. As soon as the normal, 'how was your day' polite pleasantries were out the way, Adam asked, 'So this is your first time?'

'Yes,' Ed said. 'We aren't really sure how it all happens but just thought we would like a little extra excitement, and this sounded like something we might enjoy. Have the two of you done much before?'

'This would be our sixth time,' Adam said, looking over to Julie.

'What's it like?' Sara asked Julie, who was sitting back in her chair, appearing a little shy.

'To be honest, it's pretty much how you would picture it—you have sex with a live porn show next to you, it's pretty hot,' Julie admitted.

Sara smiled back, her mind trying to picture Adam and Julie naked and fucking next to her. The thought warmed her.

'How was it the first time?' Ed asked, leaning forward a little so the other diners couldn't hear.

'We met at a hotel and went halves in a room; we took some wine and let them lead the way. They suggested we undress each other's partner and that was pretty hot, to be honest.'

'Okay, I can see how that would be,' Ed said, his eyes locking with Julie's. Julie blushed slightly and Ed could tell she'd pictured the scenario in her mind as well.

'Then the four of us climbed onto the bed and had some very exciting sex!' Adam said, looking at Sara.

'Was there any touching?' Sara asked Julie, desperately wanting to contribute some more to the conversation.

'Just a little, they knew it was our first time and didn't want to freak us out,' Julie said.

Ed placed his hand on Sara's leg under the table and she put hers on top of his. It was now he wished they had set up a code so they could get a feel for what the other thought. The conversation continued for another thirty minutes before Adam asked, 'Do you think we might be a couple you would like to experiment with?'

Ed looked at Sara, she wore a smile that answered the question before her words came out.

'I think so,' she said, a mixture of embarrassment and excitement flooding through her.

'Same for me,' Ed said looking at Julie, trying to imagine her lying naked beside him.

'I think we feel much the same,' Adam said, looking at Julie who nodded with a positive expression. 'Well, that's great,' Adam said. 'I guess we find a time and a place; we can't host as we have children but are happy to contribute to a room if you prefer.'

Ed's hand had slipped between Sara's legs, and she spread them a little. The short dress gave him easy access to her silk panties. He immediately felt movement in his groin.

'What do you have on for the rest of the night?' Ed asked, his heart pounding as he asked the obvious question.

'Nothing really,' Adam said looking at Julie, her smile radiating from her face. 'My mum is babysitting and is staying over, so we are free.'

Then Ed asked, 'Would you like to come over to our place then? We just live two blocks away.' Ed's eyes swapped back and forth to them both. Adam and Julie looked at each other and it was agreed. Now there were four hearts racing at the table. They all sat back, almost silent as they finished their drinks. Ed went up and paid the account and when he returned, he gave the address to Adam.

'We walked here so we can meet you there,' Ed said.

'We can give you a lift if you like?' Adam offered.

'That's okay, probably a good chance for us to chat on the way,' Ed said smiling.

Adam grinned, 'Great idea.'

Ed and Sara headed off in the direction of their house and Adam and Julie made their way to the car park.

'So, are you all good?' We can bail at any time,' Ed said as they crossed the street hand in hand.

'I'm quite okay, they seem very nice and genuine,' Sara said.

'Yeah, have you already pictured the whole thing in your head like I have?'

'Pretty well,' Sara said, smiling at him.

Adam and Julie were already parked at the front of their house as they turned the corner into their street.

'Well, there you go, I wasn't expecting this little bonus tonight,' Adam said as they all arrived at Ed and Sara's front door.

'Does anyone want a drink or anything?' Sara offered once they were all inside.

'All good,' Adam replied as Julie nodded in agreement.

'Okay, well follow us,' Ed said, taking Sara's hand as they all ascended the stairs. Ed dimmed the bedroom lights to a perfect twilight brightness.

The four of them stopped for the perfect amount of time before Adam asked, 'Would you like to undress Julie for me, Ed?'

Ed looked at Sara who nodded approval and the two girls turned to swap partners. Julie ran her fingers down Sara's cheek as they crossed and gave her a sensual smile.

Julie put her hand on Ed's chest and held it there for a moment, as if transferring some secret sexual energy. She started to undo the first button on his shirt and then slowly the next, her eyes fixed on his. Ed looked over to Sara; she had her back to Adam and he watched this relative stranger unzipping her short blue summer dress.

Ed looked back at Julie who now had his shirt undone and was removing it. Julie held up her arms, indicating it was her turn to lose her top. He lifted it carefully over her head and her white lacy bra filled his vision. He put his arms around her, stepped closer till their bodies touched, and reached for her bra clip. He undid it slowly as he felt what it held fall against his chest. Her nipples were now firm, and he could feel them tight against his chest. His body was responding to this erotic moment. Julie let the bra fall to the floor and she reached for the button at the top of his pants. She let her fingers feel his bulge before focusing on the button and zip. Julie lowered the zip and let him fill her hand before she lowered his trousers and underpants together to the floor. As she raised back up to stand, she placed her right hand around him and gave him two soft strokes. She leant tightly into him so he could undo the back of her skirt. The scent of her hair filled his senses, and he closed his eyes as he let the skirt fall to the floor. He slid his hands into the back of her knickers and lowered them to fall gracefully on top of the skirt. Now completely naked, she turned to face Adam and Sara, her hand behind her holding Ed's erection firmly.

Once Adam had undone Sara's zip, he turned her around to face him. His hands started at her face, slid down her cheeks, her neck, and under the shoulder straps of her dress. His fingers caught the dress, and he lowered it gently with precision. He ran his hands over her breasts as he removed it, letting it fall once it was past her hips. Sara's eyes were closed, relishing his slow sensual touch. This was far hotter than she had ever imagined.

Her body was gushing and now desperate for more. Adam reached behind her and undid her bra; as he lowered it, his hands again relished her breasts. As he removed his hands, she opened her lust-filled eyes. Adam smiled back, and she realised he was now the only one still fully dressed.

She lifted off his t-shirt and undid his jeans, his manhood bursting from the top of his underwear. Sara gasped when she saw the size of him. She carefully lowered his jeans and underwear, drawing them down with her to kneel in front of him, her face now filled with his growing arousal. He reached for her hand and placed it around his penis. Without hesitation, she slid her hand along its length a few times before turning to see where Ed and Julie were.

Julie still had her hand full of Ed when they moved over to swap back to their partners. Ed lay Sara on her back and climbed between her spread legs. He could see she was already completely aroused, sensing she was swollen and wet and desperate to have him inside her.

Julie lay next to her and took Sara's hand as Adam also positioned himself above her. Sara knew when Adam had entered her, Julie squeezed her hand so tight she thought she might crush it. Julie's head fell back as she released a loud moan from deep inside her. Sara knew firsthand what she was receiving.

Ed moved on top of Sara, kissing her neck and earlobe as he found her, filling her with an enthusiasm she hadn't felt in a long time. Sara's eyes locked onto Adam as she watched him feeding himself into Julie. Their eyes never broke the stare, and it wasn't long before Sara's mind was convinced it was Adam himself between her legs. She could see his hips rise and fall and saw him disappearing into Julie with each thrust. It almost mirrored what she felt from Ed. Adam watched as her eyes started to close and her body tightened as she came, a deep moan erupted from her. Adam himself had also imagined it was Sara he was with, and her release was all he needed to join her, filling Julie deep with his cum. Ed and Julie soon followed, making it a full house of panting and satisfied lovers.

Sara watched as Adam removed himself from Julie, still semi-hard and glistening from her juices in the dim light. Ed rolled to Sara's side and the four of them lay there naked and basking in the euphoric experience. Ed was the first to speak.

'Well, I have to say that was much more fun than I expected.'

'I think we would agree you are the best couple we have been with,' Adam said, looking for confirmation from Julie, who nodded as she threw a warm smile at Ed and Sara.

Ed hopped up and reached for a pair of track suit pants and a t-shirt. He handed Sara her dress and she slipped it back on without any underwear. Julie and Adam were soon dressed and followed Ed and Sara downstairs. Ed shook hands with Adam and kissed Julie on the cheek. Sara kissed Julie on the cheek and Adam on the mouth, a kiss that was probably a little longer than it should've been. Her eyes were locked to his as she pulled away.

Adam turned as they reached the front door. 'Hey, call us if you would ever like to do it again.'

'I think you will be hearing from us, Adam,' Ed said, as he opened the door for them.

As the door closed and Adam and Julie headed for their car, Ed turned to Sara. 'My God, how hot was that!' His look more than contributed to the statement.

Sara walked up to him and hugged him. 'That was not what I expected,' she said.

A look of uncertainty filled his face. 'What do you mean?'

'It was amazing, much more than just having sex while lying next to someone.'

'That's true, the undressing was so hot, what a great idea,' he said, taking her hand and heading for the kitchen.

'And we do it again tomorrow night?' Sara said, looking at him.

'No, just meeting them was the plan. But then so was tonight, I guess!' Ed said, holding up a carton of orange juice as if asking if she wanted any.

Sara nodded in acceptance of the drink and said, 'They're first timers, right?'

'Yes, like us, never done it before.'

Sara smiled. 'Like we used to be—we are experienced now.'

Ed smiled back. 'Yes, and what an experience! Julie didn't seem so shy once we got started.'

'I noticed her stroking you as you watched Adam and I.'

'I bloody nearly came in her hand when I saw Adam put your hand on his cock.'

'My God, he was huge, too big for my little body I think,' Sara said as she remembered the vison of him filling Julie with his powerful strokes. Her body twinged as the thought blasted a wave of heat through her again.

That night, it was Sara's turn not to sleep. The vison of Adam filled her thoughts until she finally drifted off, her subconscious continuing her fantasy in her dreams.

Ed had arranged for the meeting with the second couple at the same time at the same hotel. Sara agreed they would also have dinner again before the guests arrived. This couple were Matt and Becky; they were about ten years younger, Ed guessed probably late twenties. He only had the one photo from the messages that were sent. Matt looked tall and skinny and, to be honest, Becky looked the same. She had straight dark hair with a part down the middle. She had penetrating brown eyes and a lovely smile.

'I'm guessing this couple won't be as full on as last night,' Ed said as he sliced a piece of scotch fillet from his plate.

'No, I guess not; we are the experienced ones now,' Sara said, giving Ed a smile.

Ed saw them walk in, instantly recognising the nervous young couple, eyes searching around the bar. He wore jeans and a white t-shirt with an old retro oil logo on it. Matt was tall alright, maybe a basketballer. Becky was tall but still inches under Matt. She wore a white blouse and denim jeans that displayed her perfect buttocks and legs. Ed put them out of their misery, standing to get their attention. Matt smiled as he spotted Ed and took Becky's hand, leading her straight toward Ed and Sara's table. Ed remained standing and waited till they arrived. He shook Matt's hand and then Becky's.

'This is my wife, Sara,' Ed said, pointing to her with an open hand. Sara shook their hands, and they sat down opposite them.

'Have you eaten? Sorry, we came a little early to have a meal,' Ed said.

'Yes, we are all good, take your time, we're early anyway,' Matt said.

Sara looked at Becky, who was clearly struggling to relax.

'So, Becky, are you keen to do something a bit different or has Matt just dragged you along?' Sara said with a warming smile.

'It was actually her idea,' Matt cut in before Becky could answer.

A smile of embarrassment formed on Becky face. 'I thought we should look at something safe that might add a bit of spice to the perfect relationship we have,' Becky said, her confidence emerging.

'That's lovely,' Sara said, looking at them both and trying not to sound like someone's mother.

'Well, this would only be our second time,' Ed said, placing his knife and fork neatly on his plate.

'How was it?' Becky asked, 'You know, the first time?' She looked at Sara.

Sara looked straight at her and said, 'It was amazing, so much hotter than I ever imagined it would be.'

'Wow, really?' Matt said, as he looked over to Becky.

'So Matt, what were you and Becky hoping to get from a few hours with a couple?'

Matt again looked at Becky before he spoke. 'I guess like the ad said, have sex in the same room as another couple, maybe they watch us a little and we watch them, nothing more than that.'

'That's great, keep it simple. I like that. We are much the same, not into swapping,' Ed said.

'When are you looking to have a little fun?' Sara asked.

Again, Matt looked at Becky, and she answered. 'I guess when we find a couple like you that we warm to and feel comfortable with, as soon as we can I suppose.'

Sara again took the lead. 'Would you like to have a little taste of it tonight? We just live nearby.'

This was clearly something Matt and Becky hadn't expected.

'If you want, come over to our place. If it doesn't feel right at any time, just say and we can arrange another time if you prefer. There's no pressure,' Ed said.

Matt looked at Becky and both Ed and Sara saw her nod in approval. Ed told Matt their address and again said they would walk and meet them there.

'If you decide not to come once you get outside, that's okay too,' Sara offered.

The four of them stood and agreed to meet at the house.

'They're pretty young,' Sara commented to Ed once they were outside the hotel.

'They looked a little older in the pictures, but it doesn't matter, does it?'

'Not to me, babe,' Sara said.

When they turned into their street, the road outside their house was empty.

'Maybe they changed their minds?' Sara said.

'Maybe,' Ed said, 'or maybe they're just slow drivers.'

A small white car slowly turned the corner and arrived at the same time as Ed and Sara.

'Looks like the latter,' Ed said softly.

'I grabbed a couple of beers on the way,' Matt said.

'I have a few in the fridge, you didn't need to,' Ed said, opening the door for them.

'Take a seat,' Sara said, pointing to the couch. 'Would you like a wine, Becky?' she called from the kitchen area. The lounge room light was off but the light from the kitchen lit the lounge area with a romantic backlight.

'That would be nice, thank you.'

Ed handed Matt a beer and opened one for himself while Sara poured out two glasses of white wine. It wasn't long before they were all seated on the couch. It was a long three-seater, and with Sara leaning against Ed's chest, the four of them fitted easily. The conversation dragged on slowly, with Ed and Sara gently moving the conversation towards sex. Ed compared tonight with the previous evening. He imagined where they were at the same time, already naked with Julie stroking him. Ed realized in that moment that, as he and Sara were now the experienced couple, he'd need to get things going. With his left hand holding his beer, he started to run his hand over Sara's breasts, and it wasn't long before he could feel her nipples harden and she started to twitch in her seat.

'You like that don't you, babe?' Ed said so they could all hear.

'Mmm, yes, you can tell I do,' Sara said with a cheeky smile.

Ed lifted her top and bra to expose her beautiful breasts to their guests. Ed was sure Matt's eyes nearly fell out of his head. Ed placed his beer on the coffee table and teased both her nipples with his fingers. Sara's eyes were fixed on Becky as she relished in the tingling the nipple stimulation was providing. Matt had slipped his hand inside Becky's blouse and was also filling his hand with her small perky tits. It was now, with her nipples pronounced through the top, that Ed and Sara realized that she wore no bra. Ed undid Sara's bra and removed it and her top. Becky lifted her arms and Matt lifted Becky's top over her head; her breasts were small with matching nipples that were now tight and puckered. Matt's eyes were fixed on Sara's breasts as he continued running his fingers around his own lady's chest.

'Would you like to touch them?' Sara asked him, placing her hands under each breast and lifting them as in offer.

'That would be nice,' Matt said as he and Sara both stood. Ed and Becky watched as Sara walked up to him, allowing his hands to be filled with the delicious flesh. After a few seconds of play, Sara reached down and ran her hand over the swelling in his pants. She felt it grow with each pass of her fingers. Unsure if she was exceeding the boundaries, she reached down, undoing his jeans and releasing him for all to see. Matt's eyes closed as she wrapped her hand around him and stroked the young, throbbing appendage.

Ed watched Becky and could see that she was accepting of the arousing display in front of her. Ed slid over next to Becky and whispered in her ear, 'Would you like me to touch you?'

'Sure, wherever you want,' she said softly, clearly hornier than Ed had expected. He stood and guided her to stand. He reached for the top of her jeans, popped the button, and released the zip. He lowered the tight-fitting denim enough to slip his right hand inside her panties. He found her shaved and dripping wet. He slid his finger between the tight, firm folds of skin and found her firm bud. His finger stroked it gently, up and down. Her eyes were now closed and her body twitching with the waves of heat that were burning their way from between her legs to consume her body.

With his left hand, Ed managed to slide her jeans and panties to the floor without interrupting her pleasure. She assisted and encouraged it. Once Becky had adjusted to the guest between her legs, she reached for Ed's pants and made quick time to have them around his ankles. She took him in her hand and stroked him with enthusiasm.

Matt and Sara were kissing passionately when Sara felt her jeans hit the floor. The energy of this young man was exhilarating. Sara lifted her left leg to rest on the arm of the couch, as Matt easily slipped one, then two fingers inside her. It wasn't long before she was wanting more, especially of what was filling her hand. As she guided him toward her, he removed his fingers to let her caress herself with his knob. With him being tall he had to bend his legs to assist, but his fitness made it effortless. He felt her position his knob at her opening and, without thought, just reaction, pushed his knob inside her. The little movements he could manage were all Sara needed to know she wanted all of him. Sara looked over to Ed, their eyes met. He nodded approval.

She whispered in Matt's ear, 'Lay on the mat.' The shagpile rug that adorned most of the lounge room floor was soft on Matt's back as he watched Sara step astride his body and lower herself onto him. She took him all in the first motion and she felt him tighten as the pleasure enveloped him.

Ed looked over to see his wife, for the first time in their married life, fuck another man. The emotion that filled his mind was nothing like he expected. Not jealousy, but rather a feeling of compersion, the pleasure he felt seeing her enjoy herself. Becky had now laid back on the couch, her legs spread in invitation. Ed needed no further encouragement, lowering himself on top of her; his lips meeting hers at the same time that his knob parted the tight folds and entered her body. She wrapped her legs around him as he fucked her with vigour, her tight pussy raising his burning arousal. The sound of Becky's orgasm was more than he could stand; he'd been on the edge for the last few minutes. He pumped Becky hard as he exploded inside her. Her own orgasm matched his pounding perfectly and she screamed with the rush of ecstasy that burst inside her.

Ed looked down at the beautiful young woman he had just made love to. Her relaxed and contented look was probably the most gorgeous thing he'd ever seen. He lay above her, in awe of her beauty. He was still relatively hard and full inside her. He rocked slightly and she jumped, smiling at him and pulling him tight to her to stop him moving. Ed had almost forgotten the fact that his wife was still riding the young basketballer by his side. Ed slowly removed himself from Becky and sat upright. Becky let her head fall against Ed's chest as they both watched Sara and Matt.

'Let's help them,' Ed whispered to Becky.

Not really knowing what he meant, she stood as well, and they took the two steps toward the lovers on the rug. From behind, Ed could see Matt filling his wife with youthful and powerful thrusts. Ed knelt behind Sara and started to kiss her neck as she rode the basketballer below her. Ed could tell she was close and his fingers now squeezing her nipples would be all it would take. He watched as she built to her moment and soon let out her seductive roar that he knew came from deep down whenever her orgasm was this big. Becky had placed one of her nipples in Matt's mouth and that, combined with the older woman squeezing his cock as she came, was more than enough for him to fill Sara with his eruptive juices.

Sara fell to Matt's chest, her head next to his. Ed could now clearly see Matt inside her. Again, the feeling was of arousal, not any twinge of jealousy. The naked Becky came to stand next to Ed and he put his arm around her. They watched as the lovers on the floor slowly separated and a smile beamed from everyone's face. With Becky still under his arm, Ed said, 'Well, that was just fucking amazing—not what I was expecting at all.'

His excitement was bursting through him. Sara stood, Matt's pleasure starting to run down her right thigh. She took in the sight of her husband with a cute, just fucked, twenty-something woman in his arms. She looked at him; their eyes locked for just a second before she said, 'We don't get to keep them, darling.'

Ed smiled and said, 'But she's so cute,' squeezing Becky tighter.

Sara smiled back and they all started to dress.

Ed and Sara had become a true swinging 'lifestyle' couple.

A Boat Trip

Kate sat staring out the window, her pen tapping her teeth. *What sexy experience could I possibly create for him?* she thought.

Tim was her part-time lover—not a husband, not even a boyfriend. She didn't want a long-term partner, and he certainly could never be tied down—never again anyway. A month ago, while having sex, Kate mentioned that she would like to try a threesome, with two men. She knew Tim was completely straight and had very little desire to be involved with another man other than when they found themselves at a swing club, though even then he kept his distance.

To her surprise, he put the little event together and 'bang'— Kate had a threesome with Tim and a distant friend of his. It blew her mind. Kate had every desired fantasy realised on that afternoon. The two men wore her out. But now, it was time for her to repay the favour and surprise him. A two-girl threesome wouldn't be that special, they had already had quite a few of those, as Kate did enjoy occasional sex with women.

But, when you least expect it, ideas and solutions can become vividly apparent.

Kate's brilliant, out of the blue idea landed at the dinner table one evening. It was in fact Tim himself who unknowingly offered the idea.

Kate had been experimenting with cooking up new dishes and had invited Tim to try her latest: chicken, mushroom, and parmesan parcels, with a warm smashed potato and green vegetable salad.

'This is amazing, Kate, I love it. It's another recipe I'm going to grab from you!'

'Thanks. It worked out better than I expected,' she said happily.

'It's absolutely delicious. I love being your guinea pig. I haven't had the chance for a decent home-cooked meal for a couple of weeks now, as things are getting frantic at work again. It seems that every client we have has suddenly decided to revamp their marketing plans or have planned some new major event—it's out of control.'

'What's landing right now? Anything I can do to help?' she asked.

'I've got a trip to Sydney in a couple of weeks for an event there, quotes for three conferences here in Adelaide, all happening in March to align with delegates coming here for the Fringe Festival, and of course, the usual additional work that comes with the Fringe itself. It's the expected lead up for "Mad March" time in Adelaide, with so many festivals and events, but somehow this year it's crazy!

'I've also got a new property development client. This looks like it'll be pretty good and a bit more regular than the one-off events. But I've got to do a promo video and advertisement for a new housing development at Mount Barker. It needs to be finished by the end of next month.'

'No wonder you have no time to cook! Hey, about that video and commercial, I've got Bec doing some filming for the Open Gardens show around the state over the next couple of weeks. Would you like me to ask her about the filming of the estate for you?'

'Bec? Which firm is she with?'

'You know Bec! Rebecca Smythe. You introduced her to me. She works at Adelaide Digital Media with Holly McIntyre.'

'Oh, God, yes! The tall one with a great smile, who works as Holly's producer. Now there is a delicacy I would enjoy.'

'Bec?'

'No, Holly. I'm sure Bec's lovely and she's certainly attractive, but Holly is one of those women who's just got so much sex appeal, it drips from her. I don't know if it's just me but when she's on set, I struggle to focus on my work. A real ten out of ten!'

'You are delightfully incorrigible, Tim my dear!'

Then a little frown crossed her brow. *That was it. Holly could be the gift for him!* she thought.

Kate blinked back into the moment and said, 'Okay, let me think how I can coordinate Bec to do the promo shoot for you. It should be quite easy.'

'Sorry if I went on about Holly.'

Kate started laughing. 'Not at all. Besides, I can't control how you feel, and I want you to tell me, everything. Hell, I'd do her too! Tim, your sexy thoughts have given me so much pleasure! Now come on, you can come help me and work your charm to clear this table!'

It was Tim's turn to smile.

'Hurry up and bring me those dishes, I've just decided that you are my dessert. You can give me a taste of what you'd like to do to Holly, if you ever had the chance!'

They both laughed, loaded the dishwasher, and tidied the kitchen, before they found Kate's bed to enjoy their final, most delicious course of the day.

Kate was excited. She'd thought of the perfect gift. Tim had no idea, but Bec and Holly had shared with her over a few quiet wines that on rare, opportune occasions, they enjoyed a bit of girl-on-girl fun. Sometimes another girlfriend would join them. It was just some sexy play, and very private, especially as they had high-profile positions and both were married. Kate assumed the information may well have been an indirect offer to join them one day.

The next morning, the first call she made was to Bec.

'Hi dear lady. How is the schedule going for the Open Days?'

'Hi Kate, it's looking good. We have a few gaps, but its fine if we have a couple of hours here and there to wait around. Gives the crew a break anyway.'

'Any chance I could ask you a big favour? I've got a special treat in return if you and Holly are keen.'

'Sure,' Bec said.

Kate proceeded to give her the outline for Tim's property promo.

'That sounds simple. We can easily do that just after we go to Macclesfield.'

'Brilliant! I'll send you the details once Tim gives them to me. Hey, I've got another favour to ask. It's sort of tied up with this. Are you interested in a more intimate type of contra payment for this job?'

'I'm intrigued! Maybe? Spill!'

Kate softened her voice so no one could hear, 'Well, you know how you told me that sometimes you girls have little weekends away?'

'Yes, been hoping you might join us one day.'

'I will, that's a certain, but anyway, have you ever thought about having… shall we say, a man watches you, like a boat captain?'

'No, but tell me more,' Bec said, sounding interested.

'You know Tim Pearce, right?'

'Yes, of course.'

'He has done some amazing things for me lately and I would like to do something special and sexy for him, and he does think you and Holly are smoking hot, by the way.'

'Does he really? That's nice to hear! So, what were you thinking, maybe topless and a little girl stuff?'

'That would be fantastic. It would make his day, and mine.'

'Would you be joining in, Kate?'

'Try and stop me!' Kate was busting from the excitement.

'I'll talk to Holly, but it's a yes from me.'

'You are the best, Bec my dear.'

'Kate, you are delightful. Now, you said he was going to be a boat captain, do we have a location? It needs to be discreet, of course; our husbands don't have a good sense of humour.'

'I know. I've thought about that too. Tim owns a 48 ft Riviera, berthed at North Haven. I'm sure being taken for a boat cruise with a solo captain and a smorgasbord of delights would be quite normal for ladies of our calibre, don't you think?'

'It's perfect. Tell Tim we'll do the filming for him, and he can take us for a lunch 'n' booze cruise on his boat on the first day the weather is good as payment, the rest can be a surprise. How does that sound?'

'Perfect. You're a legend. Thanks so much. By the way, I'm going to be looking forward to seeing a bit more of you, Bec!'

'Okay, get going, I'm starting to get horny at the thought.'

'Thanks Bec, bye!'

She dialled the next number to kick start phase two of her plan.

Tim's phone rang. 'Hi sexy, what's up?'

'Tim, about that promo video you want to do for that new housing division at Mt Barker?'

'Yes?' Tim said, drawing out the reply.

'I just did a deal with Holly and Rebecca to produce it for you in their spare time at work.'

'Holly McIntyre?'

'Yes, Holly McIntyre and Rebecca Smyth. They said they'd do it, in return for a day on your boat. It needs to be the first best weather day after they finish, if that's alright?'

'That's more than alright, it's fantastic. That's a deal!' Tim replied with enthusiasm. 'Let me know what they need.'

'Email me through the brief and location details. I'll take it from there.'

'Kate, thank you. I really appreciate it, and I especially like the payment terms. I'd love to take you all on a cruise, I haven't had the Riv out in ages!'

'Always happy to please, Mr Pearce!' she responded cheekily.

Tim already had most of the footage he needed for the promo, so it really wasn't a lot of work for the girls to produce both a thirty and sixty second promo videos for TV.

He was more interested in securing the date for the contra payment!

The filming for Tim's client and Kate's Open Day went without a hitch and was completed within the one day. This was great, as it gave Kate, Bec, and Holly the next day free.

Kate phoned Tim.

'Hi! Everything's gone brilliantly today with the filming and your work is done too. Bec and Holly are with me now, just tidying up. It gives us tomorrow free, so are you up for a little cruise tomorrow? The weather looks perfect.'

'Absolutely, I'll just shuffle a couple of appointments. Shall we get an early start, have a cruise down to Glenelg, grab some lunch, and cruise back? Would 10.30 a.m. work?'

'Hang on, I'll just ask the girls, I'm with them now.'

Bec and Holly were already nodding.

'It looks like you have a date at the helm with three stunning women then, Mr Pearce!'

'Brilliant. Can't wait! See you at 10.30 a.m. tomorrow then, with the champagne. Say hi to the girls!'

Tim arrived early at the marina to remove the covers, give the cruiser a bit of a wipe over, and check that everything was going to run smoothly. He started the engines, checked the fuel, and all seemed good. As the engines warmed up, he went about cleaning the sea spray from the windows and seats.

He'd loaded the three bottles of champagne that Kate had recommended for his guests into the fridge and a few beers as well. He expected Kate might join him in a beer, knowing she wasn't really a champagne lover, but he'd brought some rosé and a bottle of red, just in case.

At 10.30 a.m. sharp he glanced at his watch, then looked up to see the three women, all dressed in white, walking side by side, almost matched in stride. His mind slowed their walk, imagining Charlie's Angels were arriving. He could see Kate pointing toward the cruiser and then all three started waving eagerly to Tim.

I can already tell this is going to be a great day, Tim thought, as he welcomed and escorted them onto the deck.

'Welcome aboard, ladies,' he said as he kissed the cheek of each of them in turn. 'Make yourselves comfortable and feel free to look around. Kate will organise a drink, while I get us underway.'

'Wow, Tim, this is not what I expected. What a fabulous boat.' said Holly, as she peeked downstairs at the galley and front bedroom.

Tim really didn't know Rebecca very well, only having met her a couple of times on shoots around town, but she was cute and maybe a couple of years older than the other two. Her smile was a lightbulb though. As for Holly, *my God, she is just fucking gorgeous,* flashed into his thoughts. Tim was barely able to respond to her first words as she complimented his boat.

There aren't many women in the world that could make Tim's heart miss a beat, but Holly McIntyre did, every time.

Kate had rallied to pour drinks for Bec and Holly and handed Tim a beer, before grabbing herself a drink.

Kate called out, 'I'll grab the stern ropes if you want?'

Tim threw her a look of wide surprise and a grin. 'Sure, thanks. I forgot you had experience as a deckie,' he said as he restarted the engines.

He disconnected the shore power and moved to quickly untie the bow ropes and tuck up the fenders. He glanced aft to see that Kate had sorted the ropes and fenders both adeptly at the rear of the boat. They were ready. He selected 'forward' on the port engine and a touch of reverse on the starboard to help pull the vessel away from the mooring. Once straight, he engaged forward on both engines and idled away, heading for the marina entrance and toward the open sea.

He really loved this part of any trip, the first moments of the sea breeze in his face, the excitement of his guests, and the throbbing of the two big turbo diesel engines as they slowly warmed at idle speed.

Kate walked up to stand next to Tim at the helm; he was staring at the waters ahead. It had been years since she'd been on the water. The spray, the rock and the pitch, the breeze, and the blue hues of the sky and sea were everything she loved. She glanced at Tim. It looked like he was doing the same. She started to relax.

Once out of the marina, Tim advanced the throttles, letting the big diesels loose. The whine of the turbos increased and the cruiser lifted its nose. The thirteen-tonne beast accelerated out into the wide-open Southern Ocean. Tim headed due west, just ocean for as far as you could see. He could hear the laughter coming from his gorgeous guests. They had cruised out for about a couple of miles or so when Tim spotted Graham, his boating buddy, out enjoying some fishing with a few of his mates. Now seen, Tim gave a quick wave and slowed to pull up alongside.

Graham was with his three mates, rods sitting idle waiting for an unsuspecting fish to commit suicide on their hooks. Tim had three ladies. It didn't take long for the fishermen to realise that Tim certainly had the better catch and the fishing rods in Graham's boat were quickly abandoned. Graham dropped his fenders so they could raft together.

Tim shared a beer with the boys, who lamely attempted to banter and flirt shamelessly with the three women. The girls were enjoying the mid-ocean attention and were probably more flirtatious than they should have been.

'Guys, sorry, but it's time for us to head off, we're heading down to Glenelg for lunch. Good luck with the fishing.'

Laughs, bravado comments, and lamenting bellows from Graham and his mates serenaded them and faded behind as Tim fired up the engines and headed off down the coast.

While Kate, in usual style, had brought cheese and other simple treats to share, the sun and flowing champagne, beer, and wine rendered all desperate for more to eat.

'Hey ladies, I've got an idea; why don't we grab a couple of pizzas to share? I can order ahead, dock briefly, and run up and collect them?'

'That sounds perfect,' said Kate, with Bec and Holly nodding approval.

Pizza was hastily ordered, and Tim was soon mooring his large boat against a somewhat flimsy jetty at Semaphore. He quickly climbed up the jetty ladder and took off for the pizza shop. The pizzas were ready, and he was soon on his way back. While he was quite hungry and wanted to offer the girls a hot fresh pizza, his speed was spurred on by fear that his knots that held the thirteen-tonne boat could slip loose and he'd find it drifting out to sea, or worse, beached on the sand. To his relief, it was all exactly where he'd left it—the boat and the three beautiful women.

He handed the pizzas to Kate as he stepped aboard and restarted the engines before untying the ropes. Tim sighed with relief. It was a smooth launch and they set sail back out to sea. It took no time at all for them to devour their lunch. While they ate and drank, he headed out to sea before turning north to head back towards the marina.

Kate replenished glasses and placed another beer in the skipper's hand. 'Just one an hour,' he said back to her with a smile.

The three girls had found a spot on the front deck to soak in the sun and warm breeze. Once seated, each took off their tops; it appeared to Tim that this may have been secretly arranged while he was collecting the pizzas.

Wow, what an impressive trio. Graham and his fishing buddies would never believe me if I told them about this! This was a dream come true. *Holly McIntyre, topless on my boat.* A smile formed on Tim's face.

The three women were still positioned with their backs facing Tim. He heard Bec suggest a 'true or false' game. 'The conventional type?' Kate asked.

'No, of course not, that would be boring. Just a little drinking game with a twist! We each make a statement about something unexpected that we've done, like a sexual experience, while pouring some champagne on our nipples. The first person to get whether it's true or false gets to lick it off.'

'I'm keen,' Kate said. Holly and Bec gave each other a subtle wink, loving that Kate was so eager to join in.

Bec started. 'I sucked my boss in the first week of my new job,' she said.

'False!' Holly said instantly. 'I'm your boss, and it took months before you sucked me!' All girls started rolling with laughter, before Holly moved over to Bec, poured the bubbles over her, before her tongue and lips rolled over her nipples and breasts.

'Holly, it's your turn,' Bec said.

'I've always wanted to be watched while I'm being fucked by a man,'

Kate looked at Holly as she spoke. She whispered hesitantly, 'True…?'

Their eyes locked for a split second. Holly nodded. 'Kate, you're right. It's okay, taste away…' she said as she took the champagne bottle, spilling enough of the bubbles to flow down from her breasts to between her legs.

Kate moved herself to be in tongue's reach of Holly's breasts. Just as she leant forward, cupping the delicate rounded handful of flesh in her hands, Kate murmured, 'I think Tim needs to join the next round.' She threw him a knowing look, before she sipped on Holly's erect nipple.

Tim could sense this was going in one direction and said, 'I think I need to take us a bit further out. Hang on.' He advanced the throttles and turned west to take them further offshore, to a spot where any other hint of life would be a horizon distance away. 'We could drop anchor and all escape the sun, perhaps you could take this game below?' he said.

Kate, who was now quite a few drinks in, moved over to sit on a step next to the helm, and without notice, swiftly slid Tim's shorts to his ankles. She'd decided it was definitely time for him to be included in their fun. Using only her lips, she took his penis into her mouth, starting to suck him in full view of the other girls. Within seconds, Rebecca joined her, adding her tongue and lips to help pleasure him. It was nearly too much for Tim to fathom, let alone control the vessel at the same time.

With two women sucking him, he could barely concentrate on driving the boat for any longer. As Kate and Rebecca were supping on him, he watched as Holly stood, slid off her knickers, and then proceeded to slip behind each of the girls in turn, removing the last flimsy pieces of their clothing. Knowing his desires and absolute pleasures, Kate took one long last drawing suck of him as she withdrew to move aside to sit at the top of the steps.

All three women were right there, naked and in his full view. Rebecca, sensing the cue, repositioned to spread Kate's legs, immediately starting to suck on her, licking her pussy with gulps of passion. Holly was now standing a little behind Tim, watching the other two women over his shoulder. Holly helped Tim step out of his shorts and jocks, then, instinctively, her hands started to run around Tim's butt cheeks and up and down his back, her own arousal rising from the delicious display in front of them. It was barely a minute or two before Kate came, crying out with resounding notes.

Tim had cut the engines and dropped the anchor with a speed that would impress the navy. 'I need to get you ladies out of the sun! Let's head below,' he said, gesturing a leading hand to all three to descend to the cabin below deck.

Holly took Kate by the hand and pulled her close; there was a momentary look before Holly kissed her. Rebecca had made herself comfortable on the bed, stretched out naked, touching herself as she watched Holly and Kate. She gave Tim a smile, a smile that left him in no doubt as to its meaning. Tim crawled between her spread legs and slipped easily inside her. Rebecca closed her eyes, arched, and relished as he fucked her. Rebecca came, and Tim had to use all his might to not be joining her. Once he felt her relax, he withdrew himself, and he and Rebecca watched Holly and Kate enthusiastically touch each other.

Tim stood to take a much-needed swig of his beer. Holly and Kate had found the bed and the three girls were all over each other.

He rested his bottle on the table and climbed onto the bed to nestle amidst the three horny women. They kissed, sucked, and licked him in every way possible. After another drink break, Kate's fingers found Holly's pussy. Holly had her eyes closed and was utterly immersed in the moment. Tim was watching closely and ran his fingers along her chest. Holly opened her eyes and looked at him with a expression of total bliss.

Holly's legs fell further apart; her hips rising, she looked at him with a look that told him his dreams were about to come true. Tim had been in lust with this woman for many years. He looked at Kate and she moved aside.

Holly's eyes watched him as he lifted himself above her; her lips were slightly apart, her legs spread wide, and she held a look of desperation.

He slid between Holly's legs and pushed up against her. He paused for no other reason than to savour the moment. Then he entered the body of this beautiful angel, deep and hard, her legs immediately wrapping around him. With her hands on his butt cheeks, she gripped him, bringing him even closer to her, deeper with every thrust. Her head fell back, her eyes closed as the moan of ecstasy filled her from her fingertips to her toes. He also came with a force that matched her own shuddering orgasm. His fantasy and her desperate need were fulfilled in that moment, totally in unison.

Tim gave her a gentle kiss on the lips and whispered, 'Thank you, Holly, that was a dream come true for me.' Tim and Holly's eyes did not leave each other till they were once again separated, each dragging every emotion from what was the climax to an amazing day.

Kate glimpsed their exchange of looks, and while a twinge of jealousy pinged fleetingly, it disappeared behind the joy she felt for having arranged the day, giving Tim his long-time fantasy goddess and remembering that by tomorrow, it would all just be a fantastic, shared memory. This was all for him, and the joy she received knowing how much he enjoyed it completely overrode any jealousy.

Holly climbed off the bed, wandered to find her drink, and ascended to the deck to find her clothes.

Tim glanced over to the bed to see Kate sitting there, clearly having been watching them. He knew she would have mixed feelings about what had just happened. Kate had gifted him so much pleasure today, yet he'd barely touched her. He swallowed hard, but then caught the knowing smile and glistening eyes, filled with the satisfaction that she'd given him. She knew she'd achieved the best gift possible for the man who had everything. He smiled back.

The next minutes were strangely quiet as Rebecca, Kate, and Tim all moved, grabbing remnants of quickly discarded clothing, each piece restoring them closer to their daily lives back on shore.

With everyone dressed and once again back on deck, Kate rallied in true hostess fashion, now fetching them drinks of water, and offering around chocolates and fresh fruit treats for the cruise back to the marina. It was a relatively quiet trip back, with all pensive about the escapades of their afternoon and soaking in the sound of the two big diesels humming and the crisp, cool colours of the vista view of the coast. As they approached the marina, Kate helped by collecting up all the empties and bags.

Once moored, Kate helped Tim secure the boat while the two girls ordered a taxi and prepared to disembark.

When the cab arrived, Rebecca was the first to initiate the goodbyes. She gave Tim and Kate each a quick kiss, exclaiming, 'Thank you for a great day.'

Holly kissed Kate, with a soft whisper of, 'Thank you. You are a truly generous and unique friend, Kate, I hope we get to see you again on one of our days away,' and then turned to Tim, offering a quick kiss and a subtle lingering look. Kate saw the sparkle in her eyes as she looked back at Tim just before turning and jumping into the cab.

As the taxi drove away, Tim blurted, 'God, her husband is one hell of a lucky man!'

'He certainly is, but not my cup of tea—more arsehole than gentleman, I think, but Holly somehow tolerates him,' Kate replied.

Tim nodded and then paused. He drew in a breath and turned to look at Kate closely. He took her hand and placed his hand around her waist, turning her to face him. 'I can't believe what you did for me today. You are the absolute best! Hey, let's not go yet. Let's grab some dinner, those pizzas were a while ago now.'

Kate nodded and their hands entwined as they turned to walk along the esplanade.

Approaching the restaurant, Tim said, 'You struggled a bit with me and Holly, hey?'

'Just a little, but the pleasure of seeing you enjoy her far exceeded the pain,' she said, looking at him casually.

He squeezed her hand a little tighter as they walked into the Tavern.

'You are one in a million babe,' he said as he opened the restaurant door.

The Massage

The siren sounded to end the football game, and Georgie could tell that her son's team had done well. Although it was an old collegian team and her son was now twenty-four years old, she couldn't help being involved with the club. Her son, Nathan—or Nat as he preferred—still lived at home with her, but he was a man now and had a girlfriend and a great job as a plumber. Georgie was helping in the canteen during the game and, being a professional massage therapist, would help if any of the boys were injured or just strained a muscle during or after the game.

Georgie was one of those parents who was always involved in her son's sport and had been since his primary school days. Nat's father had left them quite a few years ago now, basically as soon as Nat had finished school. He'd found a younger lady who was willing to perform and be involved in all the fantasies that a man having a midlife crisis craved. They were a happy married couple up until then, and Georgie had to admit to herself on those lonely nights that she, just maybe, could have tried a little harder to accommodate her husband's growing sexual needs. But that option was long gone now, so Georgie had settled for the single life living with her grown-up son. With her friends and massage work she was kept busy and made enough to live comfortably in the little country town.

Georgie was packing up the canteen now, and if no one required any massage treatment she would head over to help out behind the bar.

'Hello Mrs. Jones,' Georgie heard from the canteen's back door.

'Hello Jonno, sounds like you won today.'

'Yes, by three goals.' Ben said.

Ben Johnson was called 'Jonno' by everyone, so much so, a lot of people didn't actually know his real name. Ben had been in Nat's classes since they started school and Georgie knew his parents well. She had known Ben since he was five years old; he and Nat had started school on the same day. He wasn't one of Nat's closest mates, but they certainly had each other's backs on the footy field. Ben was probably six foot two and played full forward. He was muscly, tall, dark, and handsome—probably any young girls' idea of the perfect man.

'Any chance of a quick massage, Mrs. Jones? My thighs are burning.'

'Of course, Jonno, I'll just finish up here. I'll be five minutes.'

Georgie remembered the last time she massaged him. She had noticed he had got a little aroused, which for boys in tight footy shorts is a little hard to hide. She'd decided to place a towel over them now to help a little with their modesty. She locked the canteen door and made her way to the change rooms. There was a little room just inside the clubroom building that they used for any massages or first aid that prevented Georgie needing to go into where the boys would be changing or showering. The door was open when she arrived and Jonno sat on the massage table, still in his football gear, swinging his legs. The room was dark, and she turned on the light and closed the door.

'So, a little tight on your thighs, Jonno?' Georgie said, putting down her bag on the bench that ran along the far wall. She opened the cupboard below and took out a towel and massage oil.

'Okay, on your back, young man, and let's see what we have.'

Jonno lay back, resting his head on the little pillow that Georgie slid under his head. The muscles in his legs were perfectly formed, and after just kicking five goals for the team were pumped and hard. Georgie spread his legs slightly and poured a little oil on his hairy right leg. She reached for the towel from the benchtop.

'We won't need a towel, Mrs. Jones, it's just my thighs.'

'Okay,' Georgie said, placing it back on the bench behind her, as she nervously recalled what happened last time. She started with small deep tissue movements from the knee, working her way up. Ben complained a little as she found the sore areas. As she worked her way up his thigh, she couldn't help but notice the bulge in his tight shorts— she was a woman, after all. The nylon football shorts left very little to the imagination and if there was any movement in that area it was obvious.

Georgie now moved over to do the same treatment to his left leg, and Ben had certainly started to react to the attractive middle-aged woman touching him. Her long, wavy blonde hair had been released from the hair tie that she wore while in the canteen. It framed her face beautifully and made her appear much younger than her forty-eight years. Georgie decided to hurry the treatment along to prevent any further embarrassment for either of them. She tried to focus on the area of treatment but found her eyes looking at the increasing bulge in his shorts. *My God, he must be three inches longer than my husband,* she thought.

She was sure she felt his hand touch her bum as she started to move away.

'I hope that helps, Jonno,' Georgie said, with her back to him as he slowly removed himself from the massage table. She resisted looking at him knowing his erection would be very obvious now that he was standing, and may have even escaped from his footy shorts.

'Thank you, Mrs Jones, I feel much better,' Ben said, grabbing his training bag which he would now use to cover himself in front of his teammates. The door closed behind him, and Georgie reflected on how this incident had affected her. She'd had plenty of men get erections while she massaged them before; it is quite an intimate practice, after all. However, this time, what concerned her more was that she had felt a little something in herself. It had been so long—years—since she'd had a man, and the fact that this young handsome man got a hard on from her touch did excite her a little. *Maybe it's time I find someone?* she thought.

She packed up the room and headed for the bar to finish off the day serving the players and supporters their last drinks. It was only half an hour later when Ben found himself in front of her, ready to order a drink.

'Jonno, what would you like, my dear?' Georgie asked, realizing all too late that what she just said could be taken the wrong way.

Ben just looked at her for a second before saying, 'A beer please, Mrs. Jones.' He held out a ten dollar note and said, 'You made me feel good, thank you.' The look in his eyes caused her to blush.

'I'm glad to hear that, Jonno,' she said as she handed him his change. As she placed the coins in his hand, he let his thumb drag back along the top of her hand as she pulled it away. It made her glance up at him and their eyes locked. Georgie's heart pounded before she quickly turned away to serve another customer. She asked the next person for his order, but her eyes kept flicking back to watch Ben as he walked away. *My God, what just happened?* she thought, now aware she had no idea what her new customer just ordered.

The next week went quickly for Georgie, but each night as she lay in bed, she found herself replaying the scene with Ben. She tried to keep what had happened last Saturday in perspective. As soon as any thoughts of Ben with an erection laying in front of her appeared in her mind, she would recall his parents and the little boy that started primary school with her son, nineteen years ago.

The following Saturday was another home game and Georgie was once again back in the canteen selling pies, cakes, and drinks.

It was a busy day for her, and the sound of the full-time siren was a relief. Without a thought she started packing up, when she heard from the canteen's back door, 'Mrs. Jones, any chance of another quick massage?'

It was Ben again and she really didn't know what to say. She was sure that the relief from his tight muscles was not his primary objective.

'Alright, Jonno, but it will need to be quick because the bar is already busy today.'

'I really appreciate it, Mrs. Jones. I'll meet you in the room.'

'Okay, I'll be there shortly,' Georgie said, with mixed feelings flooding her body.

When Georgie arrived at the little massage room, the door was closed. She opened it to find Ben on the table and a white towel across his waist. She was a little taken aback, but she massaged hundreds of people a month, *this is just one more, isn't it?* She closed the door behind her and retrieved the oil from its place in the cupboard.

'So, Jonno, what do we need to focus on today?'

'My groin, Mrs. Jones, I think I strained it.'

Georgie's throat closed over. 'Okay, but like I said I can only spare a few minutes.'

'That's fine, I removed my shorts to make it easier and save time.'

Georgie felt she was stepping into the lion's den. Whatever happened from here was not going to be good.

'Lay back then and let me see.'

Ben lay his head back and she watched him close his eyes. She poured some oil on her hands and slid her fingers under the towel. He'd not just removed his shorts, but his underwear as well. She could feel the tight adductor muscle that ran through the crease between his leg and pelvis. It was only seconds before the towel was elevated by his erection.

She paused, not quite knowing what to do, as the towel was no longer covering him fully. It had been a long time since she had seen a man hard or ever seen one this big, and her hand was now only millimeters away from it. A heat flushed through her body, and a tingle rang out between her legs. Before she could react, she felt a hand on hers, a warm hand. His fingers slipped between hers, covered in oil, and before she knew what was happening, Ben had placed her hand on him and wrapped her fingers around his pulsing thick flesh. She tried to resist but his strength and her hesitation had her already stroke him twice.

The towel had completely fallen away now, and she watched, almost in slow motion, her hand running along his engorged penis. For only a split second, the woman in her wanted him, to take his hard cock and pleasure him fully. But she called out adamantly, 'Ben, stop it!' as she pulled her hand away. She didn't know what else to do or say, so she grabbed her bag and quickly left the room, leaving him naked on the table.

She rushed to her car, jumped in, and locked the door. She put her head in her hands. 'My God, what just happened?' she said out loud to herself. She recalled the feel and vision of her hand as he ran it the full length of him; she could feel his knob, so hard and defined. The muscles that held it so firm bulging as her fingers slid over its length. 'I won't be able to look at him again,' she said.

Ben had showered and dressed and was now sitting at a table with two other teammates when Georgie arrived at the bar to help.

'I can do this,' she muttered to herself as she placed her bag under the counter and started to serve the next waiting customer. Ben didn't approach the bar for the remainder of that night, but Georgie couldn't avoid a glance in his direction between customers. Ben was gone when Georgie helped close the bar and her biggest fear was that he would be standing next to her car as she left to drive home, but thankfully that didn't happen. Georgie drove home with the thought of what happened with Ben still playing over and over in her mind.

Her first thought was, *did she respond correctly, did she respond fast enough?* The fact that he had managed to have her stroke him twice before she pulled her hand away may have given him the impression that she couldn't decide whether to keep going. The thought of him, firm in her hand, brought back that tingle. She tried to push that thought from her mind, but the image was too powerful. She arrived home and the distraction of unloading the car almost cleared her mind of him.

It wasn't until she was in bed and turned out the light that the vision again filled her mind. She played it over and over—the two strokes she had performed against her will. It wasn't long before she imagined three strokes, and more. Her body was reacting naturally to the thought, and she soon found herself quite aroused. Her strong masseurs' fingers found her wetness bringing her a sense of calm and pleasure. She pictured him laying back, his eyes closed as she massaged the part of him that he wanted to be soothed the most. She imagined him moan as her hand clamped tighter, making him stiffen even more as his pleasure built inside. She imagined him call out her name, not Mrs. Jones but Georgie, as she saw his creamy juices explode and cover her hand in thick, warm fluid. Her fingers were now moving in a frenzy over and around her clitoris.

She came in that moment, the vision of him still full in her hand as the last drop of his cum pulsed from his swollen knob. Every muscle in her body clenched as the wave of ecstasy burned through her. As her panting breaths subsided, she imagined Jonno watching her as she masturbated and came. This fantasy alone had her there at the orgasmic tipping point again. This time the pleasure was so intense it almost hurt.

That's never happened before, she thought as she gently fell back to earth, each muscle slowly releasing the unyielding grip on her. She lay back exhausted, her legs still spread, and her hands flopped by her side. She was completely spent.

Somehow, it all seemed alright now. She knew she would never be able to massage him again at the footy club, but she was comfortable with the thought that this gorgeous young man found her so arousing and attractive. She fell asleep with a sense of relief that she had somehow justified and satisfied herself with the whole event.

Georgie woke the next morning and Ben hardly entered her mind. She still had a delicious tingle from her two orgasms last night and it was putting a little extra step in her walk and a smile on her face. She decided in that moment that it just might be time that she found someone to bring that enjoyment to her life on a regular basis. She was a very attractive woman and had many offers for dates. But it was a small town, and she knew everyone's business and history and they hers. She didn't want anyone's discarded husband, or the talk that would filter through the town as a result. She may need to look a little further or maybe move to the city. But what she did know was that Ben had opened a door that had been closed since her husband had left.

She made a coffee and as she sipped the first taste of her morning essential, she flicked open her laptop computer and saw that her first massage was at 9.00 a.m. She loved the new online booking system that most of her clients had now learnt to use. It saved her needing a receptionist, or worse, having to stop her treatment to answer the phone. She could see she had six one-hour sessions today, with the last at five o'clock.

She stepped into the bathroom, and for the first time in a while had a good look at her naked body in the mirror. She ran her fingers down the sides of her face and tucked her long wavy blonde hair behind her ears. Her breasts were still full, although not exactly where they used to be, but hey, she was only eighteen months away from turning fifty! With that, she gave them a tick. Her tummy was flat, which was probably what she was most proud of. Her eyes wandered lower, and she decided a little trimming was overdue. She reached for the trimmer from the bathroom cabinet, turned it on, and slowly started the manicure. Again, she felt a little sense of arousal as she trimmed herself in the mirror. Was it the buzzing so close to her still heightened area or was it the fact that she could be trimming for an unknown man to have his way with her? Either way, she was again moist between her legs. She turned the trimmer around and ran the handle between her folds, the vibration sent a flash of excitement through her as she recalled her fantasy of Ben last night.

'Okay,' she said, placing the trimmer back in the cabinet. She turned on the taps and stepped into the shower. She decided that a purchase of a more appropriate stimulator was definitely on the cards next time she was in the city.

It was a quarter to five when she heard her last client arrive in the waiting room. With only her and Nat living there, the big house easily provided the two spare rooms required for her work. Nat spent most nights at his girlfriend's house these days, but he was home enough for it to feel like he still lived there. Georgie had finished the treatment of Mrs. Wilson, who was a regular each week. Georgie stepped into the kitchen from the massage room to wash her hands and give Mrs. Wilson time to dress. When she re-entered, Mrs. Wilson was ready, and Georgie opened the door for her to exit through the waiting room. As Georgie followed her out, her eyes fell upon Ben sitting reading a magazine. He looked up at her, a smile forming on his face. Her look of shock was obvious. Georgie offered a slightly flustered goodbye to Mrs. Wilson, before closing the door. She turned to Ben.

'Jonno, what are you doing here?' she asked, in the calmest tone she could muster.

'I'm your next client. I'm sorry, I made up a name in case you wouldn't see me.'

Ben was standing now, his height a good few inches above hers. He took a step towards her. She went to step back but didn't.

'Jonno, I can't do this. *We* can't do this.'

Georgie looked out the window to the street and could see the town folk walking along minding their business.

'Come in here,' she offered, wanting to secret him inside before someone walking past saw them in a deep discussion.

Ben walked into the massage room and Georgie closed the door. The room was still quite dark, with only three thick scented candles lighting the room.

'Now, Ben Johnson, you can't expect me to let what happened at the club ever happen again, you know that, right?'

'Mrs. Jones, I'm sorry about that, but you are all I can think about. You touching me like that was the best thing that has ever happened in my life.' Ben looked to the floor, and it was all silent as Georgie desperately searched for the right words.

'Ben,' she said softly, 'you are a gorgeous young man, and you can have any woman you want.'

Ben looked up from the floor and into her eyes. 'You are the only woman I want—you're the only one I've ever wanted.'

Georgie had to look away. She'd seen a tear in his eye and realised that he truly meant what he was saying.

She reached out and took his hands in hers. 'Ben, I'm twice your age, and I'm your friend's mother. I'm old enough to be *your* mother!'

'I don't care about any of that. I love you.'
'Ben don't say that.' She said with as much seriousness as she could gather. Ben stepped forward and pulled her into a hug. Georgie didn't resist.

'I love you more than you will ever know,' he whispered into her ear. Georgie enjoyed the warm embrace and a tear now trickled from each of her own eyes. She lifted her arms to hug him back and he ran his hands through her hair.

Georgie closed her eyes, enjoying the cuddle of this strong infatuated man, the sweet smell of his masculinity filling her senses. She went to pull back and he loosened his hold. She looked up at him, their faces now only inches apart. Her eyes locked on his as he moved to kiss her. Again, she didn't resist; she couldn't. His kiss was as soft and tender as a ripe peach in spring. She closed her eyes again and kissed him back; she was past the point of no return. Her hands found themselves under his shirt and then somehow his shirt was gone. His hands effortlessly undid her bra through her shirt and then slid underneath the fabric to fill one of his hands with her breast.

The kissing didn't stop as her shirt and bra hit the floor. She reached down and felt him hard through his pants, the same thick python she only yesterday had stroked with her oily fingers. She undid his pants and helped them to the floor. He stepped out of them, now completely naked in her arms. She felt his hand slide into the elastic band of her thin cotton pants. She gasped as his fingers found the wetness that welcomed him. Her head fell back, breaking the kiss as he gently slid a finger inside her. She reached down and helped shed her pants and knickers. He picked her up as if she weighed nothing and placed her onto the massage table.

He took a second to admire her body before climbing between her now spread legs. He knelt between them; his enormous cock filled her vision. She had never had someone this big. He leant forward, his hands beside her face.

'Please be gentle,' she asked, as she felt him push against her. She felt her vulva part as the first millimeters of him found her.

He leant forward, kissed her, and said, 'I will, I would never hurt you.'

She felt his knob enter her and retract. He pushed again, a little further this time. Georgie was completely consumed; there was no other world outside this room. As each stroke pushed a little farther inside her, she gasped as her body stretched to accommodate him. She felt him now so deep, deeper than any man had ever been. It hurt a little at first, but as he started his rhythm of repetitive thrusts, the familiar warmth that she'd felt build inside her last night was pounding every nerve in her body. Her juices flowed. She could hear his breathing as the big man filled her over and over. She opened her eyes and saw that his were closed; she sensed he was nearing his ultimate moment.

His eyes opened and looked into hers with a look that was more than lust. Her climax was now close and as he pounded her harder to heighten his own orgasm, he came. The feeling of having a gorgeous young man filling her with his cum had her body explode with an ecstasy she never dreamed possible. Her vagina clamped around him as each wave pulsed through her. She finally opened her eyes to see his beautiful face smiling back at her. She smiled back, confused by the reality of what just happened. He was still inside her, but he was fading at a rate which would make the extraction gentle and smooth. They stared into each other's eyes, before he said, 'This is the best day of my life.'

Georgie smiled back at him; she had no idea how to reply. He'd slipped out of her now and sat back on his knees but still between her legs. She felt a little exposed, but in the dim candlelight it was okay. A part of her wanted him to stay there, but he hopped off the table and held out a hand to assist her. She felt the need to dress and slipped on her pants without her knickers and her shirt without her bra. Ben also dressed, and she watched him as her mind was spinning, reeling with so many emotions. *How could something that feels so good be so wrong?*

Her arms were tight across her chest, as if trying to hold in the feelings surging inside. But then, a feeling of calm engulfed her, suddenly feeling alright with what'd just happened, and possibly like his, her life would never be the same. When Ben had slipped on his shoes, he again took her in his arms and held her tight. He kissed her ear and said, 'I love you, Mrs. Jones.'

It was so tender and sincere, and her heart loved the sound of it.

'Thank you, Mr Johnson,' she whispered back.

The Piano

'Listen to that engine,' Greg said to Bill.

'Purring like a kitten,' Bill replied, as he reached for the carby throttle linkage and revved it again.

It was a fifty-year-old, big V8, big carby, and big fuel consumption. Perfect for the themed car event that was going to take them again on another outback adventure. One that they look forward to each year. The four businessmen were giving up their week to raise money for a charity that they're all very passionate about. There was to be around a hundred cars involved, most with four crew members, but some with three, and three with just two. Greg and Bill, being the two best drivers of the group, were also the only ones that had any idea about cars and engines. All the necessary equipment was loaded: swags to sleep in, beer, tools, more beer, and a comprehensive list of spare parts. The rules for the rally were that all the cars needed to be older than thirty years, two-wheel drive, and… the driver must be sober. Even though most of the driving was to be done on private property, it's preferred that the driver's not drinking… much anyway!

'I'll see you in the morning at the start line, Bill,' Greg said as he headed home for his last night's sleep in a real bed for just over a week.

The fellas all arrived early for the start and all the kids and parents lined the streets to watch the funny looking cars leave the start, one at a time. Only minutes after the start, Greg, who was driving the first stint, heard a beer can open in the back seat, shortly followed by another. Greg grinned. The two in the back weren't needed to drive today. Greg was to drive, with Bill navigating until lunchtime, then they'd swap after lunch. Tomorrow would be the turn for the back seat couple, Sean and Mark, to take over the driving and navigating duties while Greg and Bill had the day off.

There were always big nights on these events, drinking and eating to your heart's desire. Along the route, people would pull over for a snack, to stretch their legs, or a quick repair to their vehicle. On day three, they came across a car stopped on the side of the road, with four women looking blankly at their vehicle. Bill was driving and as soon as he saw them, he pulled to the side of the track behind their car. The four boys all hopped out, the two from the rear with cans of beer and the front seat crew with only a smile. Greg asked, 'What's the problem, ladies?'

Jenny replied, 'It's all over the road. I thought it was a flat tyre, it changes direction when you accelerate or brake and we are still some fifty kilometres to the next town.'

'Sounds like a broken centre bolt in the rear spring; it's the bolt that holds the leaves together.'

'The what? Anyway, I can't drive it, it's too dangerous,' Jenny said. 'Can you fix it?'

'No, not out here, but I'll tell you what,' Greg said, 'let's put one of you lovely ladies in our car, and I'll drive yours to the next town for you.'

'We would really appreciate that, thank you,' Jenny said.

One of Jenny's team jumped in with the boys and Greg joined the three girls, with Jenny seated in the front next to him.

'I'm pretty sure it's the centre bolt. It's easy enough to fix if you can get the part at the next town,' Greg told Jenny as he pulled back out onto the road.

It was a challenge to drive but Greg handled it well, cruising along at half the pace they were at before. Greg's team were happy to follow slowly along behind.

Greg looked over at Jenny and she at him, she had a look on her face as if to say, 'My hero!'

They all chatted, talking about themselves, their families, their jobs, and of course—due to the alcohol consumed—their lusts and fantasies. Jenny was now having a drink since being relieved of the driving duties but she was still a long way behind the girls in the back who were now flirting full time with Greg.

Greg was enjoying it and smiled to Jenny each time one of the girls in the back said something inappropriate.

They finally arrived at the next town, which was also their planned stop for the night. A camp site on the side of the river and dinner on a big paddle steamer that had cruised up from downstream for the occasion.

Greg parked the car at the workshop and handed the keys back to Jenny.

'Thank you so much, Greg, I hope to see you later at dinner,' she said as she stepped forward to kiss him on the cheek. Neither turned their heads very far and the kiss was half on his mouth. It was soft and offered with feeling, her eyes confirmed this as she pulled away. The smile and the lingering look had Greg's heart fluttering with interest. Jenny was shortish, with shoulder-length mousy blonde hair, not a wrinkle on her forty-something face. And her eyes… well, they were like sapphires, backlit from a light that shone deep in her beautiful soul. He stole a moment to watch her tight bum and slim legs disappear into the workshop office. He stood there for a second after she had gone from sight. He took a breath as one of the girls from the back seat, Annie, approached him for a hug, her drunk arms held out wide, inviting him to fill them.

He hugged her back and she whispered in his ear, 'Would you like to be with me tonight, honey?'

Greg was a little shocked, but his heart was elsewhere—it just walked into that workshop in Jenny's wake. He whispered back, 'I would love to, but I already have an interest I would like to pursue.'

'Good luck with *her*, buddy, she's very happily married!' she said as she smiled and took a small step back. 'Well, when you find out that you are wasting your time, I'll be here.' She looked back with a cheeky grin.

Greg couldn't wait to tell the boys the stories he'd heard in the car, including his proposition. 'I'll be following that one up tonight,' claimed Bill, which he would later the night find very rewarding.

At dinner Greg looked everywhere for Jenny, he couldn't wait to catch up now that he was showered and clean of the dirt from the dusty tracks.

Jenny did finally appear, looking absolutely stunning. Greg now understood why she was late, making yourself look that good in the middle of nowhere would be time consuming. She wore a white top that was probably unbuttoned one button too many and a dark blue pleated skirt that made her look even younger than the forty years he had guessed.

She took a plate and sat with the girls from her team, minus the one that Bill was away with somewhere. Greg watched Jenny, completely distracted from his teammates' conversation. Not once did she look in his direction. With dinner almost finished, most people left the boat for the big bonfire outside, stocked up with drinks and ready to settle in for the night.

When the dining room of the steamer was almost empty, Greg walked over to Jenny who was about to leave her table.

'You look stunning, Jenny,' he said.

'Thank you, Greg, and thank you again for today. It might be our last day on the rally as the mechanic doesn't think he can get the parts for another three days.'

'You're kidding? That's terrible news,' Greg replied.

Jenny gently placed her plate in the wash bucket along with her knife and fork and turned to Greg. She looked up into his eyes, and Greg could feel his heart being extracted through some magic invisible beam she had created with her look. She broke the stare and turned for the exit. Greg gently took her arm and turned her to face him.

'Jenny, that was not just any ordinary kiss today.'

'No, it wasn't. I do have feelings for you, which is wrong, so let's just leave it at that. No good can come for either of us from heading down that road. I'm married, Greg, I can't do this. Everyone here knows my husband.'

There is nothing Jenny could say that would stop Greg wanting this woman. But he eventually said, 'Okay, I understand.' His gaze dropped to the floor along with his heart, before he looked up to lock onto her delicious blue eyes one more time.

'No, I understand,' he said again, trying to convince himself that he did. Jenny turned to walk away, stopped, and turned back.

'Greg, I haven't felt like this before… ever. This is dangerous ground for me!'

He looked at a closed door that they were standing near, it opened to an adjoining room. He turned the knob and the door creaked opened, he reached for her hand and guided her, reluctantly into the darkened room that was closed off from the dining room. He closed the door behind them. She followed now with little resistance. The only light was from the flicker of the big fire that most people were now gathering around outside. Greg could make out a grand piano in the far corner, the rest of the room was empty. He took her face between his hands and his lips found hers. The sweet taste of her lip balm made her all that more delicious. Their kiss became passionate, her hands starting to find the bare skin beneath his shirt. Then she stopped and pulled away.

In the little light coming through from outside he noticed a tear run down the side of her face. He could see her eyes were wet but not much else. Greg's desire for this woman was only trumped by a regret about the risk of hurting her, knowing this was an unfair precipice between everything in her life before today, and what she wanted in the moment.

He kissed her softly and said, 'Let's leave it at that, I don't want to see you cry.'

'You should've let me go,' she said softly, her head now resting on his chest.

He wished he could better see her face. He knew this would be a moment that they would both remember for the rest of their lives, no matter what happened from here. She lifted her head from his shoulder, allowing him to run his finger down the side of her face, wiping away the remaining tears.

He kissed her again and suddenly, there was no hesitation from her. She kissed him with a passion that left him in no doubt that they had passed any chance of turning back. He took her hand and guided her to the darkest part of the room furthest from the door.

'Are you sure?' Greg asked in a whisper.

'Yes,' She replied delicately, like a secret wrapped in a warm breath.

He moved around to the back of the piano, and they found themselves on the carpeted floor beneath the large grand.

He lay her head on his left arm as a pillow as his right arm caressed her face and body. She undid his shirt, then ran her fingers across his chest like a sculptor admiring her finished creation. Greg's hands felt her breast through the thin white cotton top and demi bra. He would've loved nothing more than to have this goddess naked in his hands, but this wasn't the place. If it was going to happen, it had to be quick, leaving the pleasure of unlimited time for another occasion. He felt her hand undoing his shorts and then find him, her hand firm around his arousal. Greg ran his right hand up her leg to find her knickers wet beneath the pleated skirt. He slipped a finger around the band and slid them down until she could pull one leg free.

He removed his arm from beneath her gently, to quickly slide his shorts and underpants to his knees. He was positioning himself between her open legs when his head hit the underneath of the Steinway. He heard her giggle, before she reached to rub the back of his head. He smiled but she wouldn't have seen that.

He was right there, at her entrance pushing toward her, at the same time his wanting lips met hers. Her mouth was open in anticipation of the that euphoric moment of the first stroke of a man entering a woman.

Greg paused, wanting to ask her if she was sure, but he didn't. He didn't need to ask, she had already answered with her lips and her body, rising in yearning beneath him.

He pushed against her, and the moist flesh parted as he filled her. He felt her knees lift and her hips tilt to invite him further. He stopped kissing her and lifted his weight to his arms. He continued a rhythm that was slowly increasing with pace—harder, deeper, and faster. He didn't want to come before her. He held his desire. He throbbed, pulsed, and waited. Only when her moans told him she was close, did he increase the rate of the thrusts to full afterburner.

She came and it was the most beautiful thing he'd ever heard in his life. He brought ecstasy to a woman he now adored. He knew this was not a time to show off his endurance, it had to be quick, powerful, and lustful. His heat rose to boiling point quickly, and before her euphoria had receded, he filled her, his cum pulsing deep inside her. The bestowment of their lust, his gift of pleasure. The feeling of giving an angel his seed in a passionate frenzy was a feeling that no words could describe. The sound of his orgasm and the hard deep thrusts that accompanied it nearly made her come again. They settled in almost a synchronised union, like a sheet being thrown out to fall softly to the bed. Still deep inside her but not moving, he lowered himself to kiss her. He was desperate to see her face, but it was just too dark.

He removed himself with a gentleness she had never felt. With her vagina still tingling, she appreciated his thoughtfulness. He again lowered himself to kiss her and said, 'You are the most beautiful woman I have ever made love to.'

She kissed him back, but decided not to answer; this was a defining moment for her. She had become an unfaithful wife, an adulterous woman, but somehow in this moment it seemed okay. More than okay—it was perfect. No one had any idea about this encounter, and while she would carry on her life as if nothing happened, deep down she knew this wasn't the case. She'd given herself to a man she'd fallen for, a man who'd helped her in a time of need, a man who would live on in her memory, for the rest of her life.

Greg was now buttoning his shorts and Jenny had put her leg back into her knickers and had slid them back up into place under her skirt. She rolled out from beneath the piano and Greg helped her stand. They embraced tightly, holding as if each didn't ever want to let go. He eventually stepped back a little, again placing his hands on her cheeks. He took in a breath.

'I love you,' he said, the words flowing from him with sincerity.

Jenny let her head fall to his chest.

'You can't say that,' she whispered back.

'I know it's crazy, but I know I do. I've never felt like this.'

'Stop it,' she said, placing a finger on his lips. Jenny turned to leave, and he stopped her.

'You feel it too, don't you?' he asked, for the first time in a normal voice.

'Yes,' she said and headed for the door. He knew they couldn't leave together and he watched the silhouette of her walking away, the door opening and then closing softly behind her.

He didn't see her again that night, she'd obviously gone straight to bed. He assured himself he needed to talk to her tomorrow, tell her he still loved her, and that he had to see her again. He wanted just one more chance to make love to this adorable creature who had been sent from heaven above. He knew it was only the third night of eight, and that he would have five more nights to see and adore the one thing he now treasured more than anything.

Next morning, he desperately wanted to find her and tell her that his feelings were true and hadn't changed. At breakfast he found Annie, and, as casually as possible, he asked where Jenny was.

'She's gone, my love, got a lift to Port Augusta with the caterer and her husband will pick her up from there. The three of us are all going to jump in other cars 'cos we can't fix our car in time. We'll miss her.'

Annie could see the disappointment on his face.

'What did you two get up to anyway?' Annie asked, with a look far more serious than the question.

'Arrh, nothing.' He said still in shock.

'You fucked her, didn't you?' Annie demanded. 'I saw you both come out of that room.'

Greg's eyes were still looking in the direction of the road that would have taken her away from him, but Annie's question had shocked him back to the moment. He didn't know what to say.

He looked at her, a smile formed on his face, he recalled the moment when he came and left a small part of him inside her.

He touched Annie's cheek and turned to walk back to his car. It was his day in the back seat with Bill. He knew that after a few beers, Bill would be telling the boys all about his night with Annie.

'You're a lucky man, Greg Parsons,' Annie called out as he strolled off; she couldn't see the smile on his face. Greg knew he couldn't say a word to anyone, but his heart was flooding his body with warmth. He would remember the beautiful woman from car 222 for the rest of his life.

The Blindfold

It was St Valentine's Day and Dave had planned to make the day deliciously special for his girl, Tess. He wanted to add a touch of surprise and spice to it, something they hadn't done before. He booked a flash hotel that fronted the beach and ordered a special room service lunch. It was a light pasta dish of spinach, sundried tomatoes, chicken, and bocconcini; her favourite dish and one that he would often cook for her. He had visited the chef personally to provide the recipe and had ordered a bottle of that sparkling pinot noir that she loved. The hotel manager had agreed to set the table on the balcony during the time when he and Tess would be out of their room. Dave arranged for their meal to be brought to them as soon as they returned. This would be their first Valentine's Day together since they'd each left their marriages.

Dave and Tess's romance started simply with a chance meeting at a drunken office party that had found the two of them in a hotel room at the end of the night. The fire burned for them both and an adulterous fling soon turned to love and a passion neither had ever imagined possible. Dave was her boss; a few years older, wealthy, established, and confident. Tess was independent, yet sensitive, and somewhat insecure despite the fact she was incredibly attractive, with sparkling blue eyes, long blonde hair, and a smile that could melt titanium.

Dave's special date was all going to plan. They'd checked in the night before and slept in late. A quick phone call had coffee arriving at their door minutes later. After the caffeine fix and a bit of a cuddle, Dave suggested they dress and take a walk along the beach and possibly a swim as it was a glorious day.

As they strolled through the lobby with towels in hand, Dave gave a nod to the concierge who smiled and nodded back in return. This was the signal to prepare the room for lunch.

They meandered along the pristine beach for half an hour or so, before the heat of the day lured them into the cool, calm, waveless water. Tess tried to avoid getting her hair wet, but once they started playing and splashing that was impossible. A check of his watch had him suggest they start making their way back to the hotel.

Having returned to their room, Greg suggested Tess grab the first shower, so they could then make plans for lunch. She didn't notice the dressed balcony table as the curtains were still half drawn. Once he heard the shower running, Greg opened the curtains, appreciating the elegance of the setting.

Minutes later, a soft knock on the door signalled the arrival of their meal. All was served and in place, just as Dave heard the shower taps being turned off.

He'd collected an eye mask from a recent overnight flight and placed that and two scarves on his bedside table, ready for her special treat after their lunch. He quickly changed into a pair of shorts and slipped on a white, unironed, short-sleeved linen shirt, leaving it unbuttoned. Tess emerged from the bathroom, dressed in a simple soft yellow sundress. The thin tied straps, mini length, and lemon hues allowed her smooth golden skin and sheer beauty to radiate. Dave drew in a breath. His heart never ceased to be enlightened at the sight of her.

He poured two glasses of wine and handed her one as he took her hand and led her to the balcony.

'Wow, when did this happen? You never cease to impress me, babe!' she exclaimed.

He pulled out her chair and she sat in front of the meal. Dave had to admit, it was probably better than anything he'd ever cooked for her. The meal was delicious, and after it was finished, along with a second glass of wine, Dave stood and reached out to take her hand. He escorted her back into the bedroom, closed the heavy drapes behind him, and lay her gently on the bed. Without touching her he lay next to her. Looking into his eyes, she motioned to undress, but Dave reached out and stayed her hand.

'No, I want to do something new. Something we haven't done before,' he whispered in her ear.

'Okay…' she answered with a smile.

He reached for the bedside table and collected the blindfold. 'I'd like you to put this on.'

A devilish smile now appeared as she obliged, covering her eyes.

Dave continued, 'Now, feel these.' He let the silken feel of the scarves glide over her fingers. 'I'm going to tie your hands with these.'

'Okay,' she said.

He brought her hands together and tied her wrists above her head.

With a soft and seductive voice, he said, 'Tess, it will only be me touching you, but we're going to imagine we are with that couple that we met at the bar the other evening. I will talk you through what is happening, but I want you to imagine that it's Mike and Sarah sharing our bed.'

He kissed her cheek and neck before he continued in a hushed tone, 'Can you see them coming into our room? They're holding hands as they stand at the foot of our bed. They're kissing as they begin to undress. Can you see them?'

'Yes,' was all she dared whisper in response.

Dave undid the thin shoulder straps and slid her dress down, revealing her breasts. Then he whispered, 'Can you see they're both nearly naked?'

'Yes.'

'Can you see that he has his hand up her skirt and she has dropped his shorts and underwear to the floor?'

'Yes.'

Dave pulled Tess's dress down to her waist and moved his kisses from her nipples to her neck as he continued the story.

'They're completely naked now, babe, you can see their hands all over their hot bodies. Are you ready for them to see you lying here, naked and wet?'

Tess nodded, letting the vision fill her mind. He then removed her dress completely, seductively sliding it over her hips and down her legs. At that point, he quickly removed his shirt and shorts.

He moved to lie half on top of her. He ran his tongue along her neck to her ear and said, 'There's one condition. If we get involved with Mike and Sarah, anything goes, but no penetration. Do you agree?'

'Yes,' she responded softly.

He found her lips in the almost dark room and passionately kissed her. As he lifted himself above her, he whispered, 'Can you see and feel them next to us?'

'Yes.'

'They're kissing and touching each other. Sarah is next to you. She's reaching out, she wants to touch your breast. Is that okay?'

'Yes,' Tess replied.

Dave tried to imagine how the soft touch of another woman would feel as he gently stroked the side of her breast and traced his fingers around the base of her nipple. 'Do you like her touching you, babe?'

'Yes.'

Tess was soon lost in this fantasy world and could imagine and feel the sensation as if it really was Sarah's fingers drifting down her stomach to eventually find her wetness.

'Do you like her touching you there?' Dave asked.

Tess replied faintly with a longer, 'Yes.'

She heard Sarah say, 'I want to touch your pussy. Is that okay?'

'Yes,' Tess answered again.

As Dave continued stimulating her, she moaned softly and rolled her hips, obviously lost in the delight of Dave's touch and the images in her mind. Dave reached up to caress her breast with his left hand as he said, 'Mike loves your tits.'

Tess arched, raising her chest a little higher.

Dave paused and then whispered, 'Tess, I'm going to move over with Sarah but will be right here next to you.' He placed both his hands on her breasts and moved his body above her. 'Mike is over you now, admiring your beautiful body. He loves what he can see.' Noticing how she had slightly drawn her legs a little closer together, he murmured, 'It's okay. I'm lying right here next to you with Sarah.'

'Okay,' Tess replied.

'Mike is with you. Sarah has me in her mouth, and I'm loving it.'

'Mmm…' was Tess's only reply. Dave saw she was there. She felt it. The sex was in her, next to her, and surrounding her. He moved as if he was Mike and slid down to kiss her feet, her ankles, and her calves. As Dave pressed the first kiss on her flesh above her knees, her legs fell apart again, and he progressed slowly up her thighs as she physically beckoned for more.

'Are you enjoying Mike's touch, babe?'

'Yes. Very much.'

Dave's mouth found her pussy, and she gasped as he started licking her lips and scrolling his tongue around her swollen bud. Her legs quivered as she welcomed more of him, reminding Dave how much she loved that. His tongue and lips worked their way north, kissing her belly and then her breast.

'Mike loves the taste of you, babe. Can you see Sarah on top of me, rubbing herself along me?' he whispered, so the image of Sarah wasn't forgotten.

'Yes, I can, but don't do her, honey.'

Acting as if he was Mike, Dave kissed her neck as he rubbed his rock-hard cock between her spread legs. 'Mike wants to enter you, babe,' he murmured as he applied a little pressure against her. He could feel how wet and swollen she was. 'He's so ready for you. He thinks you're beautiful.'

'Oh,' Tess gasped.

'Sarah wants me inside her, babe. She's pushing against my knob, she wants to fuck me bad, just like Mike wants you.' He pushed his hardness against her again, this time almost parting her wet, swollen flesh.

'Ye—err, no,' she managed to get out. 'Don't we have a deal?' Panting, she raised her hips towards him again.

'I know, but Mike really wants to be inside you. He's right there, you can have him.'

'I want you, Dave,' Tess was now almost breathless.

'I have my knob touching Sarah... Can I please just push in a little?' He gently pushed himself against her just parting the delicate lips of pleasure. He could see Tess's hips rising, feeling what Sarah wanted, what she herself desperately wanted...

'No, you can't,' she murmured.

'Can Mike fuck you, babe?' He pushed until he could feel her resistance quiver, allowing his knob to be just inside her.

Unable to control herself, 'Oh God! Yes, I want him!' burst from her lips.

He pulled out and then pushed back inside, entering her a little more each time, teasing her, making her shake with anticipation. He continued to build on the moment. 'I'm going to fuck Sarah, babe. You're fucking Mike and she's already got me inside her. I want you to enjoy him. It's okay, take all of him, make him come in you.'

Dave kept her thoughts right there. 'Can you see her riding me, babe? I love the feel of her, she's going to make me come. Does Mike feel good, babe? I'm so turned on by seeing you having a different cock to fuck.'

Tess's reply was a resounding, 'Yes! he's going to make me come.'

Dave fucked her hard now, he too shuddering with each thrust. Within seconds, she was climaxing hard, her whole body nearly leaping from the bed as the waves of ecstasy pounded her. He kept riding her hard till she came again and then he exploded into the Sarah he'd pictured in his mind. Tess and Dave were now totally consumed in the imagery of Mike and Sarah and riding high on the thrill of sex with strangers.

As the waves of passion subsided and they both lay exhausted, the realisation of what had just happened flooded their minds. This had been so intense and was much more than Dave had expected. He moved to lay beside Tess, as if he'd been alongside her all along.

Dave removed the blindfold and untied her hands. She hugged him tight, as if wanting to apologise for her indiscretion. She'd just emotionally made love to another man. Lying cradled in each other's arms, they held each other without saying a word.

After a time, Tess whispered, 'That was such a turn on and so naughty. I felt a little guilty, but it's nice to have you back in my arms, babe.'

They spent the rest of afternoon cuddling in bed, dozing in and out of sleep as the sea breeze from the open balcony doors caressed their bodies.

When they finally arose and started to get ready for dinner, Dave commented, 'You really got off on the blindfold play.'

Tess replied guiltily, 'Yeah! I sure did.'

Dave smiled. 'I was convinced I was with Sarah. I've always been so aroused and fascinated by imagining sex with others. Maybe we could try a little same room one day?'

Tess turned and looked at him, 'I didn't get the impression that Mike and Sarah were into swinging.'

'Well babe, one thing's for sure—you can never tell what people are into just by looking at them.'

Brett's Love

*B*rett was a little nervous. He was meeting Vicky today, a girl he hadn't seen for thirty-eight years—actually, since the last day he walked out of his primary school gate. At that time, they were both only twelve years old.

It had been by sheer coincidence that in recent months that they'd made contact through a chance discovery on social media. A few messages and an exchange of phone numbers soon had them chatting, and the heightened curiosity finally brought them to an agreement to meet for lunch at a quaint Italian restaurant. It was renowned for a tasty menu and unhurried service. Neither knew how it would go; it could turn out to be awkward or they may just connect, and the conversation might just flow.

Brett arrived a little early, preferring he be the one looking around to catch the first glimpse and offer the welcome greeting to the young redhead who'd sat across the other side of the classroom, all that time ago. His mind wandered back to images of her bright smile, her long curly strawberry blonde hair, and her sweet innocence. But he was struck with the realisation that she was now a middle-aged woman, whom he hadn't seen in decades. *Would he recognise her?*

Vicky arrived shortly after the agreed time, recognising Brett instantly. While the first kiss on the cheek and greetings exchanged were somewhat tentative and awkward in the initial moments, the wine, delicious pasta, and sharing of a few school reminiscences had the two of them completely relaxed.

Vicky told him about the other girls from school that she'd kept in contact with, suggesting that it might be nice if they all caught up sometime. By the end of the first hour, the connection and conversation flowed easily, as their recounting of the years lost moved through high school, first jobs, and loves, through to their current families and lives.

Long after the plates were cleared from the table they were still talking, connected through memories and the fresh discovery of their adult selves. So easy was their conversation, it wasn't long before some intimate details came to the fore. Brett was a good listener, and in turn, Vicky's soft, alluring voice and seductive eyes kept him enthralled throughout the whole afternoon. A kiss on the lips when they parted signalled to them both that only a little time would pass before they would be in contact again.

In the months which followed, they would call each other whenever they could. Such was their rekindled bond that sometimes it was as often as three times a day. Their resonating friendship grew so strong that more and more intimate disclosures were shared, and their chats started to become quite flirtatious. One day, Vicky admitted to touching herself while they chatted, something that Brett had suspected, and secretly enjoyed. It wasn't long before they both masturbated during calls, neither openly declaring the pleasure their connection inspired.

One afternoon, Vicky started to share some of her husband's lovemaking pillow talk. She told Brett how she'd sometimes imagine it was him she was making love to, when the passion wasn't there fully with Graham.

Brett was excited knowing Vicky thought of him in some of her most intimate moments, as he braved himself to tell her that he, too, had thought of her, during sex with others.

'Really?' she replied, with a mix of disbelief and excitement in her voice.

'It's true. I often think of how I would pleasure you if we were together.'

Brett could hear a little intake of breath, before Vicky asked softly, 'So what would you do?'

'I imagine kissing you, something I am so desperate to do—long, slow, and soft. To taste your lips on mine and feel the connection we have for each other. From your kiss I realise what I suspect… that you want me as much as I want you. I would slowly unbutton your top and see the beautiful breasts held firmly in your bra, something I have only imagined. I'd slide your shirt off and run the tips of my fingers over your shoulders, following the line down from your bra strap to the top of the cups.'

'I will place my hands firmly over your breast and see in my mind's eye the hardened nipple I can feel through the material. My mouth will water, longing to savour your nipple in my mouth. I'll kiss you again, as I reach behind and release the clasp. You'll feel the release but the bra will still hang loosely in place. My lips will find your neck and my kisses continue down to your shoulder to your breast. You feel the shoulder strap fall as my tongue explores inside the bra that keeps me from the part of you I'm searching for and yearn to taste.

'My mouth will find your nipple and my tongue circle the firm erection. I draw as much of your tender flesh as I can into my mouth, while my hand cups your other wanting breast. I swap and your second nipple hardens instantly at my touch. My kisses descend from your breast, trailing kisses down to top of your jeans. My hand reaches for the button and I slide the zipper down. I fold away the denim, to let me kiss your skin down to the top of your panties.

'Now kneeling in front of you, I can smell your arousal and my own body has started twitching in desperation for you. My finger pulls the front of your panties down only as far as your lowered jeans will allow. I kiss you as deep as I can. Still on my knees, I pull your pants down and you step out of them. I continue kissing your body as I slowly lower your panties. It's then I can taste you and it drives me crazy.

'I stand and lift you onto the bed. I reach for your hand and place it between your legs and for a second, I imagine the times you touched yourself while we talked. I undress in front of you, watching you the whole time, as your fingers circle your firm bud. Once naked, I climb slowly onto the bed. Your legs fall apart, beckoning me in. You feel my hard erection against you before I lower myself to kiss your mouth again. I want to see your face as I enter you for the first time, that moment when your moist, swollen pussy welcomes my knob. I'm watching your eyes slowly close as I take the first millimetres of you. I stop, deliberately, and you open your eyes again. I want you to look at me as we become one, joined together by a lover's connection. I want to see you gasp as we mate.

'I push into you as hard as I can, busting to be a part of the woman I adore. I'm so overwhelmed that I'm able to bring you this pleasure and I'm desperate to hear you explode from the pleasure I'm giving you. I see your head fall back, your eyes close, and your mouth start to open, wider and wider till that rush of ecstasy bursts from your lungs. I pound you hard, heightening your orgasmic release. At the same time my ultimate dream is realised as I fill you deep with my warm seed.'

Brett paused the narration as he listened to Vicky coming on the other end of the phone. He smiled to himself; she'd liked his story.

Phone sex had entered both of their lives.

Despite taking turns to tell their own phone sex stories each week, Vicky never suggested that they actually do it for real, and Brett was not going to push.

One day as Brett had pulled up at his work still chatting to Vicky on the phone, she mentioned that the night before, her husband Graham had suggested during their lovemaking that he'd like to watch her with one of his mates. Vicky said that Graham had brought this up many times when they were having sex. She was clearly concerned—not by the fact that he would get off on watching her being fucked by someone else, but that he'd offer up a mate from work whom she didn't know. That was not her idea of what a loving husband does.

Brett stayed sitting in his car for another half an hour, chatting to her about what her husband may have been thinking. By the end of the conversation Vicky agreed that she would probably do it, but it would be her choice as to who it would be. Brett softly mentioned that he would love to be that person.

'Would you do it, Brett? Screw me while my husband jerks off watching us?'

'Yes, I would do anything to make love to you, Vicky,' Brett said softly, almost embarrassed that he had admitted that he had completely fallen for her.

The next day, Vicky called and told him that during sex last night it came up again and Graham agreed that he was happy with a man of her choice. A smile formed on Brett's face.

'How do we make it happen?' Brett asked.

'It would need to be spontaneous; Graham wouldn't be able to handle a long, drawn-out event,' Vicky, said making it sound rather clinical.

A few months later, Brett unexpectedly did get to meet Graham when he was at the Australian Grand Prix in Melbourne. Graham and Vicky were there for a weekend escape to watch the race. Brett had planned to spend the weekend with a woman named Rachel, who just so happened to have attended the same primary school as him and Vicky, and was now living in Melbourne. Rachel was a very attractive, yet somewhat elusive woman, who at Brett's invitation accepted to be his date for the event.

When Vicky told Brett that she and Graham would be in Melbourne at the same time he was there, he arranged for the four of them to all have dinner together at a restaurant in Chinatown in inner Melbourne.

The night was full of fun, blended with great food and conversation, shared naturally between all four. A real connection started to form between Graham and Brett. At the night's end, Brett extended a very genuine invitation for Vicky and Graham to join him for a cruise on his boat sometime when they all returned to Adelaide. While that night Brett had the pleasure of Rachel's company in his bed, his thoughts kept drifting back to Vicky and the thought of one day making love to her.

Once back in Adelaide, Brett followed up with Vicky, reminding her of his offer of her and Graham being his guests for a relaxing day on his boat. The date was set for the following Sunday.

It was summer and the forecast was for fine weather. Brett arrived at the boat early and prepared it for the short cruise off the Marina Pier at Holdfast Shores. There wasn't much to do, but Brett wanted to start the engines early just in case a battery had gone flat, give it a wipe down, and ensure it offered a pristine welcome to his guests. Graham and Vicky arrived on time with several beers and a bottle of champagne. After the greetings and a quick tour of the vessel, the champagne was opened.

Brett restarted the engines, untied the boat from the mooring, and they set off through the marina. Brett headed for a spot to show the pair some dolphins he knew were always loitering. The beers were now also flowing and the champagne mostly gone when Brett suggested that they drop the anchor and maybe have a swim. Vicky declined but Graham said, 'Sure, but what would we wear?'

After a moment of silence, Brett suggested they strip off and keep their clothes dry. 'I have towels for when we get out, we're all adults after all. Do you mind, Vicky?'

'Not at all, I'm sure you don't have anything I haven't seen before!' she said, giving him a cheeky smile. Although Vicky and Brett had enjoyed phone sex many times, they'd not ever had the opportunity to make their relationship physical, making this the first time she would see him naked.

The three of them made their way to the transom, the landing right at the back of the boat. Graham and Brett stripped off and dived in. Vicky dangled her feet in the water as the boys splashed around in the deep blue sea. After a few minutes Brett reached for the ladder at the rear, folded it down, and suggested it was time for another beer. Graham agreed and the two men climbed out, the sun glistening on their wet, masculine bodies.

Vicky handed towels to them both. As Brett stepped in front of her to grab his towel, she gave him a smile that said she liked what she saw. Graham took his, and after they'd wrapped them around their waists, they sat down either side of her.

'Now, how about that beer?' Graham asked.

'Getting it now,' Brett replied, standing and readjusting his towel. Brett took two beers from the fridge, opened them, and checked his phone for messages. On his return, as he passed one to Graham he couldn't help but notice that Vicky's hand had slipped through the split in Graham's towel and was giving him some slow easy strokes. Brett sat down next to Vicky again, as she continued to slowly pleasure her husband.

It was all silent for a few seconds, and Brett, trying to avert his gaze, took a mouthful of his beer. He swallowed it down and said with a smile, 'This boat really does make people horny!' They all laughed, and Graham's towel now fell apart, proudly displaying the attention Vicky was giving him. Graham lay back on his elbows, fully accepting Vicky's slow and firm strokes.

Brett could feel the tingle as the blood was finding its way to his groin. His own erection was also making a tent in his towel, displaying his growing excitement. Catching sight of Brett's rising cock, Vicky's eyes twinkled, followed by a cheeky smirk, signalling her delight in the ability for her one hand to singularly arouse both men. Graham looked over at Brett and could see that his erection was obvious.

'You know what, Brett?' Graham said, 'I've had this fantasy of someone fucking Vicky while I watch.'

'Really?' Brett asked, tossing a glance at Vicky who was nodding in agreement.

'Would you be interested?' Graham asked.

'Are you sure?' Brett replied, checking both of their faces for approval.

Graham turned to face Brett. 'We've discussed it before while we make love, and after the Melbourne trip Vicky said she'd like it to be you.'

'That's flattering.' Brett looked at Vicky, whose eyes were instantly blazing with passion. 'How would it work?' he asked, now looking back at Graham.

Graham took a swig, his manhood still hard; the conversation was certainly stimulating him.

'I'd like you to make out I'm not here—it's just the two of you. Imagine she has come aboard your boat expecting to make love to you. You've sailed out here, and the time has come for her to give herself to you.'

Brett looked at Vicky; lust filled her eyes. She was ready for him, alright. He looked back at her husband, and he nodded his approval.

'Okay, I can do that,' Brett said.

Brett stood, dropped his towel, and reached for Vicky's hand. She stood and Brett put his arms around her and kissed her, something he had wanted to do for a very long time. The kiss was easy, easy like long-term lovers. Brett had kissed her many times in his mind as they chatted and aroused each other with words of lust during their phone calls. Brett broke the kiss and looked into the eyes of the woman he was about to make love to. He had forgotten that Graham was there, until over her shoulder he could see him already stroking himself. *This is for real. He's getting off on this*, he thought. With that, Brett took Vicky's hand and led her downstairs. Graham followed but deliberately kept a pace or two behind; he was not to be a part of the lovemaking, he simply wanted to watch.

Vicky took Brett's erection in her hand as he started to remove her clothes. They kissed as Vicky's clothes formed a neat pile on the floor next to the bed. Graham had found a seat to the side of the bed, remaining fully naked and continued to stroke himself slowly, his eyes never leaving his wife and her—now—lover.

Brett, being an analytical, three-dimensional thinker, pictured the scenario. While delicious and spontaneous as this was, the situation needed to be handled with care. Factor one, once the husband comes, his interest in watching his wife being fucked risked dropping quickly. So, he would need to also finish around the same time as her husband's pleasure was realised. *So much for making out Graham isn't here!* he thought. He'd also need to try and make Vicky come before he and Graham did. With that, he knew he'd need to have her fully aroused before he entered her.

He took her hand, guiding her like a regal princess, and lay her gently on the bed. Vicky relaxed, her arms resting above her head and her legs partially spread in willing invitation. With the only light coming from the doorway at the top of the five stairs, the room was quite dark. He could see the wetness that was glistening from the part of her that he had been craving for months. He knelt on the bed between her legs, and she let her knees fall further apart. Brett leant down, kissed her belly, then ran his tongue down through the creases at the top of her legs.

It was only when his tongue touched her sweet juices and the delicate skin from where they flowed that she let out a familiar moan. The same one he'd heard many times over the phone. He ran his tongue either side of her now engorged clitoris. With each glide of his tongue, deep ecstatic notes escaped, as quivering pulses shuddered through her body. Brett looked up; her eyes were closed and her head tilted back. He knelt, then lowered himself onto her body, his knob finding her entrance perfectly. He buried himself inside her, as deep as he could. He had realised his dream.

Vicky called out his name shrilly as he pumped her hard. He knew it would only be seconds before she came, she was so close. Her moans grew even louder and higher as he filled her hard.

Graham watched as Brett's first stroke entered his wife, seeing Brett so hard and her dripping wet. He nearly came himself as he watched that first pounding stroke fill her. He watched Brett's bum rise and fall as he pushed into her. He could see Brett's gluteal muscles tighten with each stroke. From where he sat, he could see where Brett's hard shaft was disappearing into his wife's wet pussy, her hips rising to take as much of him as she possibly could. He could hear that Vicky was nearly there; her moans, so familiar, signalling her orgasm was building. Graham quickened his strokes; his own pleasure was also now close.

Vicky yelled as the ecstasy burst through her body, and that was all Graham needed. He blew, his cum squirting inches into the air and covering his fingers and thighs.

Brett heard Graham's guttural, orgasmic moan. He quickened his pace and pushed hard into Vicky as his own orgasm rose and exploded into her. He held her tight as he felt the last pulse of cum leave him and fill the woman he adored. He knew this would not be the last time he made love to this beautiful woman. He lifted himself so he could see her eyes, and she looked into his. Her eyes told him that she'd felt what he had. In that moment a special message was exchanged.

'That was fucking hot mate, thank you,' Brett heard from behind him. He knew it was time to leave her. Reluctantly, he gently removed his slightly softened cock from her, and he could see her twinge at the loss. Brett sat back, and just for a second, looked at the gorgeous redhead that lay in front of him, and her tender smile in return warmed his heart.

He stepped off the bed and turned to Graham who was now cleaning himself with the towel that was initially around his waist. Brett reached for a fresh towel from the bathroom and suggested to Graham they go back upstairs for a beer while Vicky dressed. Brett glanced back at Vicky, and again a warmth he couldn't explain burst through him.

Brett grabbed two beers, opened them, and handed one to Graham. As they chinked the bottles, Brett said, 'Thank you, Graham, your wife is a beautiful woman.'

'No, thank you. We've been talking about doing that for a while and my God, it was even hotter than I expected.'

Brett really didn't know what to say next, so he just smiled and took another mouthful of beer. Vicky soon appeared, fully dressed and her hair neatly brushed.

'That was so hot, babe, did you enjoy it?' Graham asked.

The smile on her face already answered the question. 'Yes, it was fun, I hope you enjoyed it too, dear?'

'God yes,' Graham said taking another mouthful of beer.

Neither Vicky nor Brett needed to say another word. They simply offered each other a small knowing glance and smile.

It was much more than just sex.

The Caravan

Jan had hardly slept last night, but it was daylight now and finally an acceptable time to rise. Her night had been restless with trepidation and excitement. She lay there for a few more minutes, letting herself bathe in the thoughts of what lay ahead on this day. Her body tingled and almost shook at the visions. Today she was giving herself to Ross, a man she'd known since long before she was married.

For years, she would lay in bed aroused, touching herself while her husband slept, imagining the scenario that would finally materialise today—at 12.00 p.m., to be exact. Her groin twinged and a sense of warmth flooded her body. She closed her eyes and imagined Ross there between her legs, his masculine weight spread gently over her body. She satiated in that moist feeling, her body ready to receive what her mind offered. She opened her eyes and carefully pulled back the covers, trying not to wake Stan, her husband of twenty years.

Jan stood in the shower, her mind racing as the warm water flowed over her. *I can't believe I am doing this!* she thought, as a small stabbing pain of guilt shot through her. *I've never been unfaithful to Stan... well, not in a physical way.*

She dropped her head to stare at her feet, looking away from the exhaust fan that was humming above her. She lifted her gaze up and over her body, appraising herself. She tried to imagine how it was going to feel when, for the first time in twenty years, another man saw her naked and touched her body.

She blinked for a moment as she thought about Stan, her husband who had always stood by her, and, other than his one small indiscretion a long time ago, had been faithful to her. He was quite a bit older but remained great company and a genuine person. However, he'd found that comfortable place, which unfortunately didn't include the sex, romance, or intimacy, something that she still wanted and her body craved. Jan knew she was at the precipice. She let a big sigh escape as the realisation hit.

There's only one question to ask myself. If I don't do this today—will I regret it? A moment passed as she held her breath, as if suspended in anticipation of her own reply. *I know I'll regret it deeply. Let's face it—I've wanted this for most of my life.* Now resolved, a smile emerged across her face as the tingling of excitement returned. She rinsed the conditioner from her hair and reached for her razor. She wanted every inch of her to look and feel as smooth and silky as she felt on the inside.

Ross had a big day ahead; a few jobs first and then his date with Jan at 12.00 p.m. His normally focused mind couldn't shake off the vision of what his afternoon would bring. In only a few hours, he'd be making love to a woman he'd known for a long time, a lifetime in fact. For years, they'd made eye contact, shared suggestive jokes, and had many lingering greeting kisses. Today would be a dream come true, something he never thought would eventuate. He couldn't count the number of times he'd made love to her in his mind. He imagined her calling his name as her orgasm enveloped her. He'd pictured her petite body under his, her head tilted back, her eyes closed as he filled her body and her soul with his deep thrusts. He shook his head. 'Stay focused,' he said aloud to himself.

Ross had finished his jobs early and now headed to his storage workshop where his caravan was parked. They'd decided against meeting at his apartment or a hotel room, as it would be too risky with her being a long-time family friend and all. They needed a place where no one could possibly see them.

Ross had thought of everything. He'd put Jan's favourite wine in the fridge and set the lighting in the caravan for the occasion. He plugged in his laptop and searched for a video that he knew was Jan's fantasy—a threesome with two men. This wasn't as easy as he first thought; it had to be long enough for their foreplay, but not take too long to get to the hot, juicy, throbbing parts. He eventually found one that suited her pleasure and his timing perfectly. It featured a middle-aged woman with two young, tall, athletic men, the exact scenario that she had told him she fantasised about.

'I'm leaving now, Stan,' Jan called out as she headed for the door to the carport.

'Say hi to the girls for me.' Stan replied.

Jan's lunches with her friends were always long.

Jan started the car's engine, which was purring much quieter than the sensations now running through her body. Her internal engine had already been running all morning, with the revs changing and upshifting with each thought of what lay ahead. As she placed the car into drive and applied the throttle, that wave of excitement accelerated through her. 'Well, I'm nearly past the point of no return,' she said aloud, now just wanting to be there and in Ross's arms.

Ross had already described exactly how the afternoon would go, minute by minute, just like the corporate functions he organised. Jan loved it all being so precisely planned; she knew how she'd be greeted and how each step would play out. Ross knew this would be the only way he could convince her. It needed to be perfect; so rather than romantic, it had to be just a date that satisfied the physical need that had been burning inside them both, as Jan had requested.

Ross heard Jan's car arrive outside, and immediately poured her a sparkling shiraz, her favourite. He picked up the glass and the red rose he'd bought that morning and swiftly walked out to meet her at the car.

Jan looked at him and smiled. As she reached for her bag, Ross said, 'You won't need your bag or phone. I'm taking you to another world where phones aren't needed.'

Jan smiled and threw the bag back into her car, locked it, and handed him her keys as she accepted the rose in one hand and the glass in the other. He'd purposely planned for no pre-chat or wasted time talking nervously while waiting for someone to make the first move. Besides, no more discussion was necessary. The script had been written. He just needed to turn their shared fantasy into reality.

It had all started about a month prior, when at a dinner party with friends, Ross and Jan found themselves sitting next to each other. Their legs pressed tightly together at the cramped table. Jan had turned most of her conversation to him, and her smiles were intoxicating. At one stage, they both had their hands on their laps and his little finger touched hers. Initially, he pulled away, but soon found the sides of their hands touching. She made no attempt to move it, instead her little finger found itself on top of his. Neither moved during this moment. Ross repositioned himself on the seat and his hand found its way under hers, his finger tips resting on her thigh. Her fingers started to run little circles over his. Both of their hearts were pounding. It wasn't until Jan let his fingers caress the inside of her thigh that the inevitable situation was formed. The conversations over the next few weeks quickly became suggestive and erotic, with many ending with two horny and frustrated callers. It wasn't long before this date was set.

Ross escorted Jan into the workshop office, before turning to lock the door. He cupped her cheek and kissed her lips; it was small but purposeful. They'd kissed hundreds of times on the cheek and once or twice on the lips swiftly, but Ross was shocked at how soft and sweet her lips were this time. He pulled back a little to look into her eyes. 'I'm so glad you're here. Are you nervous?' he whispered to her.

'Yes,' she replied, although no sound came out. She was now lost in his story and his touch.

He took her hand and the bottle he had just opened and led her to his caravan. He opened the door, holding it wide, and extended his arm to gesture her in. Her heart was pounding even though she knew exactly what would happen next, having been told every explicit detail of his plan. He'd even told her what to wear, well... suggested anyway. She'd willingly obliged, wearing a skirt and simple button-down shirt. Something about the anticipation of knowing what was to come merely heightened her arousal.

Jan stepped inside, immediately appreciating the new smell of the van, which he hadn't long ago purchased. Ross stepped in behind her and shut the door softly behind him. It was the little click of the door that signalled to her that this life-changing event had started. There was no turning back now. He took a sip of the wine and so did she, both looking into each other's eyes. They didn't say a word. There was no need.

He took the glass from her and placed it on the table, before placing both hands on her cheeks as he guided her lips to his into a long, deep, passionate kiss. Jan had not been kissed like that in a very long time. *He was right*, she thought, *he is taking me to another world.*

Ross reached down, lifted her skirt, and slipped his fingers into the sides of her panties, exactly as he had described he would in their last phone call. He slowly slid them down till they fell freely to the floor. He motioned for her to lay on the bed next to his laptop. She knew exactly where and how. The story had to unfold as she already had it held in her mind.

While she did this, he kicked off his shoes and removed his pants, shirt, and underwear. He lay down beside her, spooning her from behind. She loved the feel of him behind her. The warmth and the feel of his body was pleasure in itself. He reached over her to hit the video play on his computer. The preselected video started. It showed the two young men meeting the woman in a bar and taking her upstairs.

He could feel her wriggle as the action continued to build and gain heat on the screen. Jan could feel Ross getting hard behind her and her crotch was now swelling and moist. Ross took her right hand and guided it slowly between her legs. She wriggled herself a little to make room. Ross's hand and fingers laid on hers and he followed her every movement as she pleasured herself. He could feel exactly how she ran her index finger through the folds and across her tender bud. Ross didn't need to touch himself; his erection grew from feeling her rising pleasure.

He slid up from behind her, between her legs, until his knob touched her fingers, which were still circling and rubbing. So aware of his presence, she moved her hand to feel down his shaft to his balls that were pressing against her. He was making small gliding thrusts that stimulated her from her bum through to her pussy. It felt nice and she wanted more.

She subtly adjusted her position, making it easier for his knob to find her. She felt his throbbing hardness. She arched her back, letting him press firm against her opening. Ross could feel the warmth of her wet pussy, and although he couldn't enter her deep from this angle, his knob was consumed with the desire to enter her. She played with him for a while before tilting her hips back and pulling him into her. As he started to push, their position moulded naturally to give her more and more of him.

Ross couldn't hold back anymore. In one swift motion he withdrew and rolled her on her back. This wasn't in the script; she'd only said she wanted to be taken from behind. She'd dared not suggest a position that was where she'd be looking into his eyes, where she knew she'd succumb to his romantic allure and true lovemaking.

But she was already there. She spread her legs wide, giving him full view of her wet, glistening pussy. He lowered himself onto her, giving her the full stroke she desired. She let a cry escape. He was there, hard and powerful. Her orgasm quickly built as the man she'd so wanted from afar now filled her adulterous body. She came with an intensity and strength that she hadn't imagined possible. Her body throbbed as each wave pulsed through her slender frame.

Ross didn't ease up but kept fucking her hard until she came again. He'd held on as long as he could, but finally blew into her with thrusts that buried so deep that she almost came for a third time at simply the sound of his throbbing orgasm and the moan that accompanied it. Ross remained inside her, loving the feel of their intense connection. He didn't understand it fully, but when a woman invites you into her body it says a lot about you and her. He knew she didn't let this happen easily and she'd now sacrificed her long-standing title as an honest and faithful wife. Just this alone was very emotional to Ross. He loved the feeling of being a part of her as he held himself above her.

He moved slightly and felt her vaginal muscles clench, as if resisting their separation. Her eyes smiled at him with a look he'd remember for the rest of his life. She looked so content and so beautiful, so happy that he was where he was. He'd made love to her, there was no doubt. It was not just the scripted casual fuck they'd planned. He used all his strength to restrain himself from collapsing on top of her and bursting into tears. He wanted to stay there forever, be a part of her, a part of her body.

He lowered himself to kiss her and her welcoming lips told him that she felt the same. He eventually removed himself gently from her and lay by her side, his hand on her cheek. He couldn't stop staring into her eyes. Now a tear did appear from the corner of his eye.

'You have never looked more beautiful to me,' he said with sincerity.

'Thank you,' Jan said, her smile now a little larger.

'Jan, this has had a bigger effect on me than I could've ever thought possible.'

Jan placed her finger on his lips before he had a chance to say the 'L' word that she knew was next.

'Let's have a drink, shall we?' she offered, in an attempt to break the spell.

'Do you feel okay, no regrets?' Ross asked.

Jan hesitated. 'My only regret is that we didn't do this years ago. My God, you were amazing. I have never had sex like that before.'

A smile appeared on Ross's face, and he said, 'Neither have I.'

Jan's skirt had found its way back into its natural position, leaving her looking and feeling fully dressed in comparison to the fully naked man by her side. They lay propped on their elbows and caressed each other's body. Ross circled a finger around each nipple and, although there was a layer of shirt and bra, he could feel each nipple harden. She was soon aroused again and reached for the part of him she again wanted inside her. He was easily hard again, and she lifted her leg to straddle him. She reached under her skirt, placed him inside her, and lowered herself fully onto him. With her hands flat on his chest, her eyes closed, she rode him back and forth, his knob hard against her G-spot. This was her most sensitive area and she selfishly pleased herself.

The heat rose in her but only the tempo increased, not the depth. She could feel that warmth rising through her; her legs were starting to shake. As the first pulse hit her, she filled herself with him, taking all with pounding thrusts. Her moan was uncontrolled and free, and the explosion erupted inside her. She kept grinding, screaming, and shuddering as she came again. Her body shook and rocked as the aftershocks rattled her beaten shell. Her eyes had not opened since she placed him inside her. She eventually collapsed onto his chest, him still hard and deep inside her. He started to rock his hips before she screamed, 'Don't move, my God, I will die.'

Ross couldn't help but feel pretty good; he lay there watching her as each wave rolled through her. He had brought ecstasy to the woman he had adored for nearly a lifetime. He could feel her clench him rhythmically as he lay there still full inside her. He put his arms around her and held her close. He knew she was spent, but he wanted this moment to last. Her breathing had settled and she carefully removed herself from his still full length and collapsed beside him.

'I'm not going to be able to walk,' she said, smiling at him.

'I know you will need to go soon but... Can we do this again?' Ross sounded more desperate than he wanted. The agreed arrangement was for a 'one off.'

She didn't answer but leant forward and kissed him. She leant forward close to his ear and whispered, 'I hope so.'

That was all Ross needed to hear. He reached for his glass and emptied it in one mouthful. Jan had already climbed off the bed and was filling her panties with tissues for the trip home. Ross dressed and followed her to her car. They didn't dare kiss outside, but their smiles said everything they both wanted to express.

Ross watched her drive off. He stood there, long after she'd gone, desperately trying to analyse his feelings. Having amazing sex is one thing, but to have it with someone you have known and fantasised about for so many years is another thing all together. He walked back inside with a smile on his face; it had been a great afternoon.

Jessica's Window

Jessica Campbell was still coming to grips with her new surroundings. She had been transferred to London for a three-month stint by the cosmetics company that she worked for in Melbourne. Her boss had told her that spending some time in the office of the parent company would go a long way to furthering her career in the industry. To her, it was a paid holiday and great life experience, something her fellow workers back at home were very envious of. She loved and hated the multicultural transition that had consumed London recently. The true British life she'd grown up imagining was now hard to find. These days, shop vendors from every corner of the globe had set up business selling everything from Persian rugs to butter chicken.

She did adore the history though, and from her third-floor apartment she could see Hyde Park and Kensington Palace. Most of the buildings on Cromwell Road were four to five stories high and built close enough to each other that your neighbour's window felt like part of your apartment.

Jess had turned twenty-one a few months ago and it wasn't long after this that Peter had decided to move on.

Peter was her first and only lover; he had charmed the pants off her, literally. It wasn't long into their relationship before she realised that he wasn't a keeper, but she still loved him in a funny sort of way. He was kind, respected her, and she loved the people that she'd met through him. He was, after all, the one who had taken her virginity, and that, no one else can ever do. In actual fact, no one else has been there since.

She did miss that part of Peter, but she had no intention of rushing into another relationship. The last thing she needed was to fall for someone in London and then go through the pain of leaving him, or her, when her stint in the UK finished. The thought that she could fall for a woman put a smile on her face. It was unlikely, but she sure knew many girls who had switched preferences.

Tonight, having finished work late, her Kensington apartment was a relief to arrive home to, it was now close to 10.00 p.m. The underground had been busy, offering standing room only, and the smell of sweaty bodies still lingered in her nostrils. Her apartment was only a block away from Earl's Court station and she could cut through a small lane that sheltered her from the icy wind that usually arrived around this time of night. The front door of her building was heavy, designed to be closed before you opened the second, smartly designed to keep the warmth of the building in and the cold out. Jessica loved the feeling of the perfumed warmth that hit her icy cheeks each evening when she finally arrived home. She offered a smile to the lady behind the reception desk, who barely acknowledged her. Despite Jessica having been here for nearly four weeks, the lady still didn't know her name, and clearly wasn't one for small talk, but neither was Jessica at this time of night.

As soon as Jessica closed the door to her apartment, she kicked off her heeled shoes. Her black pencil skirt was tight, and she released the zip almost in sync with her shoes being tossed. Her bedroom faced the adjoining building, and although she could easily see to undress by the streetlights coming in from outside, she did need to hang things and find her desperately required track pants and windcheater. It was from her bedroom window that she could see the Palace, although she did need to push her face hard against the cold glass to catch a glimpse of the royal outer wall.

However, she delighted that her friends at home were impressed that she could see the Palace from her bedroom. At night, the lights lit the Palace walls and Jessica could only imagine which royal may be staying there that night.

Her neighbour in the building directly opposite was an older lady who appeared to live on her own. Jessica had nicknamed her 'Betty,' which seemed to suit a woman of her age and the Victorian décor she could see. In the apartment below Betty was a young man, who had a girlfriend, or possibly a couple, who lived there. They looked to be in their late twenties. She'd seen them walk around their bedroom, figuring their apartment's layout must have mirrored hers.

She flicked on the light and stepped towards the window. She placed her hands on the curtains to close them before she undressed—she didn't want dear old 'Betty' getting a shock. Betty's bedroom was dark; she must already be in bed, or perhaps still out for the night. She looked down to the window of the apartment below.

Suddenly, the young man, bare chested, appeared at his window to also draw his curtain. She hesitated momentarily at the sight of the almost naked man. Then, he looked up at her—almost as if he knew she had been looking. Their eyes met and he started to smile. He was dark, with brown eyes and a trimmed beard. He was tanned, as if he was from the Mediterranean somewhere. Jessica swept the curtains closed, shocked that she'd been caught looking into his bedroom. A wave of awkwardness had her place her hand over her mouth.

God, that was embarrassing, she thought.

She'd let the thought slip by the time she changed and turned off the bedroom light. But she stopped before heading out to the kitchenette to heat the evening meal she had bought during her lunch break. She turned back to her window. It was dark and her eyes hadn't yet fully adjusted. She tiptoed toward the window, the outline of the curtain now obvious. With a finger she pulled one side back slowly, her eyes knowing exactly where to look. His curtains were almost closed, but open just enough to allow her to see him lying on his bed. She spied a strip of his bare chest, enough to suggest he might be completely naked, or maybe not. Her imagination provided what her eyes couldn't see, and a warmth ran through her body. She paused; her eyes fixed on the small part of the man's body.

She remembered Peter and what it felt like to be naked and the pleasure of them making love. Jess's eyes had drifted off with that vision and when she looked back to the man's window, he was gone. She slowly closed the curtain again. Her mind still full of Peter and her body tingling. She realised now that she did miss him. She took a breath and left for the kitchen. That memory faded as she turned on her favourite playlist and prepared her dinner.

The next day at work, Jessica had the nagging feeling that she was keen to get home. It wasn't until she had walked into her apartment that she understood why. She arrived home earlier tonight, but it was still dark outside.

Jessica went straight to the bedroom and when her eyes saw the window, she knew exactly why she was so keen to get home. She stepped guiltily up to the glass in the dark. Her eyes found his window; his light was off, but she could see the bed was still made and empty—after all it, was only 7.30.

She scorned herself for her sneaky indulgence and changed in the low light of the outside streetlights; she didn't want to close the curtains.

At 8.30, Jessica left the apartment and headed down to Earl's Court Road in her track pants, windcheater and Ugg boots to get some Chinese takeaway. It was very casual dress for a Londoner, but she didn't care. Stepping back into her apartment, she couldn't help but again check the window. His room was still empty, but light now filled the room and the near side of the bed. She chastised herself verbally this time, calling herself a pervert, but the tingle of just seeing his naked body again was almost irresistible.

Jessica moved a chair to the window and started to consume the Chinese dinner in the dark. It was now 9.30 p.m. She couldn't believe she was doing this, and decided it was definitely time she found herself a man. After only a few mouthfuls she could see that someone had entered the room, noting shadows bouncing across the bed.

Jessica was now finding it hard to swallow—partly because how ridiculously naughty this was and partly because the desire of what she may see. She felt her heart racing. A shadow darkened the bed, and then she saw him lay fully naked on the bed in clear view. He hadn't closed the curtains at all this time. Jessica stopped chewing; her mouth still full of Asian greens. She could see him all so clearly, given he was probably only four metres away. She looked at the slim, muscular, tanned body; a light covering of dark body hair confirming he was likely from southern Europe. His hands were propped up behind his head. She could see him from his head to his knees, and his penis appeared to be growing as she watched. She somehow managed to swallow the mouthful of food and placed the plate on her dressing table. She leaned back away from the window; confident her face was not being lit from the streetlights.

Her eyes fixed on him, and when he reached to stroke his now aroused penis, she instinctively looked away. Her hands covered her eyes as she looked sideways towards the wall. But that didn't last long, as she again found herself staring at him. A heat started burning from inside her, her body reacting to the vision of the man masturbating in front of her.

Just then he turned his head and looked straight at her and smiled. She froze and an instant of cold dampened the burn that was radiating inside her. She leant to her side as fast as she could and fell from the chair. There was a crash as she and the chair hit the floor. She lay there, desperate not to move.

My God, he knew I was watching him, was my face lit up from the outside lights? She picked herself up and again peeked through the window. The curtains were now pulled across and through the small gap she could just see a woman's bare leg where she'd now joined him. Jessica reached for her plate of food and slowly made her way back to the kitchen. She was still in shock at what she had seen, but, more than that, at what she had done. That was it—she was now officially a pervert, a voyeur.

However, it had turned her on, that was true. Watching him stroke himself, she remembered what it felt like having Peter inside her, and yes, it made her wet watching him. Very wet.

The next day at work she was consumed with the visions of the night before. She found herself looking at the men in her office, wondering whether he would be someone she could 'do.' Just to satisfy that itch that was starting to burn inside her. But she knew a fling with someone in the office would just end up a nightmare. She couldn't wait to get back to her apartment—she wanted to see him again.

She decided that dinner would be the leftover Chinese that she couldn't finish the night before. It was a late finish, and she found herself rushing upstairs, a tingle of excitement flooding through her veins. She stepped slowly to the window and checked the time. It was now 9.45 p.m. She again found his light on and bed vacant. She kicked off her shoes and removed her jacket. Her track pants and windcheater were laying on the chair that she'd knocked over the night before. She removed her top and let the tartan skirt she had bought last week fall to the floor. She had just reached behind to remove her bra when he appeared at the window.

Jessica gasped as his naked body filled her vision. She shed her bra without barely noticing, as her gaze fixed on him. He looked up to her window and smiled. He sat back on the bed, his eyes not moving from her direction. He was naked again and this time already fully aroused. She was mesmerised as he lay back on the bed. Only now, she realised she was also naked, all but her knickers and stockings. She watched him stroke himself again, his eyes seeming to burn into her. *He was doing this just for her.* She imagined he could see her standing there, almost naked and turned on from watching him. *Hell, maybe he could see her?* That thought alone made her nipples tighten. She ran a finger around each of them in turn. She badly wanted to step forward towards the window where the streetlights would light her nakedness for him.

Then she stepped forward, her horniness taking control—she wanted to give him something back. She felt the amber streetlight illuminate her body like a burning floodlight. Her eyes were fixed on his and she could see from his expression that he liked what he saw.

Just then his head turned, and the blinds were closed by the woman who had arrived to enjoy what Jessica now wanted badly. Through the tiny gap she again saw the woman's leg climb over him. Jessica's hand was now in her panties as she watched through the small gap in the curtain as the woman rocked back and forth above him, riding what she wanted, now more than anything. She tried to imagine when each of them had come and she did as well, in sync with them. Her mind was there; it was a threesome of sorts. She imagined actually being there, in their bedroom, touching herself as they fucked in front of her. Watching the young woman take his length over and over till he exploded inside her, his eyes watching Jessica as he came.

The next night when she arrived home, she checked her watch. 10 o'clock couldn't come fast enough. The excitement was overwhelming. She tried to put it into context—*was it so wrong that she watched them now that he knew she was there?* It didn't matter to her; all she knew was that she wanted more. *What would he provide for her tonight?* She was tingling with excitement as she boiled some pasta and opened the packaged sauce. She grated some cheese and checked her watch again. It was still only 8 o'clock. Once she had finished her meal and cleaned the dishes it was 9.15.

Jessica went to her bedroom and removed the track pants and windcheater she had put on earlier. She stood there naked, her body shaking with desire.

'Get a grip,' she said aloud.

She went to her underwear drawer and put on the only matching pair she had; satin, turquoise bra and knickers that she'd bought in Melbourne to impress Peter, but she was sure he didn't even notice as he'd removed them swiftly to devour the contents.

It was 9.45 p.m. Jessica turned off the light and slid the curtain back fully—she hadn't opened it this far before. She watched his window like an animal watching its prey. The light turned on at 10.00 p.m.—she did appreciate his punctuality. She watched the shadows again on the half of the bed that she could see. Then he appeared at the window. He was dressed in jeans and a t-shirt, his eyes focused immediately on hers. He waved and smiled. Jessica waved back without thought and then immediately pulled away from the window.

'My God, we just waved at each other, why did I do that?' she said, almost loud enough for her neighbors to hear. 'What does that mean now, that I'm somehow part of his sex life? Hell, he is all of mine, I guess.'

She looked back and the light was out; the blind still open and the bed just faintly lit from the light of another room. If the apartment was the mirror to hers, which she suspected it was, the light would be from the hallway. She went to the kitchen, her underwear clad body now lit by the kitchen light. She grabbed a beer from the fridge—she needed a drink. She removed the top and took a swig big enough to put an Aussie tradie to shame.

This was insane, but she was hooked. She let out a gentle lady's burp and headed back to the window of lust. Nothing had changed, the bed still empty and backlit from the hall light. She took another mouthful of beer and had almost swallowed it when she saw a naked woman lay down on the bed. Jessica placed her beer on the bedside table. The woman was looking towards the foot of the bed, she couldn't see much more than that. Jessica could see the girl's legs fall apart, and her fantasy man place his head between them. She watched the girl's head tilt back, and felt the urge to do the same as she remembered what that felt like. Her knickers were getting wet as she watched them, her right hand now providing her own self-love. She stayed in the dark—she didn't want the girl to see her and deprive her of this blissful joy.

The man finally moved up her body and filled the young beauty that lay beneath him. At the first stroke he turned and looked toward Jessica. She moved into the light to show him she was there and then faded back to again hide from view. Jessica watched him rhythmically fuck her. She could see the muscles of his body tighten with each thrust, or was that just her imagination? It didn't matter. Her eyes had adjusted well to the darkness now, and she watched them both with burning desire. The man then turned the girl over and entered her from behind. With her facing down, the man again could look towards Jessica's window, and she again moved into the light. He could easily see her and watched her come, her face was squashed against the window in orgasmic delight, giving him no doubt as to her orgasmic pleasure.

She watched him pull out of the woman, his eyes still fixed on Jessica. She saw him stroke himself hard until he exploded onto her back, his creamy cum pulsing from him. He opened his eyes again, looking to see the young woman from next door still watching. She waved and he smiled as Jessica slowly closed her curtains and collapsed onto the bed.

This is the craziest thing in the world! She thought. *What am I doing? I now have a lover who screws someone else while I wave to him.* A smile came over her as she dismissed the craziness and thought, *well, at least it's not complicated.*

She laughed. 'Complicated, how can this not be complicated?' the sensible side of her yelled at her.

'I wonder what his name is?' she said in a whisper. She jumped up and slipped the curtain back a tiny amount. His curtain was now closed and the light was off. They must've gone to sleep.

'Goodnight, lover boy,' she said softly and brought two fingers to her lips to blow him a kiss.

It was Friday and her workmates suggested a drink after work and maybe dinner. She agreed, of course, this was the first time anyone from work had invited her out socially. Most of the girls were married and had to get home to kids and families, so a drink and meal was a rarity. The office was situated in Regent Street in the heart of the London's exclusive shopping district. They'd picked a restaurant in the nearby Chinatown area which was nice and close to the Leicester Square underground, so they could all get home easily.

Jessica loved how after just a wine or two the girls opened up, telling each other in their posh English accents about their personal lives. It was really the first time she felt relaxed with her new workmates. Jessica found herself checking her watch, and each time, the sensible Jessica told her that she didn't need to be home, it was the weekend tomorrow. But the sexy Jessica had an appointment to keep.

Robin noticed her check her watch for the tenth time and asked, 'Do you need to be somewhere, Jess?'

A stumbled reply came out, 'Oh, not really, it's just... it's just, I normally call my mum at ten o'clock.'

'But wouldn't that be the middle of the night in Australia?' Robin asked. Jessica had no idea what time it would be and wished she had more time to think of a better excuse. Jessica then found herself trying to see the time on other people's watches.

The account finally came, it was 9.15 p.m.

Jessica asked the girls, 'Does anyone know the best way to get to Earl's Court from here?'

Robin, who was probably the oldest of them all and her immediate boss, said, 'Piccadilly line from Leicester Square will take you straight there, no changing, my dear.'

'That's great, thank you.' She checked her watch again, said her goodbyes, and headed for the station. It was 9.50 p.m. when she reached the front door of her building. Her heart was racing, either from the power walking or the excitement of what she'd been waiting for all day.

Once Jessica reached her apartment, she dropped her bag and headed straight for her bedroom, again checking her watch. It was 9.55 p.m. Her legs felt wobbly as she thought about the craziness of this 'thing.' *It doesn't even have a name,* she thought.

She hesitated as she started to remove her clothes. *What am I doing, where is this going to end? He does actually have a girlfriend.* She continued to remove her work clothes, justifying to the sensible Jessica that she would be putting her trackies on. Now naked except for her knickers, she turned out her bedroom light and walked to her window, her heart about to explode in her chest. Slowly she pulled the curtain back and peeked through the gap. His bedroom light was on, but there were no other signs of him. She pulled the curtain back further, so the gap stayed without her holding it. The two glasses of wine she'd had at dinner had now made her brave and she slid the curtains back fully to each side and stepped into the light from the street. She was so excited, in anticipation of what delicious vision her mystery man would provide for her tonight.

She relaxed against the window frame, wishing she had another glass of wine. Just then she saw movement in the room below. *Was it him or her? Maybe she should step back?* The alcohol had slowed her decision making, and before she could decide or even react, he was at the window. He looked up to her and could see her there clearly. He smiled and she smiled back. She tried to imagine how he would interpret that. He turned away momentarily and then returned, holding a piece of paper,

It said something that she couldn't read. He tilted it back so that the light from his room lit the page. She could read it now. She gasped and moved quickly out of the light. 'Oh my God,' she said, her hand tight across her mouth. 'Oh my God!' she said again. His written three words ringing in her head over and over.

'What do I do now?' she said to the dark black wall. She looked back and he was gone. She went to the kitchen and poured herself a glass of chardonnay which had really been open too long, but that didn't matter. She went back to the bedroom, stood by the window, and again watched them make love. She again watched him between her legs, both enjoying what Jessica was becoming more and more desperate for. She watched his hips rise and fall as he gave himself to the woman. She watched as he came, the hard thrusts and his gluteal muscles tensing as he filled his lover. She watched him roll from the woman and she stared at the naked man that now lay spent on the bed.

Jessica wanted him badly. She was so aroused, her panties were soaked, and her body was tingling all over. She recalled the message: 'Can we meet?'

He glanced away, obviously to see if his lady had returned from the bathroom. He looked back at Jessica, and with a smile held out his hands in an expression of, 'Well?'

Jessica's heart was in her mouth, and she nodded 'Yes.'

He smiled back and stood in front of the window, his naked body on full display just for her. He slowly closed the curtains, his smile disappearing behind them.

Her sleep was restless; she imagined meeting the mystery man and him enticing her to sleep with him. She agreed that he wouldn't need to try very hard. She could nearly feel herself exactly where the woman was, him licking her before filling her swollen pussy with that glorious cock.

She awoke, unsure whether she had actually had a wet dream or was she just still wet from her masturbating. *What would tonight bring? A meeting place or a phone number?*

She filled the day with a long walk through Hyde Park, a little shopping, and some general housework. As evening approached, Jessica found herself again checking her watch constantly, and was again impressed by the man's immaculate timing. 9.50 p.m. arrived, and with a full glass from a new bottle of chardonnay, she stood naked by her bedroom window. Almost on cue the man appeared at the window, his splendid naked body again in full view. Her heart was pounding as the girl arrived, also naked, at his side, and they both looked up at her with smiles on their faces. Jessica's heart nearly exploded as the confusion of this new scenario presented itself.

After only a second, which seemed like minutes, the couple waved in a beckoning motion, as if inviting her to come and join them. Jessica froze, trying desperately to take in the moment. She was tingling all over, lust burning through her. She focused on them and nodded back, totally unsure of what she was getting herself into. The man pointed toward the street, leaving no confusion about wanting to meet outside.

She swallowed the rest of her wine, her heart racing so fast she was almost ready to faint. She pulled on her tracksuit pants, windcheater, and Ugg boots and headed downstairs. She arrived at the neighbour's building the same time as the couple opened their front door.

'Hello neighbour,' the girl said with a strong Latino accent.

'Hello, I'm Jessica,' she said, barely able to speak.

'I'm Maria and this is José or Joe,' The smile on both of their faces was infectious.

That was all the introduction needed. None of them spoke another word.

Maria took Jessica's hand and guided her inside the building, up the stairs, and into the apartment that Jessica had only seen through her window. Maria led her to the bedroom, which was backlit from the hall light, just as Jessica had imagined.

Maria took Jessica's face in her hands and kissed her. Maria's soft lips caressed hers, so delicately, yet passionately. It was nothing like Jessica had ever felt or imagined. She felt José move in behind her, his hands exploring inside her windcheater until they cupped her breasts.

Her body and soul had become theirs to devour however they pleased. She was no longer in control, but ready to ride this train of lust wherever it took her. She felt Maria's hand slide inside her pants and touch the swollen wetness with a gentleness that only a woman could. Jessica gasped at the touch, closed her eyes, and gave herself completely to her new friends.

Karen's Lover

The Boeing 787 had just touched down at Denpasar's Ngurah Rai International Airport. Sitting in seat 9A was Karen Johnson, an attractive middle-aged woman. She was filled with a mix of trepidation and excitement. Landing in a different country on her own for the first time signaled this to be the first official day of her new life.

Her husband had recently arrived home and told her that he'd met a woman that he'd like to get to know a little better. Karen figured he'd probably already got to know her pretty well, no doubt, a few times when he was late home from work. It wasn't really a shock to Karen, as since the last of their three children had left home it had become just a marriage of convenience. Over the years the intimacy, passion, and sex had faded to zero.

To be honest, she no longer saw anything exciting in him either. Nonetheless, it had still hurt like hell, and it took some time for her to work out how best to shape a future on her own.

She decided to pamper herself first, so she booked a holiday to Bali's Nusa Dua, secretly hoping to get a little overdue action. As the plane taxied to its gate, Karen rested her forehead against the Perspex porthole window and stared out across the tarmac to the balmy horizon.

The palm trees and colourful dressings filled her vision and a warmth filled her heart; it was a holiday she really needed. She gathered up her things and double-checked she hadn't left anything behind as she joined the line of excited passengers exiting the aircraft.

It was the heat that she noticed first as she departed the air-conditioned terminal. The hot, moist air was as heavy as a sledgehammer. She gasped—it was such a contrast to the Melbourne spring she'd just left behind. A waiting taxi driver soon had her in his cab and on the way to Nusa Dua.

The resort she'd booked was breathtaking, even more naturally beautiful than the pictures online. The straw-roofed foyer was completely open to the outside. Large timber fans slowly rotated across the vast open ceiling. The immaculately dressed Balinese staff cruised around and offered various types of 'hello' in their best English with their hands clasped in a praying pose. It really was a tropical paradise.

The concierge took her bag, and after a quick check in, a man wearing a white sarong with an ornate green and gold trim escorted her to room 1025. On the way, he pointed out the pool area, the three restaurants, the gym, and the spa, the place where she would get her complimentary one-hour massage.

As she stepped into the small suite, she was hit with the immediate relief of the cool air-conditioning. She scanned the room, smiling at the sight of the huge bed, seemingly the size of two doubles joined together.

A vision of a tall, dark, handsome man laying naked on it flashed through her mind. She looked away, took a breath, and tipped the porter with a ten-dollar Australian note. It was probably more than his whole day's pay. He was very grateful.

It was now mid-afternoon and the small snack on the plane seemed such a long time ago. The pool would be first though. Karen unpacked her case, leaving her black one-piece bathers on the bed. She stripped off, and for a moment stood naked, looking out her window. She doubted that anyone could see her with the unlit room and the scrim that covered the window. She still tingled at the thought of some handsome man walking past, seeing her naked, and smiling back at her, liking what he saw. She sighed and stepped into her swimming costume.

She was nearly fifty and had kept herself trim, no fat at all, but the years and three kids had reduced her shape from that of model status. Although she could probably pull off a bikini, she felt more comfortable in the low-back one piece. Her bosom filled the cups with a little to spare and her tight arse from years of yoga, gave her a look she was happy to display to a possible suitor. She let her shoulder-length brown hair down and ran a brush gently through it. *First impressions do count,* she thought to herself.

She chose one of the long white beach chairs that surrounded the pool like the petals on a sunflower. She placed her towel and slip-on shoes next to it and slowly descended the steps into the pool. The water was warm, probably her exact body temperature. It was divine. There weren't a lot of people around as it was the shoulder season. There were two couples at one end of the pool bar and a single guy, lounging back, smoking a cigarette on the opposite side to them. In the water was a beautifully tanned girl in her twenties wearing a miniature white bikini, who was busy flirting with a boy she'd either already slept with or would be soon.

Karen could see the girl's erect nipples easily through the thin material and could only imagine what was happening in the lower half of her body. That thought sent a warmth through her own body.

Karen continued to luxuriate in the water, enjoying a slow, flowing breaststroke toward the pool bar that sat in the center of the kidney-shaped pool. Once there, she sat almost next to the two couples, so she was a far away from the smoker as possible. The person closest to her was a lady of similar age. She was pretty, with long blonde hair tied back with a blue hair tie that matched her bikini, and deep, sapphire-blue eyes. Wedding and engagement rings indicated it was probably her husband sitting next to her. He was tall, greying, fit, and had a warm smile—so much sexier than the husband she had just traded in. Karen's eyes stayed with him for a little longer than they should. The other couple watched her take a seat and smiled.

'Hello, would you like a drink?' the barman asked in his broken English.

'Thank you, yes, do you have champagne?' Karen asked.

'Yes ma'am.'

Karen looked again at the two couples next to her and smiled. The lady closest to her said in a perfect Australian accent, 'Where are you from?'

'Melbourne,' Karen said, glad to have some conversation.

'We only arrived today; this is Bill and Rose,' she said pointing to the couple furthest away. 'And this is David, my husband, and I'm Angela. We're all from Sydney.' Everyone smiled a warm welcome.

Karen felt David's eyes momentarily lock with hers and she looked away quickly, more so with embarrassment than anything else. Her body for a second time gave a little tingle, thrilled that a man saw something in her. Hopefully no one noticed her blush. She turned back to Angela.

'I've just arrived today as well, I'm here for a week. Oh, sorry, I'm Karen.' She reached out to shake Angela's hand, realising quickly that it wasn't required but it was too late. She shook hands with the four of them. Again, she felt David's eyes tell her what her body wanted to hear in the second that he held her hand.

The champagne arrived and she took a sip, as a vision of David knocking on her door during the night and making love to her flashed through her mind. She quickly shook the thought away when Angela asked, 'Are you here on your own, Karen?'

'Yes, it's sort of a long story. Well, it's really a short story, you can probably guess,' she replied, not really wanting to elaborate any more than that.

'Well, we'll keep an eye out for you,' David said, leaning forward.

My God, yes please, she thought.

'Thank you, David, but I should be okay.'

Karen ordered another drink, the first having gone down far too easily. The ambient heat warmed her body, the champagne her insides, and David her heart. It wasn't that she wanted him, it was just that it was so nice to have a man think she was attractive, even if he was someone else's.

She soon finished the second glass of bubbles. She thought it best to stop before she was too drunk to find the room she'd only been to once. She said goodbye to the four, and again her eyes hung with David's as she saw him checking out her breasts. *I think he just undressed me,* she thought. She felt a flush in her cheeks rise as she turned to leave; admitting to herself, *I wish he could.* Her heart had picked up a little pace at her mind's fantasy of having him escorting her back to her room and maybe just giving her hand to get her costume off. *It's much easier with someone's help when bathers are wet,* she thought.

She found her room easily. The cool air-conditioning on her wet bathers made her shiver. She slid the shoulder straps off and over her breasts; the cold air blowing over her wet nipples had them quickly firm. She imagined David blowing on them, before putting one in his mouth. She gasped at the thought and slid the costume down to fall at her feet. She turned her nakedness to face the window again, wishing he was there watching her. Her body quickly reacted to that thought and she soon found herself on her massive bed, her fingers adding stimulation to the imagery of him there above her, ready to feed himself into her. She soon came, relaxed, and fell asleep.

Karen awoke an hour later; naked and her body still tingling where her imaginary lover had been. It was getting dark, and she was starving. She rushed through the shower and dressed, deciding to eat at one of the three in-house restaurants tonight.

She walked into the one nearest her room, knowing she'd find something delicious at whichever one she dined at. On entering, she immediately saw Bill, Rose, Angela, and David. She blushed instantly when her eyes met David's; his expression was almost as if he knew what she'd privately enjoyed. Her four new friends waved her over, which she accepted without hesitation.

Angela quickly made room for her between herself and Rose. They were about to order, but they waited for Karen to choose so they could all order together. The conversation during the meal was perfect, with only a few questions being directed to Karen. With David on the other side of Angela, Karen was able to avoid constant eye contact with him. The four of them had had a long day, with the early flight from Sydney and then the three-hour loss in time. They were ready for bed. Karen admitted to having had a little sleep, leaving out the part where she imagined David had joined her. She suggested that she might have a drink down at the sand bar that was on the beach before retiring for the night.

They gave the waiter their room numbers to charge out the meals and stood to leave. Karen realised that David would now know her room number and immediately wondered, *what would I really do if he came knocking?*

As they walked out, she heard a voice say, 'You all go, I'll stay and have a drink with Karen.'

It was Angela, who swiftly took Karen's arm in hers, and the two of them headed for the beach, waving goodbye to the other three.

Karen couldn't believe how easy Angela was to talk to. She told her about how her husband had decided to move on and that she was really here to have some fun—some sexy fun. The girls were on their third glass of wine when the waiter advised them that the bar was closing, but that they could stay as long as they liked, and to just leave the glasses on the bar when they go.

It was a still, moonless night, and with the bar lights off, their faces were softly lit by the resort's distant lighting. It was still warm, and the most gorgeous balmy breeze blew along the beach from the south.

'This is so romantic,' Karen said.

'It *is* very romantic, isn't it,' Angela said, pulling the hair tie from her hair. The soft blonde curls fell neatly around her face, framing her gorgeous delicate features. Karen couldn't resist touching it.

'Your hair's so soft,' she said.

Angela just smiled and slid her hand along the side of Karen's face, her finger running up and around her ear, tucking back her hair to clear her face. Both girls were now quite drunk and very relaxed. Karen knew she would be staggering back to her room, no doubt about that. Angela stood, swallowed down the last of her wine and took Karen's hand, indicating for her to stand, which she did. She wobbled back and then fell forward into Angela's arms. Angela held her for a moment, the delicate fragrance of Karen's hair and perfume filling her senses as she let her head fall onto Karen's shoulder. The combination of the beach, the breeze, the wine, and this gorgeous lady in her arms had Angela feel something she'd never felt before.

As Karen apologised and gently pushed away, Angela placed her hands on Karen's shoulders. She looked into her eyes and an overwhelming feeling enveloped her. She placed her hand on Karen's cheek, leant forward, and kissed her.

Karen welcomed the goodnight kiss; it was much longer than she would have expected from a woman, but when she felt Angela's tongue run across her lip, she pulled back in shock.

'What are you doing?' she screamed in a drunken whisper.

'God, I'm so sorry, I don't know why I did that, I've never done that before.' Angela's head dropped almost like a naughty child admitting they had stolen from the cookie jar. Karen felt instantly sorry for her and reached to hug her. Angela apologised again.

Although she couldn't see it, Karen smiled. 'Well, it was kinda nice, best kiss I've had today,' Karen said, kissing her on the cheek.

Karen took her hand, and they walked back into the resort. Their suites weren't too far apart, and Karen kissed Angela again on the cheek before they each headed for their own rooms.

Karen lay in bed, realising that she was only a mouthful or two of wine from having the room spinning. But it was Angela she thought about now, not David. She played the event over in her mind; the pretty face, the beautiful soft hair, and those gentle lips on hers. The soft smell of roses and the tender, whiskerless skin. She played over in her mind how Angela's tongue had brushed her lip with such tenderness and what it might've been like if she'd just let it go a little longer. Karen soon came again for the second time that day, relaxing into the huge bed with the buzz of the euphoric self-pleasure. She fell into a blissful sleep, not moving again until the sun was well up the next morning.

Karen was seated at a table for two when her four new friends arrived for breakfast. They waved and sat at another table nearby. Karen was watching Angela, who appeared as if she either had a hangover or was still embarrassed about the previous night or both.

Karen was at the toaster, waiting for her bread to become toast, when Angela appeared next to her.

'I'm really sorry about last night,' Angela said, staring at the toaster.

Karen turned to her and said, 'Don't be silly, it's fine. Actually... I liked it.'

Angela turned to her, 'Did you really?'

'Yes, it was so soft and gentle—not what I'm used to, let me tell you.'

'I've never done that before,' Angela admitted, 'not with a woman, anyway.'

They both looked at each other, smiled, and then laughed. Their toast getting cold, they collected it and turned and walked back to their tables. Karen could see that Angela's face was brighter, obviously now feeling much better about the incident.

After breakfast Karen caught a taxi to Kuta, a half-hour trip, to spend the day on the beach. There she'd get a five-dollar pedicure, a five-dollar manicure, a five-dollar massage, and a few two-dollar beers before heading back to the resort later that afternoon. A chair shaded by an umbrella on the Kuta beach sand would be her salon for the day. An endless number of locals selling their wares bombarded her. She tipped them well, knowing full well these poor people lived on next to nothing.

With her fingers and toes shining with clear nail polish, she strolled along the beach. Both Angela and David continually returned to her thoughts. She smiled at how crazy the trip had turned out so far. She had to restrain a laugh thinking that David may well be jealous that his wife had kissed the woman he had been making eyes at. After another beer, she headed for the road to find a cab.

It was hot and muggy in Nusa Dua when she stepped from the cab, and the water was the only place to be. She put on her still slightly damp bathers and headed for the pool. Her four new best friends were in the same spot they'd been the first time she met them, and even seated in the same order. She slipped into the pool opposite them and swam across to again sit next to Angela.

'Hi everyone,' Karen said.

'How was your day?' David asked with that cheeky smile and seductive eyes he'd flashed at her the day before.

'I spent the day in Kuta on the beach,' said Karen, holding up her hand for Angela to inspect her freshly painted fingernails.

Angela took her hand and said, 'That's what I need.'

Karen ordered a drink and David said, 'We were thinking about trying the Sato restaurant tonight if you would like to join us; it's just two resorts down along the beach path.'

'If you don't think I'm gate crashing, I'd love to.'

'I did book for five, just in case,' he offered with that smile.

Thank you, that's very thoughtful,' Karen replied.

After just the one drink, Karen excused herself to freshen up and change for dinner. She offered to meet them at the restaurant. She wanted to look nice, reminding herself, *dress to impress. Who knows who might be there?*

She showered and picked out a strappy summer dress, a floral mini that highlighted her figure and accentuated her slim, sexy legs. She looked in the mirror and was quite happy with what she saw. After the final touches to her makeup, she locked the door behind her, headed toward the sand, and joined the path that ran the entire length of the Nusa Dua beach. She turned right heading south and was easily at the restaurant in time.

There was a spare seat between Angela and Rose with David and Bill opposite, the two men standing as she approached. *Old fashioned, but I like it*, she thought.

'Hello everyone,' she said, taking her seat.

'Would you like a glass of chardonnay?' Bill offered, picking up a bottle from an ice bucket that sat next to him.

'Thank you, yes, please,' Karen replied.

The restaurant specialised in seafood, and Karen felt it only right that she indulge herself. She ordered a pan-seared Barramundi, apparently flown in straight from Darwin. She doubted that, although the price suggested it may have flown first class. David continued to seduce her with his eyes but not enough to make her feel uncomfortable, and she'd decided that if no better options presented, he'd be who she thought about when she lay naked in her bed tonight. The conversation with Rose and Angela became more animated by the time the third bottle of wine was finished. Karen had discovered that Bill was Rose's second husband and apparently was 'a gun in the sack,' and also that Angela and David had been together since high school.

Bill was the first to yawn. Karen wasn't sure whether it was a signal to move on or whether he was actually tired. Anyway, they soon paid their bills. Rose had heard Angela and Karen talking about how much they enjoyed their nightcap on the beach the night before and suggested that they all check it out before venturing back to their rooms.

Again, the two men decided to call it a night, leaving the three women to adorn the beach bar. Rose had only one drink before deciding to leave Karen and Angela to have another. Once Rose had left, it gave them another person to talk about, which they did, being nice of course, as Rose was such a likeable person.

At 10 o'clock, the waiter closed the bar, leaving Angela and Karen alone once more on the now moonlit beach. It was almost a mirror of the previous night; the warm breeze teasing their hair and the twinkle of the lights on the water just made the experience breathtaking. They were both silent for a while as each looked out over the water, but their minds were thinking of something else.

'About last night...' Karen blurted out, probably louder than what she meant to.

'I know, I'm sorry—truly,' Angela said.

'No, I think I liked it,' Karen said. 'I was a little horny when I got home thinking about it.'

'My God so was I,' Angela said, taking Karen's hand. They both laughed, their eyes glued to each other.

It was silent for a moment when Angela asked, 'Would you like to try it again?'

'Yes,' Karen said softly, nearly shaking from the excitement.

They both stood, looking into each other's eyes. Angela again took Karen's face in her hands and leant forward to kiss her. It was just a peck, both women holding their eyes open.

'Is that okay?' Angela asked.

Karen nodded in approval. Angela kissed her again a little firmer this time, sucking Karen's bottom lip as she pulled away.

'Still okay?' she asked again.

'Yes,' Karen said, her eyes opening slowly and a smile formed on her face.

Next was the most passionate kiss she'd ever experienced. Angela's hands were caressing her back and the sides of her breasts. Karen didn't know how to respond at first, but soon found her hands inside the back of Angela's top. Angela kissed her neck and earlobe, before again asking her how she felt.

'My pants are wet, if that answers your question!' Karen replied.

'God, so are mine,' Angela said.

Their lips joined again, and Karen felt Angela lift her dress and slide her fingers inside her panties. Karen didn't protest. Angela's lips were at Karen's ear when she said, 'I want to fuck you, Karen.'

This was a shock, and she pulled away gently to look Angela in the eye. It was clear to Karen that Angela meant what she said.

'Is that even possible?' Karen asked.

'Of course… not in the traditional sense, I guess,' Angela suggested, the desperation slightly fading from her face.

'This is all a bit overwhelming just at the minute, I'm still quite confused with the feelings I have,' Karen offered. 'Let's sleep on it and talk tomorrow.'

Angela, not wanting to come on too strong, nodded and kissed her quickly on the lips again.

Karen took her hand and turned back toward the resort. She wasn't aware that Angela was also battling with her own emotions. They kissed again and went their separate ways.

Once back in her suite, Karen flopped back onto the enormous bed and stared at the rotating ceiling fan.

'Could I really make love to a woman?' she asked herself. 'Be completely naked, kiss, lick, and suck our way over each other's bodies?'

She swung herself off the bed and headed for the bathroom. She cleaned her teeth, before removing her makeup and clothes. She lay naked on the bed, imagining Angela next to her running her soft, feminine fingers over her body.

'I think I *could* do it,' she said to herself. 'But first I want a man.'

Next morning Karen skipped the hotel breakfast and ordered a taxi to take her to Ubud, a little village in the north that sold almost everything Balinese from dresses to wood carvings. She spent most of the day in and out of shops. She ate lunch at a lovely restaurant that was part of a flash five-star hotel; it wasn't cheap, but it was delicious. It was then she decided that if she was to find a man, it would have to be at Kuta.

She shopped for another two hours before finding a taxi to take her back to the wild side of the island. The one-hour trip gave her time to catch up on her emails and message a few friends. The night before with Angela kept replaying in her mind; remembering how wet she got from her kisses and the gentle touch when Angela had put her fingers inside her knickers. Her body immediately responded to the thought, and she knew she now had an itch that needed desperately to be scratched.

Karen arrived at Kuta beach at around 4.30 p.m. Time for a beer, a massage, and then to find a club that might have some action. She was quickly ushered to a chair on the beach by a shirtless young Balinese man. A Bintang soon filled her hand, and the warm breeze added the only other requirement to make it a perfect afternoon.

She finished the beer, paid the three dollars, and thanked the very appreciative, almost naked, young man. A stroll down the street that ran parallel to the beach found an endless supply of massage options. It wasn't until she saw a young girl holding a menu for the many massages her shop offered and her warm welcoming smile that she decided to stop and indulge in an hour of relaxing bliss.

It was 6.30 p.m. and starting to get dark when she walked out from the massage. The first bar she came to was already pumping with music and holiday makers. She was wearing the same mini dress she wore to dinner two nights before and was pleased when a few men turned to watch her walk in. She ordered a beer and took a seat at a table for four near the front window.

Three of the men who had stopped talking to watch her arrive occasionally turned to look over and smile at her. One of them took her fancy. He was the one furthest away and didn't need to turn to look at her. She felt great; her long tanned legs spilled endlessly from the mini dress, her hair was down, and her make-up retouched after the massage.

With all her might she tried to resist looking at the three men, but each time she did, one or all of them were looking in her direction. She tried to imagine what they were saying about her— was it complimentary or just a 'I'd do that' statement? A few people came and went, and after she finished her beer, she decided to check out another club in the street.

As she stood, the man she liked clearly looked disappointed, his head rising to take in her departure. *Well, there's one option,* she thought. When she reached the door, turned, and looked back at him, a warm smile filled his face. Her heart missed a beat, and she stepped out onto the street and headed to the next noisy bar. She hoped he would follow her, but he didn't.

Three clubs and three beers later, Karen made her way back to the first club, hoping he would still be there. She walked in and she saw him notice her straight away. She ordered another beer and sat at the same table she was at earlier. He smiled and lifted his beer as if to say, 'welcome back.' She smiled back, and not exactly knowing what to do, she also lifted her beer. Within a minute he approached her, introducing himself as Paul. He was from Perth and here in Bali with two mates for five days. She hadn't even finished her beer before Paul asked her if she would like to come back to his room. She accepted.

As soon as his apartment door closed the pace was frantic; they were both naked in seconds and with minimal foreplay she was on her back and Paul was filling her at a frenetic rate. This is what she wanted and what she needed; the first man other than her husband to fuck her in twenty years. It felt good, really good, and she came quickly. Paul was an expert, he held himself full inside her as she rode the wave and then fucked her hard again as she descended. She quickly felt her second orgasm build and squeezed him tight against her chest, her legs wrapped around him with the intent to pull him deeper inside her. Paul picked up the pace and she could tell he was going to blow this time. He moaned slightly—that beautiful moment when the semen starts its pulsing trip from deep inside him—and then exploded into her. His increased pace had her there as well. The feeling of his cock throbbing inside her had them erupt in unison. Her orgasm was bigger this time, longer, she was crushing him with her arms and legs.

Paul then lay still, his manhood still hard and full inside her. He didn't move as she floated back to the room. It wasn't until she was completely relaxed that he slowly removed himself. He moved to the side, his head resting on one hand as he looked at her with a smile. She smiled back.

'You're a good fuck,' she said.

'Thank you, Karen, it's pretty easy when you have a beautiful woman to make love to.'

Nice line, she thought to herself.

It was obvious that Paul wasn't intending for her to stay, and to be honest, she preferred to wake up in her own place back at Nusa Dua. They laid there for a few more minutes before she said she should get going. They dressed and Paul organised her a taxi to take her home. There was no request for phone numbers or future meetings. It was just a quick fuck for them both. He was probably married, she figured, and he'd be bragging about it to his mates for the rest of the trip.

The taxi ride home was forty minutes through the busy traffic. Her body tingled from the hot sex and Paul's cum was now creating havoc in her knickers.

Karen walked through the foyer of the resort, a smile on her face, and that beautiful warm feeling between her legs.

She arrived at her door to find a note. She took it and opened the door. She fell back against it as it closed, the air-conditioning a welcome relief. She placed the keycard in the holder and the room lit up. She lifted her dress and dropped the sticky, wet knickers to her feet, kicking them towards the wall. She opened the note and read it.

Angela had searched for Karen since breakfast, and when she was been nowhere to be seen all day, Angela was near distraught. She was convinced that she had pushed Karen too far last night and that she was now avoiding her. Karen was all she could think about. She had never made love to a woman before, but she'd fallen for Karen; she wanted her naked, to touch her, kiss her, and love her. Her need was so bad she wanted to cry. It was all she could think of doing to leave Karen a note, in the hope Karen might forgive her.

Karen, I hope you aren't avoiding me. Tomorrow is our last day and I have to see you, please, just one more time. I can be free all day, we have a dinner tomorrow night though. Please, love Angela XX

Karen placed the note on the dressing table and hopped into the shower. She let the warm water flow over her, the pressure was amazing. She thought about what she should do about the Angela situation. Having just had hot sex with Paul, her sexual needs had been satisfied for the moment. But she did like Angela. There was something so alluring and naughty that had stirred unexpected feelings in her. Angela's softness, her touch, and her kisses… well, they were just divine. She reached for the taps and said to herself, 'I think I'd really like a little more of her.'

Next morning, Karen was again at the toaster when Angela appeared next to her.

'Have I upset you, Karen?' Angela said beseechingly.

Karen turned towards her, touched her cheek, and said, 'Of course not, darling one. I went to Kuta yesterday.'

A smile of relief formed on Angela's face. 'Is it okay if we catch up again, perhaps on our own?' she asked.

'How's my place at noon?' Karen said. She could see the elation on Angela's face.

By the time Karen had finished breakfast, enjoyed a swim, showered, and ventured across the road to the supermarket to buy a bottle of Riesling, it was soon 12 o'clock. Almost perfectly on time, a soft knock broke the silence. Karen opened the door and a smiling Angela walked in. Karen closed the door and kissed Angela on the lips. As Karen pulled back, she could see Angela's eyes were still closed.

'Would you like a drink?' Karen offered.

'Love one, whatever you're having will be fine.'

Karen opened the screw top bottle of wine and filled two already prepared glasses. She handed one to Angela.

They clinked glasses and Karen smiled. 'I'm a little nervous, I must admit,' she said.

'Me too, but very excited as well,' Angela replied.

Angela placed her glass on the cabinet that held the big flat screen television and Karen did the same. Angela stood up close in front of Karen and began to unbutton her blouse, starting at the top and slowly working her way down in no rush at all. Karen's bra came into view more and more with each button. It gave Angela an arousing tingle seeing Karen's underwear. Karen filled her white bra fully, her nipples obviously firm beneath the satin material. Angela slipped the blouse from her and placed it on a chair that was behind her. Angela ran her finger along the lace edge of the bra and Karen's eyes closed again. She ran her fingers along the straps that ran over her shoulders and, stepping forward, reached behind her and released the three-hook clip. Angela stepped back a quarter step to see Karen's breasts unrestrained, the bra now only a loose cover.

Karen opened her eyes, her expression now full of passion and arousal. Angela lifted the straps from her shoulders and let gravity take the garment. Karen gasped as she realised she was now alone and topless in front of a woman she hardly knew. Angela's hands found the button and zip of Karen's shorts, and, along with her panties, pulled them down over her hips and let them fall to the floor. Karen was now completely naked and almost shaking from how hot and naughty this felt. Angela took another half step back to admire the naked woman standing in front of her. Their eyes met again, glowing with the look of desperate desire for each other.

Angela raised her arms above her head as a smile formed on her face. Karen stepped forward and lifted Angela's dress over her head, revealing that she wore no underwear at all. For just a moment they stood there taking in the moment, both naked, both their bodies tingling. Angela reached and took Karen's hand and without her eyes leaving her, guided her to the large bed. Karen lay down and Angela followed. Angela was on her side, her raised head resting on her arm.

Angela's right hand started running slowly over Karen's body. Her touch was as soft as a feather. Angela traced Karen's breasts, her nipples, thighs, and the creases where her legs met her groin, until eventually feeling the wetness beneath her mound. She kissed her lips as she found the firm button that lay within the juices of lust. She was in no rush, she wanted to take Karen on a journey like none before. Angela's kiss was soft, but with purpose; her fingers had intensity, but no urgency. Her wish was for Karen to build at her own pace, no haste, how only a woman would know.

Karen was building alright—a heat was burning inside her, increasing with pressure and temperature with each second, every stroke that Angela swept across her clitoris and swollen lips.

Karen wasn't sure how this would go; this was foreign ground. She'd had explosive orgasms before, just like with Paul twice the night before, but this was different. This burn was from deeper inside her. *Was it the fact it was a married woman whose husband was probably only metres away in another room? Or was it more? Did she hold feelings for Angela, a love she had never known she would be so desperate for?*

She let her thoughts go as the heat continued to build, the pressure soon reaching a limit she could no longer control. Angela's kiss became more passionate, her fingers a little firmer.

Karen's insides were boiling—she was no longer in control of her body, Angela was.

Karen felt that first pleasurable pain, the first uncontrolled convulsion, the spark that would ignite the explosive charge. Angela slid two fingers deep into Karen. Karen's head flew back from Angela's lips, as she released something between a moan, scream, and a yell. It filled the room, a sound that any other nearby guest would be left in no doubt as to its source. A second moan coincided with the next convulsion. Karen's body jumped in time as each wave pounded through her body. Then those couple of seconds as the thread of silk is dragged through your soul, and then the falling feeling as the electrifying charges start to equalise—then there was silence, a complete stillness, not a finger moved, not a word spoken, just the feeling of her inner being descending back from heaven to her earthly body.

Angela watched and had a smile to greet Karen as she arrived back. Removing her fingers would be the last part of her trip. They were covered in the orgasmic fluid that had flowed from Karen.

Karen lay there, exhausted and spent, but physically satisfied like never before. Karen's eyes opened slowly, a smile taking a while to form on her shattered face.

'My God. I was on another planet,' Karen said.

'Yes you were, my beautiful friend.'

'I've never felt anything like that before,' Karen said, nearly recovered.

Angela removed her fingers with the gentleness of a eye surgeon, but still it made Karen cringe.

'I'm sorry, but you can't keep them forever,' Angela said softly.

Angela continued to caress Karen, as they kissed, talked, and kissed some more. Karen had never licked a woman, but she really wanted to taste the sweetness of the person her heart was now open for.

Karen lifted herself, indicating for Angela to lay back. Karen knelt over her on her hands and knees. Her breasts rested against her lovers' as she kissed her, that feeling alone sending shivers through her. Karen couldn't believe how beautiful Angela looked, her blonde hair falling across the pillow and her seductive blue eyes full of the lust that she now also shared. Karen kissed Angela's lips, her neck, and each nipple before working her way south.

She loved how soft Angela's skin was; no man could ever feel or taste this sweet. Karen kissed all around her pubic area, teasing her, making Angela groan with anticipation. Karen continued to tease her with her tongue and lips. She felt Angela's fingers in her hair and decided to give her what she was now so desperate for. The first stroke of Karen's tongue over her firm bud, made Angela moan. Karen felt Angela's hips rise as the tip of her tongue continued to circle her, before sucking the firm flesh into her mouth.

Angela had never been with a woman before, not like this. She'd kissed a couple at drunken parties, and sure, it was nice, but Karen was different—the lovemaking felt so natural and so right. When she kissed Karen, she didn't need to try, her emotions and her desires just knew what and how to do it. Having a woman touch her with such softness was blissful. She knew she was in love with this woman. As Karen licked and sucked, Angela felt her feelings surrender to the moment and this person. Angela's orgasm was well on the way when the first tears formed in her eyes. Her climax would be so different to Karen. It was more emotional than physical—she came for Karen; she came because a woman she loved more than anything in that moment was performing an intimate sexual act on her. Angela's burn was from her heart. Probably more powerful and certainly more dangerous.

Angela reached down and pulled Karen on top her, hugging her tight. Not enough to crush her, but nearly. Karen's head was buried in Angela's beautiful blonde hair when she realised she was crying. Karen pushed back on her arms.

'Are you okay?' Karen asked with the softness of a caring lover.

With tears flowing freely into her hair, Angela said. 'I love you, Karen; it's not lust, I truly love you.'

'But you don't even know me!' Karen protested.

'I knew the second I saw you,' Angela said.

Karen moved to lay beside her and wiped the tears from her face. She didn't know what to say. When she finally spoke, the words formed and were delivered without any consultation with her sensible side.

'I think I love you too,' Karen admitted.

Angela burst into tears again and hugged Karen.

'I can't believe how right this feels, how can it be wrong?' Angela said. 'I've known you five days and you have taken my heart.'

Karen could see the clock from where she lay and knew Angela would need to leave soon, but she couldn't let her go home like this.

'Let's have a shower?' Karen suggested.

'I can't get my hair wet,' Angela protested.

'You need to let the water flow over your face. Say you've been in the pool and will need some extra time to dry your hair.'

They spent most of the time hugging and caressing. There was no time now for any more lovemaking, but both women enjoyed the moment immensely as they soaped each other's bodies.

Angela dried herself and slipped her dress back over her head. She slipped on her flats and kissed Karen again. Angela pulled back, taking Karen's face in her hands, and said, 'I'm so in love with you.'

She turned, opened the door, and was gone. Karen stood there still wrapped in the white hotel towel staring at the closed door, trying to understand the enormity of what had just happened. She lay back on the bed, avoiding the huge wet spot she herself had caused. Karen's heart was pounding, she placed a hand on her chest, she could feel it. Eventually a warmth came over her and she said in a soft voice, 'I love you, my darling Angela.'

Next morning Karen was early to breakfast, 7.30 a.m. She knew Angela, David, Bill, and Rose were leaving today and she decided she had to spend every second possible with Angela. She hadn't yet got her number, she didn't even know her last name, and she simply had to see her again. 8.30 a.m. had come and gone, then 9.30 a.m., and a cold panic engulfed her.

No, no, she can't leave me like this! her head screamed.

By 10.30 a.m. Karen was the only remaining person in the restaurant. She watched the staff clearing away the breakfast items and start to prepare for lunch.

Karen stood up, in a daze, with nothing feeling right. The sun was too bright, the temperature too hot, and the birds too noisy. She tried to think. *They must've left early, maybe their flight had changed? She told me she loved me; I know she meant it. Surely, she would've left me a note at reception.*

Everything was starting to become clearer now, and she headed for the front desk. New arrivals were everywhere waiting to check in. She waited till a clerk had become free between guests and pushed in.

'Sorry, just a quick question,' she said apologetically to the next couple waiting to be served as she stepped up to the desk. Turning to the desk clerk she asked, 'Excuse me, I'm Karen Johnson, room 1025, do you have any messages for me?'

The clerk, looking a little frustrated, pulled open a large dark timber drawer that was below the immediate counter. He flicked through a few papers before saying, 'No, Miss Karen, nothing. Sorry.'

Karen mimed a 'thank you,' turned and walked slowly back toward her room. She knew the resort wouldn't share any personal details.

As the hours went by, she missed Angela even more. The next morning, she herself would be checking out and flying back to Melbourne. Then, there would be no connection to the woman she now loved, just ships in the night. It was her turn to cry, and through her tears and broken heart, she called out, 'How could you do this to me?'

She reached for the pillow on which only yesterday the head of the woman she had made love to lay, her blonde hair spilling carelessly in all directions, her blue eyes seductively eating into her soul. She could smell her, the scent of the perfume she wore as they made love. It was some time before Karen stopped crying and fell asleep.

The next morning Karen awoke feeling numb, with a heavy heart, like a close friend had died. She tried to pull herself together and did. She focused on the good parts of the holiday. She now had a tan that everyone in Melbourne would kill for. She screwed a man in Kuta, and that's what she'd came for, after all.

She packed, picked up her case, extended the handle, and headed for the door for the last time. As she opened it to exit, she stopped and looked back to the bed where the woman she now loved had laid with her. She took a deep breath, turned, and closed the door. It was quite a walk back to reception and the queue for checking out was about six deep. She waited her turn calmly, as her flight wasn't till later in the afternoon. There was no rush.

She checked out, really a simple case of handing over her credit card and paying for all the charges to her room. Three taxis were waiting outside. She was heading for the first one when she heard, 'Miss Karen, there's a message for you.'

The Runner

It was nearly Christmas and parties were happening almost every night, with a constant stream of invites to social, family, and work functions. Sandy used to be a party girl but that was a while ago now. She was middle aged and divorced with grown-up kids. She now relished her life as a single woman and had no intention of changing that—well, not any time soon anyway. She loved her work; she was able to spend time with some very interesting and famous people. To be honest, she just loved that everyone really liked her, valued her contribution, and trusted and respected her as an important cog in a very big wheel.

She was a runner in the film industry. She'd pick up the cast and take them to set, she'd drop off rushes after each day of shooting—basically, she was the ultimate 'Girl Friday.' Whenever someone wanted something done, it was always, 'Get Sandy to do it.'

She was really looking forward to tonight. It was a dinner with a few friends in her street, at Mary's house to be exact. She'd be the only single person there, but she was more than happy with that. Sandy was a 'glass-half-full' person; she appreciated the advantages of being with someone as well as the advantages of being on her own. Alone, she would indulge her own fantasy—about a special man being with her to caress her, kiss her, make love to her, and cuddle her till the tingles of ecstasy subsided. But that man was forever fictitious, made perfect only by her imagination. No real man could be just right for her, to leave her be when she needed to be alone, or at those times when she wanted to console herself. Not to pester her about why she was sad or incessantly ask if something was wrong just because she didn't feel like smiling.

Her imaginary man would always simply smile at her, give her a hug, and whisper in her ear, 'I love you.' He was perfect.

Tonight's choice of dress was aptly summer; it was bright and screamed of fun and sunshine. A white, full-bottomed, twirling, light fabric, adorned with large crimson red hibiscus flowers with dark green stems and leaves. It was short sleeved, with a bodice that tapered to her waist. While perhaps maybe a little low cut and tight for her full bosom, she liked the way the little protrusion of flesh made her feel and added a little hint of sexy. The skirt flared out to just below her knees and she wore white, strappy, wedge-heeled sandals. Sandy matched her lipstick boldly to the hibiscus on her dress and let her shoulder-length hair flow naturally and softly, with only a brush and a little touch of product.

As she headed for the door, she grabbed her purse and phone, stealing a quick glance in the hallway mirror for a final check. She stopped and looked at her reflection in the darkened passage. She looked at her eyes, still recognising the spark and deep alluring colour that the fifteen-year-old Sandy's gaze held all those years ago. A smile appeared on the face of the forty-five-year-old that looked back at her. She quickly scanned the rest of herself with approval. *You look all right, woman,* she thought as she cupped her breast and centred her bra. Then, although the words never actually formed in her mind, she fleetingly wondered if Clint might think she was pretty, sexy, and flirt with her again?

She frowned at herself. She couldn't allow even her imagination to indulge these thoughts, as Clint was Mary's husband. Although nothing had ever been said, or even that she'd ever dare go there, they'd quite often found each other holding their stare for a second longer than they should. Clint always listened intently to her conversation and was always keen to hear stories of her adventures in the film industry.

The flirtatious moments were flattering and fun, but simply fuel for her fantasies. Sometimes, at home after seeing him that day, she'd lay in bed and allow her thoughts to bring him there with her. She'd imagine his smell, his taste, and his touch, as she indulged herself in some self-love.

She turned away from the mirror, reached for the door, stepped out, and listened for the click as the lock engaged. The lock badly needed adjusting because without a hard pull the tongue wouldn't lock into the striker plate and a firm push would have it easily open. 'Damn it! I really need to get this door fixed,' she said out loud after three hard slams. After finally securing the door, she walked toward Mary and Clint's house with a hint of music beneath her feet.

'Clint, are you nearly ready? Everyone will be here soon!' Mary called out from downstairs.

'On my way,' he called back.

Clint was always excited to have guests over, he was a true entertainer. The fact that Sandy was coming tonight gave him an extra tingle; she just oozed sex appeal, which he desperately wanted to be covered in. He'd imagined many times Sandy giving herself to him, and how he would make love to her over and over. He would sometimes imagine Mary was Sandy when they made love, and his enthusiasm would boil over in orgasmic pleasure. In fact, he was sure one time he'd called Mary 'Sandy' but luckily, she mustn't've heard him. He would do almost anything to have her, often dreaming about her walking up to him, reaching out to touch his cheek with her fingers, and then whispering in his ear, 'Have your way with me.'

Clint shook his head to wipe the image from his mind and headed downstairs. Halfway down, the doorbell rang.

'I've got it,' he called out as he opened the door to Shane and Vicki from next door. 'Hello,' he said as he kissed Vicki on the cheek and reached for Shane's hand. They shook and Shane presented Clint with a bottle of red wine.

'Thank you. Come on in,' Clint said as he held his arm out, gesturing in the direction of the lounge room.

Mary had appeared just at that same time, smiling with similar greetings. The doorbell rang again, and Clint excused himself. Soon after, Michael and Kath entered and the greetings continued. Clint looked at his watch to check the time—Sandy was the only one not here yet.

Clint set about pouring drinks for everyone and Mary chatted with the girls about their children and their Christmas preparations, while putting the finishing touches to a cheese plate.

They were all good friends. Their lives had been spent knowing and growing alongside each other for years; everyone was relaxed with no one overly trying, or really needing, to impress anyone.

Clint checked his watch again as the doorbell rang. He put down his drink and headed for the door. He opened the door to finally see Sandy smiling up at him. Their eyes locked for what seemed like an eternity, making Clint feel like he was in a trance. *Did my heart miss a beat?* he thought.

'You look... stunning, Sandy,' he said as his eyes moved from hers to her bosom, and then scanning the rest of her body and that dress. 'Please come in,' he said, only allowing enough room so that she had to rub against him as she passed. He sucked in her scent as she brushed against his chest.

Sandy walked up to all the guests in turn and kissed each on the cheek before settling in the kitchen with the other women. She felt a hand touch her back, quite gently, yet firm at the same time, as a voice asked, 'What would you like to drink, Sandy?'

She turned to Clint and replied lightly, 'Bubbles would be great, the same as the girls, thank you.'

As Clint handed Sandy her drink, she was careful not to make eye contact. She somehow felt a heightened attention rising in him tonight. After all, she told herself, she can't go there, and she mustn't give him any further encouragement.

The night went well, everyone had had plenty to drink and eat. Sandy entertained them with stories about antics on set, while Mary told them all about her week endured with her kids at camp and how her own children were so embarrassed by her singing karaoke on the last night. It was a night filled with laughter, so relaxed and enjoyable.

Shane and Vicki were the first to go. Sandy didn't want to be the last of the guests to remain, so she announced it was time for her to depart too, and there was a minor protest from Clint. She'd avoided looking at him for most of the night. She didn't want Mary or anyone else noticing *'that look,'* the one that would be so obvious—especially to a suspicious wife. Mary was her good friend, so Sandy was more than happy to just leave Clint in her thoughts, as always. Sandy kissed and thanked Mary for a great night and they agreed to catch up in the morning to go shopping.

Clint walked Sandy to the door and reached to kiss her lips. Sandy quickly turned her head to offer her cheek. It was a messy kiss from Clint as he'd really had a lot to drink. His hands brushed her breast as he went to give her a quick hug. It had been some time since any man had touched her and she instinctively stepped back.

'Thank you for a lovely night,' she said as she stepped away and headed for her house. She looked back to see Mike and Kath saying their goodbyes as well and could see Clint watching her walk away. She could feel the skirt of her dress sway from side to side as she walked and imagined what that might look like to Clint.

The wine had aroused a sense of desperation in Clint that was almost uncontrollable. He'd convinced himself that the clumsy touch of her breast was not only enjoyed but encouraged by Sandy, as he also believed that given the opportunity, she would fall into his arms and make all his dreams come true.

He stopped, looked around, and listened. Mary was already upstairs cleaning her teeth and getting ready for bed.

'I'll just tidy up a bit more,' he called out to Mary.

'Sure, don't wake me,' Mary called back.

Sandy reached her front door, unlocked it, stepped in, and leant back against it as it closed.

My God, what am I doing? I must talk to him and tell him nothing can happen, she lamented, having felt and carried Clint's watchful eyes all evening. She shed the thoughts with a sigh as she kicked off her shoes and headed for her bedroom. The zip at the back of her dress was much harder to undo now, but she eventually managed and slipped it off, along with her bra. It was a warm night so she decided on wearing just her knickers. After spending a while in the bathroom, cleaning her teeth and cleansing her face as best she could, she hopped into bed and thought about the night, and Clint.

Clint had put a few bottles out and finished stacking the dishwasher. All he could think about was that Sandy would now be undressing, and wondering if she would be thinking of him while she removed her clothes. *Was she wishing he was undressing her?*

He pictured her laying naked on her bed as he slowly moved between her legs. The thought had made him aroused; he touched the bulge in his pants and whispered quietly to himself, 'It's for you, Sandy.' He went upstairs and through the bedroom door he could see Mary fast asleep. He stood there for a second before deciding he needed to tell Sandy how he felt, how she's all he thinks about. He turned and quietly went downstairs and out the front door. He was shaking with excitement.

His thoughts were rampant, filled with wanting. *She may be naked and waiting for me, maybe she has already started without me, maybe I can arrive just in time to fill her as she comes?*

Clint stood outside her front door. All the lights were off.

My God, what am I doing? He countered his own hesitation. He placed his right hand on the door and looked down at his feet. He pushed himself away from the door, and it swung slowly open. The striker hadn't locked when Sandy got home.

He stepped inside and closed the door gently behind him. He slipped off his shoes. He knew where her bedroom was, he'd been in her house many times before, mostly when she was still married to Phil. Her bedroom door was open, and in the dim light that cascaded from the streetlight outside he could see her almost naked body. She was on her back, obviously asleep, her breasts lying flat on her chest, her large nipples laid at rest, rising gently with each breath. His eyes moved to her knickers and her legs that were just slightly apart; she looked so delicious and inviting. His heart pounded. He was so close to the thing he wanted most in all this world.

For the second time tonight, he rubbed his erection through his pants. He felt for the zip and undid it. He slid his jeans quietly to the floor, his shirt and underpants following quickly. He stood there, completely naked, his erection in his hand, as he watched her breasts rising and falling with each soft breath. He stroked himself slowly as he looked at her smooth, parted legs. He was now desperate to be between them. He eased himself to sit down softly on the bed next to her and ran a finger softly between her breasts. He wanted to give her a slow and gentle awakening that would lead to her saying, 'Oh Clint, I've been waiting for you.'

Sandy was in a deep sleep, and, to be honest, she alone would state that she could sleep through World War III. She started to wake slightly, with the subconscious feeling she wasn't alone. It wasn't in a scary way, just that she was aware someone was there. Her first thoughts were that she had a lover who was caressing her. As she woke more, without opening her eyes, she realised she'd gone to bed alone. Her eyes flew open, enough to recognise Clint in the faint light.

'What are you doing here?' she screamed as she grabbed for the sheet that was down around her feet.

'I want you, Sandy, and I know you want me too. I've seen the way you look at me; we are here now both naked, let's make each other's dreams come true.'

'Clint! Are you crazy? I'm not going to sleep with you—not now or ever. My God! Your wife is my friend.' She clutched the sheet tighter to her, desperately trying to sit up against the bed head.

'Have I read the signs wrong? I was certain there was a little something special between us.'

'There is, but I'm not going to sleep with you! How on earth did you get in anyway?'

'The door wasn't locked. I thought that it may've been an invitation.'

'No, it wasn't, and you need to go before someone sees you here.'

Clint stood up slowly. Sandy could see he was completely naked, but no longer armed with what he was so desperate to give her. She watched him dress and walk from her bedroom. He stopped, turned, and said, 'I'm really sorry, Sandy, please forgive me.'

Sandy didn't answer, nor did he wait for her reply, now consumed with embarrassment and shame. She heard the front door open and close. In a flash, she jumped out of bed, went straight to the door, and pushed it hard until it clicked.

'I need to get that door fixed,' she murmured to herself.

The Dress

Andrew Stephen's approach to planning was always ten steps ahead of anybody else, so when it came to spoiling his new lady, Robyn Coats, it had to be perfect. He sat back in his office chair, pen in hand, and a plan was created.

He drafted a minute-by-minute schedule of the most exciting twenty-four hours anyone had ever had for their birthday—well, anyone outside the billionaire status anyway. It would need to be based around a dinner, of course, but not just any dinner. She loved duck, and so did he. A quick search of the internet found a couple of special places; one in Melbourne and the other in Sydney. He decided on Sydney and a restaurant booking was made, and so started his creative plan. Next was to ask her to keep the weekend free and let her know she would need an overnight bag; nothing special, just the bare essentials.

He booked two business class flights from Adelaide on Saturday, 30th of August—which was her actual birthday—around lunchtime and returning back about the same time the next day. He'd arranged accommodation at the five-star Shangri-La Hotel, right at the Harbour's edge, for the night. The timing for what he'd planned was going to be tight, however the hotel, restaurant and shopping area were all close by.

To make sure she would feel spoilt from the start, before they even departed Adelaide, Andrew visited the airport and spoke personally to the staff at the airline lounge. He explained his surprise gift for his lady to the two women on duty at the lounge front counter and asked if he could have a free entry pass for Robyn, so she could meet him inside without needing him to escort her as his guest. His romantic plans hit the spot, along with some charm and a cheeky smile. He secured a pass without a blink!

Next, he had to arrange getting Robyn to the airport. He sat and penned three separate messages, placing each note in an individual envelope. Then he booked a limousine to collect her from her unit. Andrew had arranged specifically to meet the driver who would being chauffeuring her on the day. Andrew explained the importance of the trip and handed the driver the three envelopes. The driver listened carefully and noted the instructions regarding exactly when they were to be handed to his passenger. The messages were clear, simple, and intriguing.

The first: *Happy birthday! Grab your bag.* This was to be handed to her when the driver arrived at her door.

The second envelope was to be given to her as the driver approached the city. It read, *please join me for dinner at Australia's number one duck restaurant.*

The third was to be handed over once the driver reached Sir Donald Bradman Drive, when it would become obvious she was heading for the airport. It simply contained a boarding pass and the lounge pass.

The day had come. The driver arrived perfectly on time and with a simple, 'Hello,' handed Robyn the first envelope. He watched her smile as she opened it and read the message. With a grin, she picked up her bag and hopped into the rear of the S-class Mercedes Benz. The driver handed the other two envelopes as instructed. It was only a twenty-minute trip to the airport, so it wasn't long before she was thanking the driver and watching the big black car drive away.

Once through the security she mildly panicked, worried that she may be far underdressed for whatever he had planned, but reminded herself that Andrew had stipulated 'bare essentials.'

She found Andrew sitting in his favourite seat in the lounge, two glasses of champagne on the table in front of him. He stood as she approached, her radiant smile and beauty almost bringing tears to his eyes. She was breathtaking. He kissed her softly and invited her to sit.

'Happy birthday, gorgeous,' he said.

'You're a wonderful and most naughty man. I loved the envelopes!' she said.

Robyn resisted asking the questions she badly wanted to ask, as she knew he wouldn't tell her anyway. They were the envy of any woman that could see them; Andrew, completely engaged in his lady, a constant smile and animated reaction to any comment she made. How he constantly touched her, stroked her face, her hair, and a hand always on her leg. His eyes never leaving hers as they spoke and that smile that most married women can only just recall as a distant memory. The smile of two people completely in love.

'QF738 to Sydney is now boarding at gate 22,' came over the speaker.

'That's us, babe,' he said.

They finished their champagne and picked up their bags. He kissed her as she stood, driving a stake through the hearts of the many women that had been watching them.

They boarded the plane and took their seats, 1A and 1C. They were served another glass of champagne and lunch was soon ordered and served. They spent the flight talking, touching, and enjoying the excitement of what else was to come. Their infatuation wasn't wasted on the flight attendant as she presented them with a bottle of wine and said, 'I've never seen two people so much in love, you've made my day.'

Andrew smiled and offered a, 'Thank you.' Robyn wanted to cry; it was all such a fairy-tale.

The plane landed on time, which was essential to Andrew's plans. They both had carry-on luggage, so within minutes they were in a cab and on their way to the harbour-view hotel. Andrew checked in, and as soon as they entered their room, Robyn was so ready to have him, tear off his clothes and have her special man inside her.

'No, no, no!' he said. 'We don't have time for that now. We still have a lot to do before dinner!'

Robyn was rather surprised; he'd never turned down that offer before. But she was even more excited to find out what was still to come. Andrew was resolved; they were leaving straight away.

Andrew led her out of the hotel, his hand in hers, and headed towards the city—the Westfield Tower to be exact. He knew this was where all the exclusive dress shops that a girl could want were located.

Andrew checked his watch; they were a few minutes ahead of time. They stopped to grab a drink at a little bar along the way, but they didn't linger to enjoy another, as Andrew wanted to maximise the shopping time.

Once they arrived at Centrepoint, Andrew led her to level two, where all the designer boutiques were in one place. He stopped, standing in the middle of the tiled landing, outstretched his arms, and turned around slowly. 'Okay, visit as many places as you want. Find a dress for tonight. *This* is your birthday present.'

Her smile erupted and didn't leave her face for the next two hours. She visited several stores and tried on many dresses with lots of banter, giggles, and fun shared between them, but she found it hard to choose. Andrew thought she looked beautiful in them all. Eventually, they'd found themselves at Max Mara, and Robyn tried on a simple, sleek, mid-length, sleeveless, champagne-coloured dress. The minute she walked out of the change room to show Andrew, he said, 'Wow! That's the one—you look divine. Do you like it?'

'Yes, I love it, babe,' she gushed.

'Okay, but before you take it off, you need shoes to match.'

Robyn just beamed, and after trying on several pairs, a choice of some elegant pumps, the same colour as the dress, was made.

Checking the time again, Andrew said, 'Hell, we really must get moving. Our booking at the restaurant is only just over an hour away.' Andrew paid and they rushed downstairs and hailed a cab. They needed to be back to the hotel to shower and dress in under thirty minutes. *They could do it*, he thought.

They raced up to their room. Robyn stripped off and headed for the shower first. As she entered the bathroom, Andrew called out, 'Hey babe, there's one more thing. Tonight, you're only allowed to wear what we bought today—just the dress and the shoes!'

'Okay!' Robyn called back in a long, drawn-out tone.

They arrived at the restaurant only ten minutes late and were quickly seated. With all he'd planned for the day, and to end up only ten minutes over schedule, he was pretty happy.

A bottle of wine and a full serving of Peking duck was ordered. They sat next to each other, enjoying the view from their seats that faced the second story window, the position perfect for Andrew to run his fingers up and down the inside of her leg. Despite his fervent temptation to touch her, he decided to only tease her throughout dinner.

The meal was amazing. The waiter carved the duck at their table and assembled the first pancake for them both. Andrew relaxed, knowing he'd made the day a memorable experience for her. She looked absolutely gorgeous in the new dress, and knowing that what was under it would be his final course for the night had him almost shivering with anticipation. They sat back, their stomachs full; it had been a big day. As Robyn consumed the last mouthful of wine, they both knew there was no more fun to be had in the restaurant. Andrew called for the bill.

Luckily, a taxi was waiting at the ramp outside—with it being the last day of winter, neither wanted to be standing in a queue for very long. Once in the cab, Robyn turned to Andrew and whispered, 'Thank you,' placing her palms on his cheeks as she brought her lips to his. The soft, slow kiss soon turned hot and passionate, with their hands frantically feeling each other's body. So consumed by passion, they were oblivious of their surroundings.

Andrew's fingers were soon up her dress and he found her sweet spot. She was so wet. She spread her legs further, inviting him to pleasure her more. That was the moment, with the cab driver frequently checking his rear-view mirror, that Andrew realised Robyn was quite turned on by a bit of voyeurism. She didn't hold back, letting moans escape and allowing her body to writhe in delight at Andrew's touch.

The cab arrived at the hotel, and before he alighted, Andrew threw the cabbie a knowing nod with a generous tip, certain that he'd enjoyed the ride nearly as much as they did. Upstairs, they were again soon locked in an embrace and kissing before the door had closed. Andrew reached behind her and slid the zipper of her dress down, allowing it to fall to the floor.

Robyn had Andrew naked within seconds. They held each other tight, their naked bodies feeling divine as they kissed. Robyn's kiss was full of love, passion, and anticipation of what she now wanted more than anything. Andrew laid her on the bed, their lips not parting for one second. Robyn's legs were spread wide, and he positioned himself easily between them. This was not a time for arousing foreplay, teasing, or sexual build up. They had been there all day. Robyn wanted the man she loved more than anything inside her. Her body was ready, literally dripping for him. Her orgasmic tingles were intense, and only one thing was needed to complete this amazing day. She felt him touch her, so thick and hard, and as he parted the swollen lips, she broke the kiss. Her breath was full, and she exhaled hard as his length filled her. It felt so deep, he was now a part of her. He thrust into her hard again, stimulating every erotic nerve in her body. She was in orgasmic heaven, electric pulses shooting from her vagina to her heart as if his cock touched it with each thrust.

'I love you,' he called out between breaths.

Robyn replied with a moan—it was all she had. She was there, every nerve stimulated to breaking point, and then it arrived, the release, that feeling as if her entire insides were going to exit her body from between her legs. Her orgasmic moan exploded from her as the greatest of human pleasure consumed her body. She felt Andrew pushing deep and through her own indulgence felt him throbbing inside her, his cum pumping so deep she could almost taste it. The moment of total ecstasy seemed to last for much longer than the few seconds of reality. They both fell together like two people holding each other tightly as they descended softly through space and back to earth. As each organ in their bodies slowly returning to its original rested state, neither moved until each had landed.

Andrew lifted himself to look at her. She had never looked so beautiful. He stayed there, looking at the woman he had just pleasured to her ultimate limit. Her eyes were still closed, her look completely relaxed; not exhausted but of total contentment. He watched her eyes open slowly and a smile start to form on that beautiful face. He realised in all his life he would never see another thing more beautiful. His heart could just explode at any moment.

'My God,' she said. 'That was huge.'

He was now fighting back tears, unable to speak, but answered her with a kiss. His head fell beside her face and now he let the tears flow.

He could never love anything more.

Railway Line

*P*roducer Grant Sheppard's scheduled five-day shoot for a new Ford 4x4 TV commercial being filmed in the 380-million-year-old Flinders Ranges had arrived. The welcome change of scenery to this stunning countryside was such a contrast to the big cities he mostly worked in these days. It was a five-hour drive from Adelaide to the unit base at Parachilna, a town he'd always felt something special about. A thriving hotel nestled by the side of a deserted country road. The town's residents basically consisted of the hotel staff. That was until a movie or TV commercial came to town.

The shooting location would be a short drive deep into the Ranges, a favourite spot for film crews. The jagged vertical continental plates that over millions of years had been forced skywards created a breathtaking pre-historic background.

Grant woke at 6.00 a.m. to the sound of the first unit and grip trucks starting to roll in from Adelaide. His eyes opened slowly, taking in the strange new surroundings. He soon knew where he was. He took in a deep breath and quickly dressed. After grabbing a coffee from the bar, he soon joined the location manager to greet the crew with directions for bump in.

It was a constant stream of vehicles for the next few hours, with the usual quiet and stillness of the outback replaced by the bustling sounds as everyone parked, unloaded, and settled into their accommodation. Call sheets had been handed out with the details of the day's shoot, which was scheduled to start later that afternoon. As always, the actors were the last to arrive, and once they did, the second AD would have them quickly attended to by wardrobe and makeup. The storyline was simple, but there was a lot of country to cover.

The TV commercial was aimed to promote a new model four-wheel drive, showing a happy family that would easily travel the challenging roads of the Flinders Ranges.

Grant noticed the runner arrive with the 'on-screen' family of four: two kids, both around ten, a father in his thirties, and an attractive mum who could have been a little older than her on-screen husband. After wardrobe and makeup had fussed over them, they were ferried off to set for the first shot of the week.

Once on set, Grant greeted the actors. 'Hi, I'm Grant Sheppard, the producer,' he said as he shook hands with the lead male actor.

'Hi, Grant, I'm Mark. This is Sam and Bec and this is Anita, my "wife" for this week,' he said with a smirk.

Grant turned to Anita and shook her hand.

Anita was one of the most beautiful women he had ever seen. A striking mix of beauty, class, and a touch of shyness. She was of medium height, and her beautifully svelte and proportioned figure was obvious through her tightly-fitted wardrobe outfit.

Despite her shape and near perfect form, it was her smile, her eyes, and her shoulder-length silky blonde hair that made her instantly breathtaking.

Over the first few days, Mark, the 'film dad,' drove the car on his own in the long camera shots where the full family weren't required. As producer, once shooting commenced and with little else to manage, Grant found himself able to help the crew by ferrying Anita and the kids from location to location. Due to some long distances, Grant knew the kids would get bored easily, so he thought of the ways he had survived the long car trips with his daughters when they were young. While those instances were two decades ago, he was sure his road trip games would still work a treat.

He was right. The four of them became engrossed in his animal game, where one person would think of an animal and each other person could ask one question in turn, until someone correctly guessed what animal it was. They all bonded, and the car trips were soon filled with laughter and fun. During meal breaks, Grant would take Sam and Bec over to the mountainous rock face and explain how they were millions of years old.

'Guys, do you want to see something that no other human has ever seen?' Grant asked.

'Cool! Yes, please,' Sam replied with the wonderous excitement only a ten-year-old could exude.

Grant broke off a layer of rock and explained how a dinosaur could have walked on that piece of rock when it was flat on the ground.

Later, when Grant had dropped the cast for their next scene, Anita hopped out of the car then turned to him and said, 'Can I just say, you have been so amazing with these kids. You've made these long, boring drives so much fun for them.'

'Thank you. They're good kids. These days on set can be so tedious for them, and besides, I enjoy it, it reminds me of the old days with my kids.'

'I've loved the games and stories too and your very easy company.' She paused for a second and turned back to face him, 'Also, it's made a pleasant change from having people hitting on me. I want to thank you for that too.'

'Thank you. But I'm sorry to hear that,' Grant replied.

'Don't be, I'm used to it.' Anita smiled, before turning away and walking off briskly with the second AD.

Grant's chest rose, filled with a warm glow as he watched Anita walk off to prepare for the next shot. He was pleased he'd made her feel relaxed, and more especially, how she'd told him how much she liked being with him.

By the third day, Anita, Grant, and the two kids would seek each other out between filming and often sat together at meals. The kids especially were now excitedly brimming with questions, wanting to hear more about Grant's other film productions and experience in the Ranges. It was soon day four of the five-day shoot, and the caterers had excelled, setting up a Thai banquet for lunch with Massaman red beef curry, green chicken curry, Pad Thai noodles, and rice. They'd set up their outdoor makeshift restaurant in a canyon surrounded by mountainous rock walls that would seldom see sunlight. The layered walls were three hundred feet high, with gigantic gum trees that reached desperately, searching for a drop of sunlight, while a mossy creek gently cascaded with crystal clear water glistening beneath. The backdrop was spectacular.

Grant never took for granted how lucky he was to be able to see and work in these locations in Australia, especially in his own state's backyard.

They all filled their plates. Anita sat comfortably next to Grant, which was now a common sight. They'd just finished their meals when Anita turned to Grant and asked, 'I've got a knot between my shoulder blades. Could you please give it a quick massage for me? I don't think my back is used to all these bumpy roads.'

'Sure, my pleasure,' he replied, as she straddled the bench and turned her back to him. He placed his hands on her shoulders, and his thumbs kneaded the delicate muscles between her shoulder blades. Grant couldn't believe how comfortable this woman made him feel. He suddenly became aware of the eyes of envy that watched from around the marquee. He nodded to the second assistant director.

'It's time to get back to work,' the second AD called out, and Grant gestured for the TV 'family' to move into the car to be ferried back to location.

The last day of the shoot involved only one location in the morning, which allowed Grant to stay behind at unit base and finish up some paperwork before they wrapped the shoot and prepared for home the next day.

Lunchtime was a wrap for the shoot, and the director was very happy with what he had 'in the can,' coining the phrase from the old days when they shot on film.

Grant spent the afternoon tidying loose ends and thanking the crew as they sorted their equipment and packed their trucks. By 7.30 p.m., most were ready for the wrap party drinks that were put on for the cast and crew by the production at the end of every shoot. Grant was talking to the first assistant director when he noticed Anita arrive at the Prairie Hotel's front bar, her long blonde hair tucked behind her ears and falling down her back.

Until now, she'd only ever been in costume attire, so this appearance was a whole new sight. She caught everyone's stare, wearing a thinly strapped mini dress, white with pastel coloured flowers splashed all over it. The volume of the bar dropped instantly by more than half as most of the men stopped, stared, and were rendered speechless to watch her pass by. Grant did a great job not to stumble his own words as she breezed past. While petite in stature, she certainly had a resounding presence.

Grant made his way around the bar room, thanking each person for their contribution to the filming. He couldn't help but glance over at Anita every now and then, seeing her constantly swamped by admirers. He felt himself recoil from their obvious ogling desperation, remembering her comments about how all too frequent and distasteful this sort of attention was for her.

The two kids, Bec and Sam, had been picked up by their parents and thankfully were already on their way home. Grant knew that a wrap party was no place for kids, even if they were the stars of the shoot. It wasn't unusual for a wrap party to get a bit out of hand after such long days, especially when it was an open bar. Grant sat back for a minute or two, admiring how Anita made small talk, pleasantly engaging with everyone who'd come up to her to chat. Every now and then, their eyes would make contact as they each moved around and through the throng of people clambering to catch a word from each of them.

There was a small window of opportunity where he found her alone, finally catching a moment to sit.

He walked up casually. 'How are you coping with all this attention? Do you want to get out of here before it gets out of control?'

'Yes, please!' she replied.

With that, she hopped off her stool and headed for the door. Grant stepped ahead, holding it open for her. Grant checked his watch as they strolled towards the railway line that ran just behind the hotel. It gave carriage solely for the coal train that each day brought the coal from the Leigh Creek open cut mine to the Torrens Island power station which supplied electricity to the city of Adelaide.

It was a warm night, still over 30 degrees Celsius. Grant checked his watch again and said, 'Hey, come with me. I want to show you something amazing,' as he took her hand and guided her to the seemingly abandoned railway station platform.

He sat her down only a foot from the edge of the platform, and within a minute or two, they could hear the rumble of the approaching coal train. Grant could feel Anita getting nervous.

'Is that a train coming? Aren't we too close?' she said, starting to edge back.

'Do you trust me?' is all he replied.

She slowly nodded, moving back next to him with a little reservation.

Soon the light came into view, growing larger and larger, until the blinding beam eventually burst past them in a whirl of hot air, explosive noise, and the pungent smell of diesel. Anita screamed as it flew past at a hundred kilometres an hour only a foot in front of them. She grabbed for Grant, shielding her head behind his back, all the while hugging him with all her might. She stayed frozen, expecting to be sucked into the train at any second. She did trust him, but held him tight until the last carriage of the one-kilometre-long train had rattled past. Grant caught the sweet perfume of her shampoo above the oily diesel smell of the train.

As the taillights slowly faded into the distance, Grant stood and held out his hand to her. He raised her to her feet, then gently patted down her hair which had gusted everywhere, asking, 'Shall we walk?'

She stood, still with her hand over her mouth. 'That was the scariest thing I've ever done. Thank you, I must look a fright!'

'You look perfect. Even with a touch of wild hair!' Grant grinned in reply.

She breathed in. 'Yes, I'd like a walk, I'm not in any hurry to go back in there!' she said, pointing in the direction of the bar.

They continued down the platform and then onto the tracks, heading south in the same path of the train that only moments ago had flown by.

'Are we safe to walk on the tracks?' she asked timidly.

'Absolutely. There's only one train a day and that was it!'

The red taillights of the train had faded long ago into the distance, again restoring the outback to its dark tranquillity, silent only for the few small animals rustling in the bushes and occasional thumping of kangaroos as they jumped away unseen. It was a raven black background behind the millions of stars. Grant was always astounded at just how many stars you could see out there, deep in the middle of the country—like nowhere else in the world, he'd been told. It was late; the sun had been gone for hours, but the quarter moon lit their way enough so they could step safely from sleeper to sleeper and avoid any brown snakes that might be out looking for a feed.

They walked for a good ten minutes before Anita said, 'Tell me, are you married, Grant, or do you have a lady? I see you don't wear a ring.'

'Well, I have a wife, but we're separated, and a friend who ran away.

'A friend who ran away? Do you want to talk about that?'

'I'm not sure where to start, but I was living in a relationship with two women, and…'

'What?!' said Anita, stopping and looking back at him.

'Yes, and the whole relationship was going great. It started with an old school friend called Cathy, and then other woman joined us. Her name was Megan, and she became our lover.'

Anita stopped again and paused for a moment. She glanced at Grant, suspicious that he was only teasing. The look on his face spoke to the contrary.

'I didn't think you could surprise me anymore, Grant Sheppard, but I'm speechless! If it's okay, I'd love to hear more about what happened?'

'It started as an equal three-way relationship. We shared everything and each other openly. However, Megan secretly wanted more. She'd evidently been trying to have me to herself, all along. I woke one morning to find Cathy gone. I found out later that Megan had been conniving and hurtful to make Cathy believe I didn't want her. She'd gone so far as to tarnish her reputation with her colleagues and ruin her career as well. Once I found out, I set out a plan to find Cathy.'

'Is Megan still with you?'

'God no! She'd been playing too many nasty games. I think she's gone back to her husband. Poor bastard!'

'Have you found Cathy?'

'Yes, but not without the help of a private investigator. We're just friends with benefits now, that's the best way to describe us.'

'That is the most unbelievable story I have ever heard, I must say.'

Grant quickly steered the conversation away from him to focus on Anita's life.

Anita told him about her young children and her husband of nearly ten years, but he picked up on a little something when she spoke of him. She admitted that he didn't like her going away on her own and Grant could see why.

Eventually, Grant suggested they turn around and head back to the now distant Parachilna. They had probably walked four kilometres and could only just see a faint light haze from the town above the few sparce trees. They were really on their own in the middle of Australia, so still and dark, their little trek illuminated by the blanket of beautiful stars and a perfect set of tracks to lead them home.

The walk back appeared quicker, as it always does. It was almost midnight, but still the temperature hadn't dropped much. They entered the hotel area, strolling past the dimly lit, deserted swimming pool. They could easily hear the noise from the bar now.

'It's sounding messy in there,' Grant said.

'It's still so warm. What about a swim?' suggested Anita.

'Sounds good, but what would we wear?' asked Grant innocently.

'Nothing,' said Anita as she lifted her dress over her head, swiftly in one clean action.

There she stood, naked except for a pair of white silk knickers, which she quickly removed before diving into the pool. Grant was momentarily taken aback, not only by her unexpected boldness, but moreover the first sight of her exquisite body.

It was only a second but felt like ages before Grant replied 'Okay' to himself, now that Anita was already underwater. He stripped off and slipped into the water, trying to not attract any attention from the bar. *This is not where I thought this would end up,* Grant thought.

Grant didn't move around, preferring to float and enjoy the cool water around him and the naked Anita. She started diving down and swimming up in front of him, then away and back again, almost teasing him. Grant couldn't believe how the attraction for this woman had now surged. He could feel himself falling for her.

Quickly, he checked himself, realising that he shouldn't really be caught here like this. After all, he was the producer. Skinny-dipping with the young, beautiful lead actor would not take long to filter through the industry. Gripping his composure with all his might, he jumped out of the pool, searching quickly to thankfully locate a stack of towels. Wrapping one around himself tightly to quieten his exposure, he walked over to hand one to Anita, also now emerging. The droplets of water themselves clung to her sculpted nakedness as she stepped out and she reached for the towel. He couldn't help but hold his gaze upon her naked form, so naturally stunning and now standing so close. She was completely breathtaking.

Without a word, they dressed and headed back to the bar. The look on the entire crew's faces as they walked through the door, both with wet hair, was to die for. Anita continued to comb her hair with her fingers as each male stood, gazing in disbelief. Grant bought two drinks and handed one to Anita.

As she accepted the glass from his hand, she leant in and whispered in his ear, 'I really want to get out of here. I'm going to exit quietly now to my room. I'd love to have this last drink with you if you'd like to follow me.'

Greg nodded with acceptance.

They snuck off through the rear exit separately under the guise of bathroom visits before they slipped into room 12, some fifteen minutes later. Grant sat on the end of the bed of the small room, Anita sitting next to him.

'That was so much fun tonight, thank you, Grant,' Anita said with a tantalising laugh.

'It sure was, I can't believe we didn't get sprung in that pool! Not a good look for a producer and leading talent,' he laughed.

They both fell quiet for a minute before Anita stood up slowly and moved to stand directly in front of him. He looked up, catching the intensity of her stare, making him rise instantly to stand face to face, only inches apart. Their eyes locked, suspended in the longest, deepest intake of each other. Anita was the first to break, simply falling into Grant's arms, nestling the side of her face on his chest. 'Oh, Grant, I can't believe how you make me feel. I've held myself back with your slightest touch or look, every day. Tonight, I'm actually trembling with you here so close, and my body is doing things it shouldn't.'

He started to reply, but she kept talking, stepping back a little as she lifted her head to look him straight in the eyes. 'Please don't say a word. I really wanted this and you, right now, more than anything. It was my desire to have you, and all of you, here in my room tonight. But I'm married, and I love my husband. Even more than that, you could never be just a one-night stand for me. I'm so sorry. I thought I could do it, but…'

Tears were now streaming down her cheeks. Grant just looked at her. He was speechless, caught by both her desire and the heartfelt despair in her words.

Anita again spoke softly, 'You have penetrated my heart and soul, and that really scares me.'

Grant finally replied. His words came in barely a whisper. 'Anita, it's okay, I completely understand. There was never any expectation. You are a delightful woman, and we both know something very special has happened here between us. I have loved every minute I've spent with you.' He stepped back and placed a hand on either side of her face, her tear-soaked eyes revealing her every emotion. He moved to kiss her, knowing that, if nothing more, he could not depart without at least a kiss to cherish. Grant hesitated for a split second, knowing this could also be their undoing. He fought with himself between doing what was right and what he so desperately wanted.

Anita also knew that if she kissed him, any resistance would be gone. Her body's needs were already screaming for him. She took a breath and let the euphoric feeling engulf her. She closed her eyes and her head tilted back to receive his kiss, knowing it would lead to her giving herself to him.

As their lips touched, there was a knock at the door. Anita pulled away and looked into his eyes. She wiped away the tears quickly with a towel and walked to the door. Julie, the production co-ordinator, was standing behind it, wanting to confirm her flight and travel details.

'Are you alright?' Julie asked, darting looks between Anita's red eyes and Grant standing awkwardly in the middle of the room. She shot them both a questionable glance.

'Tears of laughter,' Anita said and smiled. 'Grant and I have been sharing lots of stories about our experiences. It's been a fun night.'

Grant said quickly, 'Yep, it has. Well, I'll leave you two to it. As I said, I've got lots to finish before I take off early in the morning. Hopefully I'll see you down the track somewhere, Anita. Thanks again, you've done a great job this week.'

He walked up to her, kissing her casually with a peck on the cheek, at the same time sneaking a soft whisper in her ear. 'I'll never forget you.' He then turned, smiled at Julie, and walked briskly out of the door.

Anita blinked to quell the tears and swallowed hard before throwing out an Oscar-winning, seemingly light-hearted response.

'Goodnight Grant, and thank you.'

Anita's eyes followed him, her heart squeezing with his every step as he left.

She drew in a breath. 'Thanks, Julie, can I catch you first thing in the morning for the details if that's okay?' Anita managed to get that out without bursting into tears.

'Sure, all good. Catch you in the morning. Goodnight,' said Julie.

Anita closed the door, immediately turning to head for the bathroom, only then releasing the first deep sob that then continued like a river, with fresh tears fuelled by the heat of passion and regret that flowed uncontrollably through her. She was returning to her home, far from South Australia, tomorrow.

She knew they would not likely ever meet again, but also that a little piece of her heart would always stay behind secretly in these ranges and the man she so nearly gave herself to.

As Grant lay back in his bed that night, he thought long and hard about Anita and how intimately, without intention, they'd both been caught, spellbound, by each other. It was as if each other's hearts and souls had entwined and a special magic had been cast between them. Grant knew he could have easily returned to her room that night. But somehow, it wasn't right and the spell would be broken. The encounter itself was enough for them both, forever poignant and memorable just as it was. But even more than that, he felt a little relief that in the heightened second as they stood on the precipice of giving into their desires, it had been broken by that knock on her door that rendered them back into the space of conformity with the rest of the world. He acknowledged that saying goodbye at that moment was the right thing to do. To honour her beyond his own desire, considering how he also knew how she might regret their actions rather than remember the momentary feelings they'd shared.

Something magical *did* happen, and she would forever be a lady he would never forget.

Tracy

Mark woke at 7.00 a.m.; the sun that had already risen above the Pacific Ocean backlit the cheap blind that separated him from the outside world. Its golden rays were desperately trying to fill his room. He slipped out of bed, and while still naked, lifted the heavy blind. It was a glorious day. He gazed through the hotel room window that directly overlooked Merewether Beach. There was no rush this morning, everything was almost set for the event.

Today would be just a supervisory role and his only real commitment was to meet the client. He would have a quick breakfast, meet his team around 10.00 a.m., and then head to the location. His client was a speedway team pitching a sponsorship proposal to a few wealthy local business owners. This was a much different event than what he normally ran. He certainly wouldn't be receiving the sort of fee he'd usually receive from a big corporation, but it wasn't a hard job, and he *was* addicted fast cars. He'd done a bit of driving himself, a long time ago, and was quite successful back then.

So, this appealed to him, a fun event between his much bigger corporate jobs. He called Chad to join him for breakfast. Chad was the one who'd been co-ordinating the setup at Brough Park stadium, as the client was a friend of a friend.

After their hearty breakfast, Mark and Chad met the rest of the crew, who were still busy erecting the presentation marquee, at the speedway stadium. They walked over to the pit garages to meet the team manager and the person in charge of promotion.

'Hi there, we are looking for Skip Barbera,' Chad asked one of the mechanics as he walked past.

'Just over there,' he said, waving a spanner to point them in the direction.

Skip turned his attention to Mark as they approached and said, 'One of you must be Mark Rainsford?'

'That's me,' Mark replied, 'and this is Chad Mills.' They shook hands as Mark noticed a beautiful woman walking towards them.

'This is Tracy Bell, my promotions guru. This was all her idea, she will help you with whatever you need,' said Skip.

Chad instantly caught what was happening between Mark and Tracy. The longer than needed handshake, the extended look, and a little twinkle in her eyes, was enough for Chad's own eyes to roll. *Here we go, Casanova Mark is at it again!* he thought.

'Tracy, we almost have the marquee up, and the tables, chairs, will be arriving in the next half an hour. The gourmet BBQ catering will be here tomorrow at eleven and is all contained. It will be done outside and brought in, so no real set up for us there. We will set up a projector and screen and a cordless mic, it should all be complete in an hour or two,' explained Chad, turning to Mark. 'Anything you can think of, Mark?'

'What, ahh… No, no, that's about it, I think,' stammered Mark, finally breaking his eyes away from the mesmerising Tracy.

'Okay, let me know if you need anything, otherwise I'll see you later. I've got cars to prepare, so I'd better keep moving.' After a slight hesitation, Skip turned and left.

Tracy looked at Chad and said, 'I'll be your contact for the event, so let's try and keep Skip in the pits, shall we?' As she turned, she gave Mark a little smile.

Chad and Mark had turned back towards the marquee when Chad said, 'What the fuck was that?'

'That was love at first sight, my friend,' Mark said with a smile he couldn't shake.

'Tell me you aren't going to screw the client, surely?' Chad asked.

'Of course not,' Mark replied quickly, 'Skip's not my type!' He laughed as they turned and walked away.

Chad just shook his head, with a secreted grin.

However, that night, Tracy was all Mark could think about. Her smile, her long blonde hair, her figure, her eyes. She was absolutely beautiful. She had been instantly captivating.

Next day, Mark and Chad arrived early, and as the caterers arrived, they helped them set up the power and the new amended timetable. Throughout the morning Mark and Tracy caught glimpses of each other and warm smiles were the only messages exchanged.

The VIPs or special guests started to arrive around 11.30 a.m. It was all going to plan and almost time for Mark and Chad to step back and let Tracy and Skip do their sales pitch.

Mark was completely in awe as he watched how well Tracy spoke, telling everyone how the team worked and the corporate advantages of being involved with motorsport. Skip's team was a two-car team with chassis' and engines from the USA; actually, just about everything was from the US on these cars. He'd also organised a purpose-built sponsor ride car that had two seats, so they could really show people what the thrill of a ride on a track was like.

After the presentation and gourmet lunch, it was time for the twenty guests to have a first-hand experience of the Formula One of dirt. They did two laps each and not one person exited the car without a resounding, 'Wow!' on their face.

Mark found himself standing next to Tracy as the rides were being conducted. Well, truth be known, he'd made sure he was standing next to her. They talked a little about the team and her involvement. Mark found out that she lived in Newcastle, had a partner, and everything about how she'd loved putting this event together. The conversation was smooth and flowing. No awkward questions, no difficult answers, just easy.

Skip approached Mark and Tracy with a greasy rag in his hand. 'We'll fire up the race cars after the last guest has a ride in the two-seater and the boys will do a couple of really quick laps.' Skip looked at Mark and asked, 'You've driven one of these, haven't you?'

'Yes, but it was a while ago.'

'Would you like to take the two-seater for a spin after everyone goes?'

'You bet I would! Thank you,' Mark replied.

Skip turned away and headed back to get the race car engines fired up.

'Wow, he must like you—he doesn't just let anyone drive that!' Tracy said, taking a step back for effect.

'Have you ever been for a ride in the two-seater, Tracy?'

'Oh no, and don't want to either, those boys are crazy!'

'Why don't you come with me?'

'No, no, no,' she replied.

'Do you trust me?' Mark said in a serious voice.

'Sure, but that's a different story.'

'I will only go as fast as you're comfortable with. I have nothing to prove.'

Tracy looked at him and he could see her considering it. She was always being asked if she'd been for a ride, so this might just be her chance to tick that box and not have to sit with one of the young racers that were trying to prove something.

'Alright, but you must promise to stop if I say, and not just one more lap?'

'I promise,' Mark said holding up his right hand, as if standing in the witness box in the Supreme Court.

Tracy shot him a glance, filled with temptation and trepidatious delight, as she walked off to do the final presentation to the guests and hand them all a gift pack with a team shirt, cap, and details of the various levels of sponsorship available.

Skip waved to Mark, signalling for him to get suited up for the drive.

'Skip, I asked Tracy to come with me, is that okay?'

'Yes, I heard.' He paused before adding, 'Be gentle on her will ya? She's like a daughter to me.'

Mark smiled back and said, 'I promise.' Knowing full well it wasn't just the car ride he was referring to.

Most of the guests had left and Mark received a rundown of the controls in the car while Tracy donned her racing suit and helmet. Mark was already seated and buckled up when Tracy arrived in a race suit that was two sizes too big for her. The two-seater was basically a single seater with two small seats fitted side by side. Their shoulders touched, helmets only inches apart. Mark gave Skip a thumbs up and the push start procedure was commenced. Once up to speed, the engine would fire and the 700 horsepower would burst into life, one cylinder at a time then the car would accelerate off like a rocket with a roar that nothing on earth could compare with.

Mark heard Tracy's first scream as he entered the first corner, half expecting the 'I've had enough!' cry and whack on his leg. It had been ten years since he drove one of these as a guest driver at Avalon Raceway in Victoria. It came back to him like it was yesterday. He backed it into the corners like a pro and was sure at one stage the front wheels were in the air as it hooked up out of the corners. He completed about five laps and pulled back into pits. He was so absorbed in the thrill of reclaiming the sensation of the ride, he had all but forgotten Tracy was there. He loved the feel of the car drifting up to the wall and then throwing it at the next corner, the throttle flat the whole time. He shut the engine down; the vibration and roar of the engine had now turned to a perfect silence, just the buzz of adrenaline pounding in his head. It was a second or two before the excitement faded enough for his limbs to now return to some sort of normal operation, remembering the other duties he was there for.

He lifted his visor and looked at Tracy; her face was a mixture of 'I thought I was going to die', and 'I'm so glad I did that.'

Already the mechanics were around the car, plugging up the air intakes and undoing their harnesses.

'You've still got it, ol' boy!' Skip said, still wiping his hands with the same oily rag he'd been clutching two hours before. Mark just grinned in reply.

Mark hopped out first, then helped Tracy. They stood facing each other as Mark helped remove her helmet.

'After the first lap, I thought I was going to die, and after we survived that, I started to think, well, I may actually live to enjoy this,' she said.

Her eyes were still sparkling from the adrenaline that was pumping through her veins. Mark just stood there looking at her with the spots of mud on her face that had sprayed off the front wheels. Something about the mix of innocent raw excitement and dirt-blotted face made her just look so cute.

Skip and the two mechanics started to push the car over to the transporter, leaving Mark and Tracy alone in the middle of the pit paddock. Mark gently wiped a bit of mud from her cheek, and with his heart pounding blurted out, 'Will you have dinner with me tonight?'

'Will it be as dangerous as the last time I sat next to you?' was her instant reply.

'Hopefully not!' Mark replied with a smile, assuming she'd just given him a 'yes.' 'What's the best restaurant in town?' Mark asked as they turned to go and get changed.

'Scratchley's on the Wharf is somewhere I have always wanted to go,' she said as she walked into the ladies change room.

'I'll call and book now, message me your address,' Mark yelled out as she disappeared.

Mark pulled out his phone and booked a table, one the restaurant guaranteed would overlook the Pacific Ocean. His phone beeped with a message. She'd sent him her address. A smile formed on his face—his heart was racing.

Mark arrived outside of Tracy's house at 6.45 p.m. as arranged. It was a small, single fronted terrace building with all the houses joined together, much like you see in inner London but without the sub level. She must've been watching, as she emerged from the front door before he'd got halfway to it. He noticed a curtain move and a little face peek through from the bottom corner. Mark smiled to himself, excited to be spending an evening with this interesting woman. She was already a fascinating delicacy, and he wanted to know more. Tracy stepped down the five steps to the footpath in a pale blue fitted dress, a white denim jacket draped over her shoulders, and white slip-on shoes. Her long blonde hair was straightened and tucked behind her ears. Everything about her look was simple, natural, and understated, but oozing absolutely gorgeousness at the same time.

Mark met her at the bottom of the stairs, took her hand, and kissed it. 'Wow, you look absolutely stunning,' he said, guiding her to his rental car. 'Hey, I saw some little eyes through the window watching you leave.'

'That was my daughter, Becky. I don't go out very often so it's a pretty big deal,' Tracy said, turning to look at Mark as he rounded the corner in the car.

'I find that hard to believe,' said Mark, looking back at her. 'Aren't men knocking your door down?'

She laughed and said, 'doesn't mean I go out with them and I do sort of have a boyfriend.'

'Fair enough,' Mark said with a little smile, as he turned into the restaurant carpark which was only a couple of minutes away from her house.

They were seated at their table as the sun was starting to set; even though the sun was setting on the opposite side of the country it was still an amazing view as the orange sky sat neatly above the dark blue ocean. They ordered wine and a delectable seafood dish, which they shared. Tracy opened up to Mark, telling him all about her life, her failed marriage, and her beautiful daughter who consumed most of her time, and who she clearly adored. Mark just sat, listened, and admired the beautiful flower opening up in front of him. He could feel his heart really falling for this lovely lady.

The food and drink were soon consumed, and Mark asked Tracy if she would like a walk along the esplanade. He sorted the bill and put Tracy's jacket around her shoulders as she stood.

Tracy was feeling great. Mark's company, the lovely food, and the delicious wine had placed her in a most comfortable state. She couldn't wipe the smile from her face. She couldn't think of a more enjoyable occasion in her life. Mark had certainly charmed her.

They strolled along the path; the seagulls overhead, still visible in the darkness, and the gentle splash of the waves on the beach, combined with a balmy temperature, added to the perfect night. This time Mark led the conversation, telling her all about his work yet resisted bringing up the ride in the sprint car that afternoon. They found a seat further up the beach, a little past the restaurants and hotel. There was a distant streetlight but the moon was providing all the light needed for this romantic event.

They sat close and Mark put his arm around her as if to add a little unnecessary warmth. Tracy enjoyed it and wanted Mark to be close; she could smell his aftershave, which aroused her sense of safety and longing. A strong, confident man to protect her from the world. To Tracy, there was no world past this beach. Mark kissed her cheek and Tracy felt a shiver tingle through her; he kissed her earlobe and then her neck. Tracy closed her eyes and was unaware of the soft moans that were escaping her. She turned towards him and found his lips; there was no warmup as they melted into a deep, intimate kiss. Tracy's body was responding to this passion and so was Mark's. They stopped for air, Tracy with her head back, eyes closed, and still reeling from the lust that was overcoming her.

Mark found her ear and whispered, 'I want to make love to you.'

'I can't. We only just met and I've never ever slept with someone on the first date, and… I have a boyfriend.'

'I'll be gone tomorrow morning and we'll never know how good this night could have been.'

'I'm sorry, Mark, I want to, but I'm just not like that.'

'Okay. I understand. I'm sorry for pressuring you, it's just that being with you has been so wonderful, I wanted this night to be a highlight of my life.'

'To be honest, you made my heart miss a beat the moment I saw you, but it's just not me.'

'Alright, well at least I am thrilled knowing that, shall we stroll back?' he said defeatedly.

They walked back along the track, stopping to kiss in the dark spots. The kisses were getting longer, deeper, and more passionate. Mark could feel the back of her bra with the heel of his palm, and imagined the beautiful flesh that filled it. They reached the car and again they embraced, Mark gently biting her neck as his hands placed on her bum pulled her against him. They pulled apart and she stared into his eyes, with a serious but lust-filled look.

'Oh Mark, I'm so torn,' she whispered.

Mark gave her a peck on the lips and then opened the passenger door for her.

Tracy reached for her seatbelt, knowing she may well never see this man again.

Tracy's resolve was failing. She was feeling hot from the kissing and her body had already fully prepared itself for a foreign visitor. Today had already been the best day she could ever remember, from the fast laps in the race car to the invitation to sleep with the driver, it had been the most amazing day. She knew she'd lay in bed tonight and touch herself as she relived the kisses and his desire to make love to her. If that was the case, how would it be any less faithful to physically have him? Her boyfriend would never know and Mark would be gone, just an amazing memory.

Without a word, in that moment she was willing to accept anything he offered. Mark pulled up opposite her house. She made no effort to leave. He removed his seatbelt and turned to her. He looked at her staring out through the windscreen, deep in thought. He gave her all the time she needed. She eventually turned to him and with a serious look said, 'Mark, I want you to make love to me.'

She closed her eyes, and he kissed her again. He then refitted his seatbelt and restarted the engine. Mark's hotel was only five minutes away. He held her hand, but didn't say anything. From her last comment, he understood that only actions, not dialogue, were the next course. He parked and led her into the hotel. Nothing needed to be said, just a touch and kiss. She offered neither a word nor any sign of hesitation.

He opened the door to the room, glad to see Chad wasn't there. He was now wishing he hadn't agreed to share a room to save a few dollars for the race team. They embraced, kissed, and undressed each other with a desperate haste.

Tracy enjoyed the feeling of being naked and vulnerable with this man; she wanted him to take her, be firm, and have him selfishly force himself onto her and into her.

'I'm a bad girl, Mark.'

'Yes, very bad?' he replied.

'How will you punish me?' she said in a soft deep voice.

Mark's mind was racing, this was unexpected and it had been a long time since a woman has wanted some rough play.

Mark took a handful of hair, pulled her head back in a firm but gentle jolt, and bit her neck. After drawing on her flesh hard and deep, he stepped back and looked her straight in the eyes.

'Get on the bed, you bad girl, on your hands and knees.'

Once on all fours, her smooth round bum cheeks facing him, he hesitated. This was a sight too beautiful to harm.

She called out, 'Smack me, I'm such a bad person.'

He smacked her bottom with an open palm, leaving a red mark. She moaned; delight in her tone. He slid two fingers inside her, trying to be rough but not too rough. She was so wet and now groaning as the forceful play had clearly captivated her. He reached forward and again took a handful of blonde hair, he pulled her head back with a little more force this time, as his erection searched for her pussy. He found her with ease, so wet and swollen. He started to pound into her with rapid, hard thrusts. She came quickly. Mark slowed his pace, to gaze and fully admire the beautiful body kneeling in front of him. She lay flat as she receded from the high of her orgasm.

Tracy rolled over onto her back, smiling back at him. He returned her smile, his eyes not leaving hers as he moved to lay down beside her.

'It was actually tough for me to be rough with you,' Mark said in a voice that was half an excuse, in case she was disappointed that he wasn't dominating enough. 'I must say, being rough with pretty women is not my normal style, Trace.'

'You were great. I do love it, but I've only done that a couple of times. It's hard to find a man I trust to be honest.'

'Well, thank you, but can we do it my way now?' he asked.

'I would love that.'

Mark knelt above her, his legs either side of her. With his weight on his elbows, he still managed to cup both his hands on her cheeks. He had decided to make this extra sensitive, so it was a complete contrast to her preferred rough play.

He kissed her lips softly, taking little sucks pulling her lips with his. He kissed her neck and her earlobe, the little purrs which escaped her signalling she was certainly enjoying it.

He lowered himself to quickly run his tongue around each nipple, giving each a little bite as he headed south. He kissed down her tummy and found her crotch with her legs together. He licked what he could reach, her slit and the creases where her legs join. He placed one leg between hers and then the other. She spread her legs wide, not only allowing but wanting him to taste her. He teased her with kisses inside her thighs and the manicured landing strip that led to utopia. His tongue found her delicate crease and parted her lips as he continued licking back and forth from her clit to her vagina. She was already so wet and he just loved the taste of her.

Tracy held the bedhead tightly, imagining her hands were tied, while this beast of a man devoured her delicate womanly flesh.

'I've been bad,' she said to herself, 'getting what I deserve.' Then she came, hard, squirting her pleasure into his mouth, as she lifted her legs to the sky.

Mark eased the motion as he could feel her explode in his mouth. He'd never tasted that before. He wiped his mouth with the back of his hand, positioning himself back on top of her and between her legs. His knob teased her before sliding inside her, she was now so wet. He rode her hard this time, planning to come with her.

At that moment the door burst open. Chad and a girl he'd picked up stood in the doorway laughing together at something funny. Chad then noticed Mark and Tracy; he took a split second to admire the naked form of Tracy with her legs wrapped around Mark as he filled her. Tracy looked at the silhouette of Chad and his girl as Chad called out, 'Sorry!' before quickly closing the door behind him. Mark had only slowed his rhythm for the couple of seconds during the interruption, resuming straight back to bringing Tracy to her next orgasm. Tracy also recovered, and within a few more seconds was building to her final eruption. Mark could feel her come and he followed with a moan that could be heard from another floor. His cum filled her body as her fluids again gushed from her.

Mark whispered in her ear, 'Can I please spend the rest of my life in this position?'

Tracy laughed and said, 'I wish you could!'

'Would make meetings difficult, I guess,' Mark said, now completely relaxed and content. He'd made love to this beautiful woman and was confident he'd contributed to an amazing day for her.

They lay together naked for almost another hour talking about their lives including the little interruption by Chad. 'I'm guessing Chad had to go get himself another room,' Mark said with a grin.

'Lucky we were here first,' Tracy said.

They eventually dressed and Mark called a taxi for her. He walked Tracy to the foyer, and as the cab arrived Tracy turned to kiss him before asking, 'Will I ever see you again?'

'I certainly hope so,' he said.

'You definitely will,' he said to himself.

Mark returned to the room and stripped the bed that had just accommodated the passionate lovemaking. He hoped it may dry out by morning, and jumped into the second bed that Chad would've had.

He woke early, showered, and packed. The memory of the night before still buzzing in his body and soul. He shivered in delight at the thought of her beneath him, her juices flooding him as he filled her with his.

As he arrived at the restaurant for breakfast, he saw Chad. He tapped him on the shoulder as he sat down and said, 'Good night, mate?'

'Fuck yeah,' replied Chad, 'A real fucking goer. Sorry about walking in on you.'

'All good, we didn't miss a beat.'

'Fuck, you won first prize with that one, mate,' said Chad, filling his mouth with a whole rasher of bacon.

'Who was the girl with you?'

'Just a girl from the bar here at the hotel,' Chad said pointing to the bar behind him with his thumb.

'Did she cost anything?' Mark asked with a smile.

'Yes, a bloody lot of drinks,' laughed Chad.

'I'll grab some breakfast and we better hit the road,' Mark said as he headed for the food.

Mark was so happy with how the night had turned out and found himself drifting back to the special parts of the day; the laps in the sprint car, the dinner, the kisses on the esplanade, and, of course, making love to the beautiful Tracy. Although he initially thought he would never see her again, he knew he had to, one more time, not so rushed. The warmth of the thoughts of her kept a smile on his face for the entire flight back to Adelaide.

Tracy was a different person when she woke that next morning. She stared at the ceiling, took in a deep breath, and then let it out slowly, as if she was performing a yoga move. A feeling of peace filled her body and a smile formed on her face. The breath took in all that had happened in the last twenty-four hours, the exhale was her accepting it. Her heart sped up as she recalled the amazing time with the event co-ordinator from Adelaide.

Her vagina still tingled from the lovemaking, her first for quite some time. She took in another deep breath as if she might drown in the thoughts, her full lungs trying to hold her heart from jumping from her chest. It was a bittersweet experience. Mark was like no man she had ever met before. He was smart, kind, and courteous, he was rich and good looking. He was a bit older than her, *but hell, that didn't matter.*

She placed one hand on her bare chest just to see if Mark had maybe taken her heart, because it certainly felt like it.

As the day progressed Tracy realised that Mark, the only man she'd ever slept with on a first date, had not only penetrated her body, but also her heart. He was all she could think about. She knew she would never meet another man like him and she was desperate to see him again. She had to realise, that to him, she was probably just another conquest that he and Chad screwed while traveling around the country. A few days passed without a word from him and she realised that Mark—and her heart—were probably never to be seen again.

Mark returned to Adelaide and to a workload that had exceeded his normal capabilities. Every now and then Tracy would slip back into his mind. He would stop as he recalled this glorious woman below him, her eyes closed and her breasts rocking as he thrust into her, filling her body with his love. He desperately wanted to do that again, to kiss those lips, feel that smooth soft skin on his, to smell and touch that beautiful blonde hair. He would then shake his head and return to the present, as she faded from his mind's eye like a ghost and event layouts filled his view.

It was a Friday night after Tracy had returned home after a drink with the race team boys when her phone beeped with a message.

> Hi Tracy, I'm sorry I haven't contacted you sooner?
> Can I please see you again?
> Would you join me in Sydney for a weekend? Mark.

Tracy read the message and started to cry. She could hardly breathe; only now did she realise how much of her heart he had actually taken. Through the tears she replied.

Yes, I would love that.

A weekend was arranged. Mark booked the Novatel at Darling Harbour for the Friday and Saturday nights. Tracy was to drive down from Newcastle and Mark would fly in on Friday morning, attend a meeting first, and would be at the hotel when Tracy arrived.

Tracy was excited and very nervous—it's one thing to have a fling, a one-night stand with a stranger, but to spend a weekend with him in another city, sharing a room, waking up next to him, that was another story. Tracy wanted this badly, to see him, touch him, and have him again between her legs. They would kiss passionate kisses as he filled her with his thrusts and she would enjoy it—no, love it. She thought about that for a minute. She had known him for one day and he had touched her heart, deeply touched it; he held it in his bare hands. What would a weekend do? *He can't be as amazing as he seems, or can he?*

She was now even more nervous, almost shaking at the thought of her giving herself to him completely. She noticed she was now taking shallow breaths and her heart was racing. She took in a huge breath and sighed, saying to herself, 'I've been with men before, hell, I have a boyfriend… but why is this so different?'

She knew what was different—no man had ever touched her heart like Mark did.

My God, what if he asked me to marry him? she thought. *Shit, I would probably say yes.*

Mark had finished his meeting and was waiting in the foyer for Tracy to arrive. He'd arranged a park in the hotel's underground carpark, directing her to the allocated spot as soon as she arrived.

Once parked, Mark met her at her car door, kissed her, and said, 'Welcome to Sydney!' He took the larger of her two cases and they walked to the elevator.

'It's only two nights,' he said, looking down at the cases.

'It's a girl thing, all right,' she replied smiling.

'Let's get you settled in and then maybe go for a walk?'

'That sounds great.'

Her smile was delicious; it was all quite surreal as he thought that in only a few hours he would again be naked and making love to this incredible woman.

Mark watched her unpack, admiring the grace with which she moved, the tenderness as she touched and placed things, the way she flicked her hair with a toss of her head. *God, could he ever get sick of seeing that?*

They walked out from the building and across the walkway that brought them out at the Harbour. Mark reached for her hand and she turned to him and smiled. It somehow made them a thing, a couple or something, more than just a fling. Her hand felt so perfect in his and a crazy urge to just kiss her right there flashed through his mind.

They found a bar that looked over one of the most beautiful harbours in the world. Mark had many corny comments to make about a beautiful woman in a beautiful place, but luckily forced himself to stay cool.

They chattered about how successful the sprint car sponsorship event was, and she told him that a gold and silver sponsor had been achieved from the program.

'Well done you, that's great news.'

They watched the shadows work their way along the Harbour as the sun started to disappear behind the buildings in the west. They had a great table, so decided to have dinner there as well.

Tracy had caught him staring at her while she relaxed to take in the view. She loved that he thought she was a bit special, and not just a score while on a job. She knew this was dangerous for her, laying her heart out for this man to step on at any time. Before she left home she'd told herself that it was just a fun weekend and to enjoy it and expect nothing more, but she knew that once the lovemaking started it would change everything. Tonight, she would invite him again into her body and they would be joined in lust and passion. The thought sent a tingle through her body.

She looked at him; he was relaxed, watching the last rays of sun disappear as he sipped his beer. She thought about her daughter and could only imagine how amazing he would be with her, the father figure she never had. He was the complete package. She felt her heart sending out tingles through her chest and a sense of submissiveness overwhelmed her. She knew she was heading down a one-way street and her brakes were failing dangerously.

'This is just glorious, isn't it?' Mark said, still watching the golden haze in the west. He turned to her, expecting an answer, and could see she was deep in thought. He wondered, *was she thinking about this apparent boyfriend she has or has she somehow changed her mind?* He touched her arm and said, 'You okay?'

She turned her head towards him and said, 'It's just perfect, Mark, too perfect; you, this... I don't know what to think.'

He took her hand and she looked up at him, her smile was gone but she was still adorable. He didn't say anything, but reached over and kissed her. It was soft but long and she felt the brakes slip further as she belted down that one-way road to who knows where. She wanted to cry, but somehow resisted.

Mark had no idea of what a turmoil she was in and just said, 'It is perfect, you beautiful thing, now let's order some dinner, hey?'

They asked a passing waiter for menus and ordered. It was getting dark, but the heat of the day still radiated from the floor and the walls.

Mark felt relaxed; the few beers, the location, and the company were just sublime. 'You know, from where I'm sitting, in every direction, all I can see is beauty; from the million dollar boats to the right, to the Pyrmont Bridge to the left, but the most beautiful of all is sitting right here in front of me.'

Tracy went a shade of red with a blush you would expect to see on a teenager on her first date.

'Thank you,' she mouthed, unsure any voice would come out right.

'Do you go out much at home, Tracy?'

'No, not really much at all.'

'I don't get why men aren't lining up?' Mark asked, looking confused.

'They do,' she said. 'But I have a sort of boyfriend and I'm not interested in anyone in Newcastle.'

'Can we talk about the "sort of boyfriend"? It's no big deal if you don't want to.'

'I was waiting for you to ask,' she said smiling. 'We just go out sometimes on dates, no sleepovers. It helps keep men away if I tell them I have a boyfriend.'

'Yeah, that's pretty well what I figured; lucky I didn't take any notice of that.' He threw her a smile before swallowing the last of his beer.

Mark paid the bill and they walked slowly back to the hotel. Mark stopped and turned her to face him. He took her face gently in his hands and kissed her, not a peck and not a pash, but a kiss that spoke a hundred words. It was a couple of seconds before Tracy opened her eyes after he had pulled away. He watched them open and that is when Mark realised where Tracy was. She was gone, gone to that heavenly place called 'in love.'

They arrived back to their hotel room; the lights of the Harbour filled the main window. The blind was open, but Mark slid back the scrim so that the outside could become a part of the room. The room's only light was from the thousands of coloured illuminations outside.

Mark took Tracy in his arms and kissed her, slowly at first, then overwhelmingly passionate, the way only people truly in love would kiss. They hurriedly undressed each other; their bodies were soon naked and pressed together. Mark's hands explored her body. Her breast filled his hand, her firm nipple pressing into his palm. His mouth found her neck and he sucked it hard as his fingers squeezed her nipple. Tracy let out a moan and Mark was sure she had nearly come at that point. Her head was back and her hips pressed into him. He laid her on the bed and his fingers found her.

She took his two fingers easily and moaned with each push inside her, but it wasn't till he again bit her neck that she came, the ripples of ecstasy rocking through her body like a wave machine.

Tracy was in heaven all right, this was the man she'd always dreamt about, but never believe existed.

Mark's right hand caressed her body and his tongue found her breast. He teased her with licks, sucks, and bites. As she settled, he placed himself between her legs. He pushed up against her; they were now both desperate for him to again become a part of her. The soft, delicate folds parted as he pushed and slid inside her. It was then that Mark felt his heart falling for this woman. With each stroke he was consumed, wanting to be so far inside her only his feet were left. As Mark increased his speed, she came again. He could feel her juices charged as they flowed around him. He let her rest for only a few seconds. Still buzzing from her ecstasy, he took her hand and guided her to stand at the window, the view spread out over the Harbour. He pushed her against the glass, taking both her hands and holding them behind her back with one hand. His other hand grabbed a handful of hair and pulled her head back.

From behind her he whispered in her ear, 'You are a very bad girl, what would your boyfriend think with you here fucking me? You should be punished.'

He spread her legs apart with his foot and probed her hard till he found her; this time it was fervent and fast, each thrust pounding her into the glass window. She screamed and again came vibrantly, and so did he, filling her with the gift of their passion. His face rested on her shoulder as they both spent the next minute panting and enjoying that exultant pleasure.

Tracy turned to him and hugged him tight, her head buried in his chest. She wanted to tell him, those three words, so dangerous but so right. Before she had the chance, the words on the tip of her tongue, he moved and kissed her. He took her hand, leading her to the bed. He cuddled in behind her and was soon asleep. For Tracy sleep would be a while away.

The next morning, after another session of lovemaking, they dressed, then headed to a nice café for breakfast. Next Mark suggested it was time to explore the shops. Tracy couldn't believe it—she'd discovered a man that liked shopping. Yes! Mark did love shopping. He had more clothes than any other man he knew. He owned way more than he needed, but that wouldn't stop him from trying on pants, shirts, and jackets.

A little after midday they had high tea in a lovely tea house positioned in a blue and white tiled arcade deep in the city. It was glorious, she didn't want it to end.

They'd agreed to have dinner again on the Harbour after dropping the many purchases back to their room. Tonight, Tracy turned the conversation to Mark's past and asking about his future. Tracy was careful not to say too much, but Mark was getting nervous. He knew she was almost perfect, but he wasn't ready for another full-time commitment—not yet. When they arrived back to the room the lovemaking was even better than the night before. Now so relaxed in each other's company, Mark was even a little rougher with her, knowing she loved it.

He woke with her in his arms; the smell of sex filled the room and her perfumed hair splayed inches from his face brought a warmth to his heart. This had been a weekend he would never forget.

Mark's flight was quite early, and soon after breakfast they packed. Tracy had agreed to drop him to the airport. The twenty-minute drive was quiet, as neither really knew what to say. Tracy pulled into the drop off bay at the departure terminal at Kingsford Smith Airport. She turned off the engine and looked at Mark, a tear already making its way down the full length of her face. Her heart was breaking.

Mark didn't want to drag this out; he would desperately love to take Tracy with him, and he'd certainly be having a good think about the relationship. He knew that with her it would be an all or nothing situation. He kissed her quickly and hopped out, as this was not the time or place for a passionate and emotional goodbye. He opened the back door and retrieved his bag.

'I really don't know what to say, but you are one hell of a lady, Tracy, and whatever happens you will be deep in my heart forever,' Mark said, before closing the door and walking into the terminal.

Tracy watched him go until she couldn't see him anymore, the tears now flowing down her face, her mascara adding black lines down her cheeks. She drove away, consumed with love and a loss she couldn't explain.

The Cruise

*G*reg had seen the ship in pictures, but now, standing on the wharf, the sight of this enormous vessel towering above him was breathtaking. He was accustomed to boats, having his own Riviera parked in a berth in the Hawkesbury River, but this was a majestic, floating city.

Greg and Kara had talked about the cruise on the plane ride from Sydney to Miami. They combed the brochures, talked about which shows they might see, and the parties they might go to. This was, after all, the premium of 'swinger' cruises. It was almost booked out with hundreds—no, thousands—of people of all ages, shapes, and sizes wanting some of this exciting action. Although there would be a few singles, it would be mostly couples.

The fact the cruise promoted so many opportunities to openly signal that 'sex was on the menu' was so exciting. Just knowing that guests were allowed to wander topless or naked in many areas and that connection and fun were encouraged all over the place, was already very arousing.

They'd been able to secure a booking in one of the suites, which was incredible, giving them near carte blanche to all on offer during the five-day escape at sea. The offerings were amazing, with fine dining, clubs, shops, and a smorgasbord of events that promoted sexy encounters. They had two days on the ocean before the stop in Jamaica which was clearly a highlight, and then the two-day cruise back to the USA.

Kara stood next to Greg, matching his gaze and awe at the sheer monumental size of the ship. She'd never been on a cruise, or any boat much larger than Greg's Riviera. This was now, suddenly, quite overwhelming.

She gripped his hand tightly as they ventured to the gangway to embark. 'Don't lose me, it might take me five days to find you.'

Greg laughed. 'I'm sure once we get to our suite, find a pool, a bar, and meet some of the other passengers we'll find our way around pretty easy.'

'Yes, but my God! This ship holds more than double the population of my hometown! It could take all five days just to find our suite! We can't waste time getting lost when there is so much fun to be had!' Kara said.

'Kara, you really are funny. We'd better get aboard then—no time to waste!'

Greg had studied the map, it was just a case of getting to the right deck level, then find the room number, proving to be not that difficult for an analytical person.

As they stepped out of the lift on level 5, Kara grabbed Greg by the hand again. 'How was that for another kinky experience?'

Greg looked at her quizzically. 'What are you talking about?'

'We've just been on an elevator at sea!' Kara giggled.

He smiled. 'Well, hold on tight then because I'm sure we'll have a lot more fun than that!'

As Greg opened the door to their suite, his first glance took his breathe away. It was a small room compared to a hotel, but for a ship it was all you needed. The cabin's décor and added amenities instantly exuded the trip's primary pleasure. The artfully folded 'swan towels' were placed on the bed, which was dressed like a red-carpet tuxedo. Crisply made, with silken white Egyptian sheets, a simple black quilt, and a mountain of pillows, upon which a single long-stemmed red rose rested gracefully.

Kara explored, exclaiming at her findings of all the subtle, sexually inspiring touches in the gloriously appointed suite, but it was the balcony alone that truly sparked Greg's interest. Like Kara, he too, had never been on a cruise ship, but had many times fantasised about sitting naked with a glass of wine, while watching the world sail by.

He'd sat with lovely naked ladies before on his boat, but this was to be a dream come true. What was the most surprising about this whole adventure already was that there were so many people—thousands, in fact—on board, who all had a similar sexual appetite to the two of them.

Greg watched Kara unpack, rushing in fact, to get this adventure started. Greg smiled to himself at her initial excitement. *This is priceless!* he thought. *She's already caught the vibe of this trip. I'm sure if that woman had her way, she would've had sex three times before the ship had even left the wharf.*

'Hey sexy, when you're finished, why don't we go for a stroll and check out this floating city?' Greg said, as Kara emptied her bags onto hangers and into every available drawer.

'Yes, okay—I can't wait!'

'You brought a lot of clothes to a holiday where we aren't expecting to wear much!' he commented with a smirk.

'You know how it is, I like to have options!' She grinned, already knowing she'd really packed way too much. 'Besides, we do go ashore on one day!'

'Sure,' Greg replied, 'to a tropical island.' His grin widening, he now turned to watch the last of the people boarding from his balcony. 'I wonder where I can get my hands on a beer?' he said, but he was out of Kara's earshot.

'I'm all set. Let's go explore,' she finally said.

In keeping with the cabins, the whole ship was remarkably appointed, with the crew wearing pristine white uniforms, chandeliers lighting the corridors, and every inch polished, exuding luxury and pleasure.

Their fellow passengers were openly engaging and friendly, more so than on an average cruise they figured, their looks filled with, '*Maybe I will see more of you later,*' than just a throw away glance.

'Hey Greg, just look at the crew. I bet they aren't chosen for this voyage for just their seamanship!' Kara laughed.

Greg took a second glance at the two stewards, one male, one female, holding open the door to the promenade deck. Kara was right. They looked more like they stepped out of the pages of Vogue magazine than off a dock. Greg whispered to Kara, 'I'm sure you're right there. Although the crew aren't meant to get involved with the passengers, but by all reports, it does happen,' Greg said.

'I can see why!' Kara said slowly, her eyes glued to the young seaman. 'Do you get the feeling we are being qualified as we walk around?' Kara whispered back.

'Oh yeah, I think a few fellas have already undressed you.'

'You think? My God. I've been watching a lot of women giving you the "lingering lustful look" and have put you on their "fuck me later, please" list for sure!' she smiled.

Greg grinned. 'Well, I'm sure we will both appeal to someone. That's all we need. Besides, even if we don't play with everyone we meet, it's a great way to make connections for later.'

'Absolutely. Who needs the club scene when there are thousands of like-minded people in one place!'

'I wonder what the percentage of first timers is compared to those who do this regularly?' he asked.

'That's exactly what my husband and I were saying!' came a voice from behind him.

Greg and Kara stopped and turned to see a tall, slim woman with a shock of long, light auburn hair, gripping the hand of a slightly shorter, stocky, yet muscular guy.

'Hello there. I'm Greg and this is Kara. Are you first timers like us, then?' he asked as he extended his hand to greet them.

'Tom, and this is my wife, Mel,' Tom said as smiles, handshakes, and greetings were exchanged.

'Yes, we're first timers to this cruise. We've only done this once before on a much smaller ship. This is nearly ten times the amount of people, and it's almost too much to take in!' Mel said.

'For sure!' Kara exclaimed with a grin. 'So where are you both from?'

'We're from LA, but Mel's English, and I'm from Sydney. We've been working in LA for a couple of years. We have such short vacation times from our work, this is a perfect escape,' Tom said, alternating his gaze between Kara and Greg with a warm smile.

'Kara and I have come from Sydney as well, Hawkesbury area. We've not cruised at all before. Anyway, how about we grab a drink, and you can tell us about your first cruise? We'd love to find out more.' Greg said.

While obviously a little younger, Greg and Kara felt the interest and subtle advances that Mel and Tom exuded toward them within the first moments. Greg ordered two beers and the girls a champagne each, now grateful for the drink package he'd paid to have included in their booking. They all clinked glasses with 'cheers' as Greg said, 'So what can you tell us?'

Mel looked at Tom and said, 'We aren't here to just screw as many people as we can, we're hoping to find a couple or two that just really do it for us. A couple we can meet over the week, flirt with, play sexy games, and who we can really make love to. We're looking for genuine couples, not only to enjoy bodies with, but people we can connect with.'

'Wow!' Greg said, 'You know, I never really thought about that, but that's really nice. I really do hope you find that couple.'

'So do we, but it doesn't matter if we don't. We get off on watching as well, and already it looks like there's plenty of opportunity for that,' Mel said. They all laughed.

The four of them went on to discuss their lives before getting ready to leave the bar.

It was no surprise when Tom shared how he'd started his working life as a boilermaker and was now leading a crew, building tankers for a chemical company. Greg instantly picked they were a hard-working couple, who'd made good of their lives. Both he and Kara caught their youthful vibe, gauging both clearly as having had done life tough at some stage. They conveyed an underlying rawness and naivety, indicating that for the most part, they'd scraped and sullied, battling against the elements of their youth. Nonetheless, Mel and Tom's open and friendly approach made them attractive in their own natural way.

They all shook hands and kissed on cheeks, when Kara said, 'Even if we aren't the lovers you're looking for, if you ever just want someone to chat or have a drink with, give us a call, here's my card. Apparently, phones work on board.'

'That's great, thanks,' Mel said, accepting the card with a smile.

As Tom and Mel strolled off, Greg turned to Kara and said, 'That's interesting. The safe way of swinging is to not to fall in love, I thought?'

'Oh well, it might work for them perhaps, but yes, it's dangerous I would have thought.' Kara said.

Their chat was suddenly broken by the long blast of the horn, signalling the cruise liner's imminent departure.

'Come on, let's grab a spot outside and watch the land disappear!' Greg said, as he grabbed Kara's hand and swallowed the last of his beer.

Standing there, highly heralded above the docks below, they barely felt the ship move. They could just sense the gentle vibration of the huge engines humming through the hull. It was as if two pieces of land were being separated, gliding apart with grace and strength. There were thousands of people on the dock waving as the ship departed. He wondered if their relatives knew what type of cruise their loved ones were taking.

The dock was soon behind them and the open ocean was now dead ahead.

Most people had gone now, but Kara appreciated that Greg was enthralled. He finally said, with his eyes fixed on the disappearing land, 'I can't believe this thing even floats, so heavy and so high out of the water… I wonder what the draft is?'

'The what?' Kara asked.

'The draft. It's the distance from the waterline to the bottom of the hull that shows how much of the ship is physically in the water.'

'So why is that important?' Kara asked, not really needing an answer.

'Knowing that allows the crew to determine the minimum depth of water the ship can safely navigate.'

'So, helps us avoid being on the next *Titanic*, you mean?'

Greg laughed. 'Yep, basically, that's it!'

'Alright Captain, come on, enough of the detail, let's get ready for dinner,' Kara laughed as she dragged him away from the railing.

Back at their cabin, Greg picked up the information folder and sat back on the bed.

Kara glanced out from the ensuite, asking, 'What are you doing?'

'Checking the menu,' he replied.

'This ship has five restaurants, you know,' Kara called out.

'It's not the food menu I'm looking at!'

'Oh, I see,' Kara replied.

'Did you know the playroom is open every night from 6.00 p.m.?'

'Yes, I did.'

'Did you know the pool at the rear of the ship is naked from 11.00 a.m. till 10.00 p.m.?'

'Yep.'

'Did you know that only a little touching is allowed in the pools?'

'Yeah, read that!'

'Why am I looking at this then? Do you have a plan?'

'A loose one, but you looked at all the brochures on the plane as well, I thought you'd have one already!' Kara answered, as she turned on the shower.

'I only looked at the pictures. Hey, there's a leather and lace night as well!' Greg called out over the shower.

'You'd look sexy in lace!' Kara laughed.

'They were a nice couple,' Mel said to Tom as she put on her lipstick, staring into the little mirror that perched above a matchbook-sized vanity. Mel and Tom thought that as they'd only be sleeping and showering in there, it wasn't worth spending double the money on a flash cabin they would spend little time in.

'Who's that?' Tom replied. 'I've seen a few.'

'Greg and Kara, the ones we had a drink with at the bar.'

'Oh yeah, they were. She had that sexy look, but I got the feeling they were just doing a bit of window shopping.'

'Yeah, you're probably right. Bit like us!' Mel laughed in reply, before smooching her lips together to squeeze out her lippy to a perfect line. 'Okay, I'm ready. Let's see which place offers the best dessert… and food too!' she giggled.

Greg and Kara decided to have dinner in the big restaurant; it was a huge room set out with large, immaculately dressed tables of twelve. Chandeliers lit the room as impeccably dressed waiters rushed from table to table. The carpet was a navy blue with large golden anchors and the excitement in the room was electric. The food was delicious, almost anything your heart desired.

Greg and Kara met their fellow table mates, who were all first timers as well, and although the topic of sex never came up, the eyes around the table suggested it was certainly on everyone's mind. The time had come, and they were both keen to get to one of the bars and get amongst it; being their first night and all.

There were three bars, named Swell, Whitecaps, and Tsunami. The Tsunami bar was clearly designed for those interested in more than just a piano bar. *More likely body language only,* thought Greg. The bar was dark, the music loud but not so much that you couldn't talk. Colours flashed throughout the room from multiple LED lights, revealing the faces that turned to check each new arrival as they entered. It was clearly for those interested in more than small talk.

Initially Greg felt awkward, but he quickly decided to treat it like any other bar. He reached for Kara's hand and guided her to one of the few vacant tables. He noticed that all the tables were for four or more, and a smile trickled across his lips. *Of course!* he thought.

'Bubbles?' he asked, as he retrieved the drinks card from his wallet. Kara nodded as she looked around the room. *If a girl couldn't get laid in here, there's something wrong,* she thought.

Greg returned with a champagne and a beer. He leant over and kissed her as he sat down.

'Have you found anything you like yet?' Greg asked.

'Well, there's a couple that have been throwing smiles in our direction since we arrived,' Kara said.

'There's plenty on offer alright, I must say I'm a little surprised at the number of singles here too. Do you think they're one of a pair or have come along on their own?' Greg asked.

'I wondered the same thing. Maybe they're a couple, but also play as singles?'

'That's an interesting thought.'

'Hey, someone's coming over,' Kara whispered, giving Greg a slight tap on the knee.

'Hi, we're Mike and Carol, may we join you?'

'Sure, of course,' Greg said, standing and extending his hand. 'Greg and Kara.'

It wasn't Mike and Carol's first cruise, and they started telling Greg and Kara a little about some of their past adventures. Carol was a petite little thing, slim, with long blonde hair, too perfect to be natural, much the same as her perky rounded breasts. Mike was a much larger man than Greg, not fat, but solid, easily passing as a rugby or gridiron player. They were both pleasant enough. Mike did most of the talking, while Carol gave the impression of being a shy, shadowing wife. It wasn't until they had all downed a couple of drinks that the soft vanilla chat started to warm up.

Mike, suiting his stature, made the bold move. 'So would you two like to have the next round in our cabin?'

Greg looked at Kara, and she smiled back with a willing nod.

They finished their drinks and rose to Mike's invitation. Kara and Carol chatted along the hallway, while Greg and Mike walked in single file behind of them. Mike opened the door to their cabin, which was similar to Greg and Kara's, just a little smaller. There was a two-seater couch, with nowhere else to sit, other than the bed.

Carol jumped on the bed, beckoning for Kara to join her, while Mike strolled toward the table to open a bottle of wine. He invited Greg to settle into the plush couch. Mike remained standing after he'd handed everyone a glass. A silence fell as they all took their first sips. It was Mike whose voice broke through the thick, awkward suspense.

'Why don't you two ladies get started?' Mike said, pointing at Kara and Carol with his glass, trying to act casual.

Carol's eager eyes turned to Kara, as she slowly traced her right index finger to slip a strand of hair back from Kara's face. They held in an intense stare for just a moment, before Carol leant forward, pressing her lips against Kara's. Their lipsticks blended into the colour of a blood rushing kiss, taking only seconds before

Carol's hands began exploring Kara's body. With each touch and movement, their clothes started to be discarded.

Swinging at sea had begun.

Mel and Tom had found themselves at the more conservative bar, Swell, which was well-lit and serenaded by a pianist in the centre of the lounge. The fellow patrons were much less forward.

'Anyone you like, babe?' Tom said.

'Not overly, no one is jumping out at me. What about you?'

'God, I could do that Asian chick over there!'

'Calm down, grandpa, she's not even half your age!' Mel replied with a smile.

'Well, in the words of Hugh Hefner, I may get older but the girls I like don't,' he replied, his eyes glued to the Asian beauty.

'Why don't we go and talk to *them*?' Mel said, pointing to a couple sitting quietly at a table by the window.

'Who?'

'The couple over there,' she whispered as she gave a quick glance in their direction.

Tom looked across to the far side of the room. 'You mean the Stetson and his trophy wife?'

'Stop that!' she smothered a giggle. 'He looks like a nice gentleman, and she's a honey.'

'That she is, but I'm not sure they're our type, babe. Definitely an à la carte couple who probably aren't into smorgasbords like us!'

'Cafeteria you mean... Come on, you never know. They do look a bit out of place, I bet they are new to this scene, so they might appreciate some company.'

Tom looked over at the couple again. Mel was right. She was gorgeous. A vision that drew all eyes to her, like an exquisite art form. Her silken, dark chocolate brown hair fell in large soft folding curls, cascading down to below her shoulders. She was wearing a deep burgundy coloured dress, that teased from her shoulders down a low-cut back and a v front, artfully encasing her breasts like beautifully formed pendants. Obviously, they were designer items too, ordered and made specifically for the dress.

Everything about her, the creamy complexion, makeup, jewellery, and style spoke of impeccable haute couture, no expense spared. She gleamed and glistened like a priceless diamond. Her engagement and wedding rings were the only rivals to her glow. Bold opulent statements in themselves, their magnificent sparkle could be seen from the other side of the room.

'Sure, let's go, but I think they're well out of our league,' Tom said with a grin as he stood and started to walk over. Halfway there he took Mel's hand. They arrived at the table to a couple of welcome smiles. The grey felt Stetson, proudly worn high above the snakeskin riding boots, blazed Texan pride, long before they heard his welcome drawl.

'Would you like some company?' Tom asked.

'Well yeah, of course. Y'all just come 'n siddown,' Keith said with a strong Texan accent as he rose from his seat. He removed the Stenson from his head and used it to gesture Mel to sit in the seat beside him. 'Sit 'ere, lovely lady,' he said.

He extended his hand. 'Keith Madison,' he said as he offered a firm grip to Tom. 'Meet the love of my life, Jennifer.'

'Jennifer stood and rested an elegant hand in both Mel and Tom's, offering a much softer, yet similar welcome. 'Please sit down. It's lovely to have some company, this is our first time on a cruise like this, I wasn't sure we would fit in,' Jennifer offered.

Keith was impeccably dressed in a crisp shirt and designer moleskin pants, complete with a gold-clasped and leather-braided bolo tie. He had a distinguished presence that commanded attention, rather like a fourteen-point stag head mounted over a mantle—you couldn't help but stare. His hair was soft grey, while everything else, including his voice, conveyed contented tycoon pride, wealth, experience, and confidence. Then there was Jennifer. It was almost as if she was his finishing touch, like exquisitely crafted crown jewels

Tom swallowed an awe-filled gulp. 'We guessed that you were newbies,' he said, his eyes fixed on Jennifer.

Turning to look at Keith, Tom continued, 'Well sir, I hope you don't mind me saying, but this doesn't seem like your kind of cruise?'

'Yeah, it's a bit of surprise to me too, big fella. Yah know, we've 'bout covered mostuv the world over, so it was Jennifer's idea for somethin' a bit different. You picked it all right. Expect we do kind a look like a bass on the bank of the Brazos River! We're only here for the sightseeing, ol' boy.' Keith said with a roar. 'So don't be gettin' any ideas, you young whipper snappers!' His mouth was smiling, but his eyes weren't.

Mel blinked and looked at Jennifer, who blushed ever so slightly and nodded.

'It's not our first cruise like this, but same here. Meeting people and enjoying the trip is the main thing. Extra fun only happens if it feels exactly right for us both,' replied Mel, throwing Jennifer a knowing smile.

'Well said there, lassie!' said Keith, raising his glass.

Tom grinned at Mel's tempered comments, as they all chinked glasses. From there, the conversation started to flow. They told each other about their lives and Tom realised that Keith was far wealthier than he had initially thought.

Greg could feel the pressure building in his pants with the two girls now topless. They sucked, licked, and kissed away on the bed. It was when Carol lifted Kara's skirt and slid her hand inside her

panties that he realised how hot this really was. He looked over at Mike to see him starting to unbutton his shirt.

Kara was lost in the magic that Carol was performing with her fingers. She rolled onto her back, giving Carol full access. With her legs now spread wide, Carol slipped two fingers inside her. It was within only seconds of her G-spot being tantalised that Kara succumbed, and the blissful shudders came.

Mike moved towards the bed, now completely naked, and started to remove the remainder of Carol's clothes. He was huge, wielding probably the biggest cock Greg had ever seen. Carol lay on her back, stretched out, her hand in Kara's who was still floating back to earth. Greg had now removed his clothes and had moved to Kara's side of the bed to lay next to her. He kissed her ear as he whispered, 'How was that?'

'My God,' was her reply. He wasn't sure whether that was a 'My God' from the orgasm she'd just had or from seeing the size of Mike's dick.

Mike was kissing Carol feverously; his fingers worked at pace between her legs. Her legs were now bent at the knees and spread wide, her left leg spilling over Kara's. Kara placed her hand on Carol's inner thigh, feeling her body arch and tremor as Mike's fingers thrust deep inside her. Greg continued to watch, giving Kara a moment to rest a little.

Mike moved to mount Carol, who then almost disappeared beneath his bulk. Her head flew back with her mouth open wide, her body arched, and she let out a noise, almost a desperate scream that must have been a combination of pleasure and pain. Mike fed his massive shaft deep into her body. She looked so small beneath him as he rode her hard, her whole body rocking several inches with each thrust. Kara could only picture a huge sea creature devouring its helpless prey. Carol soon screamed with orgasmic shrillness, as Mike withdrew from her and blew all over the chest of his spent wife. Both Greg and Kara were shocked at the volume this bloke sprayed, covering her from chin to belly button. It was only then that Kara saw the true size of him.

She grabbed Greg, whispering a hasty, 'Climb on me, now.' Her urgent need for him inside her had escalated from watching Mike and Carol. Greg pumped her fast and hard, as the contented Mike and Carol watched, only inches away. A deep guttural moan escaped from Kara as her second wave of joyous bliss erupted. This heralding sound was all Greg needed and he soon emptied himself into her. As their waves of passion subsided, Greg slid out and off Kara slowly.

Mike walked over to find his glass, swallowing most of it in one mouthful, his manhood dangling low between his legs.

'God, that was fun!' he bellowed. 'Maybe next time we can swap?'

'Yeah, let's see how we go,' Greg replied, also standing to have a drink. The two girls were now sitting up, resting back against the bedhead. Kara's thoughts were scrambling. *We really need to get out of here—before he tries to get that python anywhere near me.*

Keith was full of questions, keen to know what Tom and Mel had done in the past. 'Tom, my boy, tell me, how does it feel, watching someone screw your lovely lady here?'

Tom looked toward Keith, who was now leaning back in his chair with a look of superiority. Tom hesitated with his reply. 'If it wasn't a two-way street, it would be different, but to tell the truth, it turns me on seeing it.'

Keith nodded, confirming in his mind that no one would be screwing his wife. 'I see,' he finally replied.

'What have you done in the past, Jennifer?' Tom asked, trying to break the silent pause. He shot a second glance back at Keith who was still leaning back in his seat, before fixing his eyes back on Jennifer. 'Have you thought about starting with "same room?"' Or just watching another couple perhaps? Or maybe you'd just like being watched by someone?'

'Same room?' asked Keith.

'He's referring to two couples having sex in the same room, on their own beds or side by side, but just having sex with their own partners. Just watching each other and not getting intimate with the other couple at all,' Jennifer offered.

Her words spoken like a textbook. *She's been researching*, Mel thought.

'I see. That sounds like fun,' Keith said, somewhat cautiously. 'We haven't thought too far ahead. We've talked about some of the naughty stuff, but it's just pillow talk if you know what I mean, ol' boy.' He let out a little laugh. 'I know that stuff gets her going and that's why we've come to check it out, ya see,' Keith offered.

Mel saw Jennifer shift in her seat as a flush rose in her cheeks. Mel put her hand on hers, saying, 'It's completely normal to get aroused by those thoughts.'

'I just can't believe we're here talking about our sex lives to strangers, though,' Jennifer said in a soft voice, now blushing even more.

'Well, if you can't talk about it here, my dear, where can you?' Tom said with a winking laugh, as he also leaned back in his chair.

'Do you imagine being with a stranger when you masturbate?' Mel whispered to her.

Jennifer covered her face in her hands to hide her shock, the sparkling diamonds on her left hand outshone by the bright red glow bursting from her face.

'Sometimes,' Jennifer whispered back through her fingers. Her eyes shot to her husband whose expression was completely neutral. Her whisper was loud enough that they all heard.

Jennifer slowly slid her hands away from her face, 'My God, I am so embarrassed, I can't believe I just said that.'

Mel tapped Tom gently on his thigh and threw him a look, as if to say, 'Do something.'

Tom jumped to Jennifer's rescue, saying, 'Don't be embarrassed, luv. It's just sex. We all think about it, want it, and fantasise about it. I figure if we've paid all this money to come on a sexy cruise, this is exactly the right place to talk about it, look for it, and enjoy it. Now, who's for another drink?'

Jennifer released a small sigh, threw him a thankful smile, and rested back into her chair. Keith's expression was giving nothing away about whether she had overstepped the mark or not. How would he take finding out that she had thought about being with another man, fictious or not?

The conversation turned to more of fragments of their lives and the other features of the cruise over the next round of drinks. They promised to catch up again before the cruise was over.

As the door closed to Mike and Carol's cabin, Greg took off running, laughing, as he darted behind the first bulkhead and waited for Kara to come running around the corner. He grabbed her, pulling her into a safe bear hug, saying, 'I'll save you from that massive serpent.'

'Fuck! Did you see the size of that bloke, my God! How does he not split that poor girl in two?' Kara said in a screaming whisper.

Greg laughed. 'I saw your face when he suggested a swap next time…'

'Why do you think I near pumped you into a frenzy, to make you come so fast? Sorry, but we won't be swapping with them, let me tell you! It could ruin me for the rest of the cruise, or my life!' she said, grabbing him by the hand and near dragging him toward the lift.

As they reached the promenade deck again, they were still laughing. Greg asked, 'Bed or another drink?'

'If you don't mind, I think I've had enough—perhaps let's call it?' Kara replied.

'You read my mind. Let's just find our cabin and enjoy a cuddle.'

They'd chatted, caressed, and cuddled and were soon asleep.

The next morning unfolded a welcome to a beautiful pristine day. As Greg stepped out onto the balcony, the warm sea breeze caressed his naked body; he felt a twinge at the thought that anyone on a close by the balcony would see his nudity. *Quite a turn on to start the day*, he thought as he sipped his cup of tea.

The sea was smooth, with not a speck of land to be seen in any direction, at least from his side of the boat anyway. He went back inside, pulled on a pair of shorts and a t-shirt to go and find coffee. He glanced at the bed and relished his warm amusement at the sight of the sleeping Kara. On her side, her hair spilled randomly, she cradled one pillow in her arms and had one leg on top of the quilt, bent back at the knee. She slept gently. It always made him smile. He closed the door carefully, trying his best not to wake her.

Tom had awoken with a hard on. He wasn't sure whether it was from the sexy environment or just what men call a 'piss fat,' either way he wasn't going to waste it. He looked over at Mel, her beautiful auburn hair scattered across the pillow. She was naked, of course, from their lovemaking last night, which was fuelled by him asking her who was she going to pretend he was.

'Be that Greg, the first guy we met at the bar with the dark-haired girl,' she'd said. 'I want him to fuck me tonight.'

As Tom recalled the event, he felt the twitch in his groin. He replayed the conversation that she wanted to be with another man and tried to picture him on her. This was firing him up even more. She then asked him, 'And what about you? Who am I going to be in your mind?'

'Perhaps you could be that little Chinese girl we saw at the bar.'

'The young one?'

'Yeah, the young one.'

'Do you want me to whisper Mandarin in your ear as well?' Mel asked with a smile.

'Nah, just clench your pussy tight!' he said with a laugh.

Mel whacked him gently across his chest. 'Come and do me, Greg,' she said, pulling him closer to her.

The recollection of the banter that incited such hot sex last night only enhanced his arousal this morning. Tom ran his fingers around her nipples until she stirred. She opened her eyes and smiled at him.

'Are you still horny?' she murmured, through a sleepy voice.

'Always, my love,' he replied as he lay beside her, his hardness pressed in behind her. Her eyes had closed again, but she reached out, wrapping her fingers around him and started a slow, deliberate stroking of his erection. Once fully hard, he mounted her; he found her easily and rode her hard and fast. Morning sex was always about quick pleasure, not a marathon, and that suited them both.

Mel could feel his eruption rising. She pushed him back, 'Blow on my tits.'

In a split-second response, he withdrew, repositioning to kneel above her. She wanked him till his cum sprayed over her chest. She squeezed his cock as the last drop fell onto her warm bare skin. Releasing him from her grip, she rubbed his semen into her breasts. Tom watched her, then rolled away to lay back, basking in contentment as his stiffness subsided. He rolled her to her side and spooned her from behind. It was another hour before they both woke again.

Kara had heard the door click shut; she hadn't opened her eyes yet but realisation of where she was brought a smile to her. She opened her eyes and let the visual cues contribute to her sense of contentment. She slowly blinked in more of the day, then vainly attempting to smooth her hair before the coffee arrived, she knew exactly where he would be. Greg soon returned to the cabin with two large coffees in hand, happy to see Kara now wide awake, and that his timing for delivery was perfect. The top sheet fell away as she reached for that essential morning brew. He loved the sight of her casual nakedness, so carefree.

Kara was aglow this morning. She was in paradise, relishing in the sight of the vast ocean beyond the balcony rail as the world steamed by at thirty knots towards Jamaica. This day brought an even richer flavour with thoughts of more sex to come. Maybe she will see him pleasure another woman, or the possibility of enjoying Greg watching her being with someone that she hasn't even met yet. *How good can it get?*

'Shall we try the naked pool after breakfast?' Kara suggested as she took another sip of coffee.

'Great idea, but it's not open till eleven,' Greg responded.

'Not open for nakedness—that's all!' Kara laughed.

Jennifer spent most of the night trying to imagine the different scenarios that Mel had told her about, to help introduce and soften her entry into this exciting lifestyle.

She'd pictured herself and Keith sitting on a spare bed in a room watching another couple together, seeing up close for the first time another woman's vagina, wet and swollen. A young man's penis penetrating the woman with that glorious first stroke. It made her tremble at the thought, now feeling her own body's heat rising and tingles from her groin. She then imagined the young couple watching Keith undress her in front of them, standing fully naked within their reach, seeing every part of her. She saw the young man's resplendent hardness rise again at the sight of her body. She led her thoughts to her legs spreading wide over Keith, as she lowered herself onto him—never taking her eyes off the young man. She pictured them, poised naked close beside her, watching her every rise and fall. She could sense the young man's intense presence, his eyes wanting her, before holding out his hand and asking her to come to him.

He'd lay back on the bed, never letting go of her hand, guiding her to straddle him. She'd lower herself onto him and feel him slide so deep inside her, further than any man had ever been before.

Jennifer came shortly after that. Keith lay snoring by her side. It was one of the biggest orgasms she'd ever had, the bed now wet below her. She moved closer to the edge to avoid it. *God, I could come again.* she thought.

Keith didn't care what type of cruise she'd asked for; such was his ignorance. She knew his only love was money, not her or her growing needs. Knowing now what she really craved, she lamented. There was no chance she would have the pleasure of any fulfilling sex in these next four days. Perhaps, just maybe, Keith would be inspired to do more? But in her heart, she knew it was all a fantasy, the chance of Keith watching her with someone else and them actually living to tell the story was unimaginable.

Kara and Greg were having breakfast when Tom and Mel arrived in the dining room. Tom whispered to Mel, 'Hey babe, the bloke you "screwed" last night is over there.'

Mel's head spun around. 'Can we join them?' she said, with way too much enthusiasm.

'They might want to be on their own,' Tom replied.

'Don't be silly, we're all here to meet other people, let's just ask!'

Mel took him by the hand to change direction and headed for Greg and Kara's table.

'Like some company?' Mel asked.

'Sure, you're more than welcome,' Greg said.

Mel's eyes locked onto Greg's as she pictured him making love to her, just as he had in her fantasy sex last night. Greg noticed the look, then casually threw a smile back at her. Tom had already headed for the buffet, but not before giving Kara a flirtatious look.

'Did you see the way she looked at you?' Kara whispered softly as Mel also headed for the buffet.

'Mmm, I did. I think she may have found that special person,' he said.

'Of course she has. How can any woman resist your superpowers?' Kara giggled.

'That's enough of that, Wonder Woman!' came his playful retort.

When Tom and Mel returned, Kara asked, 'Did you get up to much last night?'

'We had a drink with a first-time couple, maybe a little over their heads on this trip,' Tom said between mouthfuls of eggs and bacon.

'What about you two?'

Greg looked at Kara and said, 'Well… We did go back to a couple's room to play; it was just a bit of same room, but it was fun.'

Mel couldn't stop looking at Greg. He had a way of looking at her that made her melt. She decided in that moment to devise a plan to make love to this couple before the cruise was over. She remembered they would land in Kingston tomorrow, for a day ashore on the Jamaican Island. She was now desperately keen to spend it with Greg and Kara.

Are you going ashore tomorrow?' Mel asked.

'We certainly are!' Kara said.

'So are we. Perhaps we might see you somewhere, or catch up for lunch or something?' Mel spoke the words, but her thoughts were still caught in Greg's gaze.

God, I want him. I want him to keep his eyes open the whole time he fucks me.

'Mel, they might just want to be on their own,' Tom said.

'That sounds like a great idea,' Greg said, as he looked straight at Mel.

Mel's heart was pounding. *Now I'm sure he wants me too.* Mel was convinced.

'We're going to head to the back pool shortly,' Kara said, trying to break the look between Greg and Mel.

Greg soon stood and reached for Kara's hand to help her stand. Mel's eyes never left him.

'I'm ready,' Kara replied with a grin, taking Greg's outstretched hand.

'Which one?' Mel asked. Both Kara and Greg noticed the swift bump Tom gave her leg under the table.

'The naked one at the rear,' Kara said, smiling at Mel and Tom's embarrassed looks.

'Okay,' was all Mel dared to say.

'We might see you later, hey?' Kara said. Greg gave them a wave as they turned and strolled away.

'I think you're in trouble. You're definitely a wanted man, mister!' Kara said to Greg as they left the dining room.

'Yep, I think you're right!'

Jennifer awoke and a shiver of excitement rolled through her as she realised where she was and the place her imagination had taken her last night. She looked over to Keith to find he was gone. She looked through the sheer curtains to the balcony. He'd made a cup of tea and was on the phone to whom she could only imagine was Jerry, his second in charge at the cattle ranch in Texas.

Their cabin was a massive suite, the most expensive on the ship, it was ten times the size of a standard room. She climbed out of bed; painfully aware her side of the bed was still quite wet.

I've never done that before, she thought, quickly trying to think what to do. *If I make the bed, it would still be wet tonight. If I leave it open, it will be too obvious.* She realised that she had only one choice, to strip the bed. She could just tell Keith that she wanted clean sheets. She put the kettle on and then quickly went back to pull the bed apart.

It was only on hearing the kettle boiling that Keith's attention shifted away from his phone call. He glanced up over the top of his glasses, smiled at Jennifer, and returned to the call. She made her cuppa and then strolled out to join him on the balcony. The warm Caribbean breeze caressed their faces as the ship sailed closer to the equator and deeper into the tropical paradise. Jennifer's sky-blue silk Donna Karan nightshirt danced softly on her perfect body, displaying momentary glimpses of her amazing figure as she leant back against the railing.

'Good morning, my darlin',' Keith said, ending the phone call.

Jennifer reached down and kissed the top of his head. 'Good morning, darling husband.'

'What would you like to do today?' he asked her.

'Why don't we have a walk around the ship and check it out? You know, they have what they call a "playroom" here as well.'

'I don't think you'll be needing that, my dear,' Keith said with a jovial spirit.

'No, of course not, but maybe we could just take a peek? We should at least see what this cruise is all about and when we get home you could tell me more stories,' she said with a cheeky grin on her face.

'Well, yeah, maybe,' he replied, as he lifted his phone back up to read a message. Jennifer turned her back to him, letting the warm breeze embrace her.

She closed her eyes as the wind pulled and teased the silk of her night dress tight against her body. She wore no underwear and the silk caressed her delicate skin wherever it touched. Her nipples became hard as the fabric slid back and forth over them. Her imagination slipped back to her dream. He was there with her now, his warm hands caressing her all over; her lips tingled as she imagined his lips on hers. She felt the moisture form. She opened her eyes. Her inner heat burned and her groin now aching to be touched.

'I'll jump in the shower,' Jennifer said and walked back inside.

'Okay, my dear,' he called back, oblivious to the erotic pleasure his wife just had while standing right in front of him.

Jennifer slipped off her nightdress and stood facing the full-length mirror, her groin still tingling as she imagined him watching her naked. She ran a finger through her wetness then took a deep breath and stepped into the warm stream of water.

Greg and Kara arrived at the pool to find quite a few people already there, almost all the girls were topless or completely naked. Kara pointed to a couple of lounges where they could sit. Greg sat down and watched Kara remove her top and then her bra.

'Is it too early for a drink?' Greg asked.

'Never! Bubbles please, sir!' Kara said.

Greg soon returned with the drinks and sat back on the lounge next to her. He resisted removing his shorts—for now.

'If Mr Big turns up, I'm out of here,' Kara said, and they both laughed.

They spied a couple in the water at the far end of the pool, both naked and kissing passionately.

'I know how that's going to end up,' Greg said. 'It's surprising how many singles there are here, I can't work out if they came alone or maybe split up for the day to do different things,' he added as he noted a few people sitting on their own.

'I suspect the cruise might screen the guests, a bit like a club, don't you think?'

'Yes, I would think so. Hey, but imagine how much fun it would be for someone young and single?' Greg said.

Kara thought about that for a minute before suggesting, 'Hey, what about one night on the way home we go out separately, see what we find, and then tell the other all about it the next day? But it's not to be a competition.'

'That's very naughty, Kara. I love it."

Two drinks down, they decided to get the rest of their gear off and have a swim. Being naked in public never ceased to be a turn on for them both. They faced each other and stripped slowly, and then walked to the pool and slipped into the tempered water. The rules were that touching was allowed, but penetration was frowned upon. However, in the water it was often a little hard to tell if anyone followed the rules exactly. The young couple in the corner were clearly considering that rule as more of a guideline.

'You wanted to watch another couple, my dear, well look at the young ones there in the corner,' Keith said, nodding towards the pool. Jennifer was already watching them.

'Would you like to take your top off, darling?' he asked.

'Really, Keithy?' she answered in surprise.

'Sure! This looks like the best place to flash those beauties, and besides, I'll certainly enjoy looking at them. To be honest, you are the only one with a top on from what I can see.'

'Okay, thank you. When in Rome, I guess.'

The young couple in the corner had finished their water play, so to speak, and were leaving the pool. The young fella's erection was only half subsided as they walked back to their lounges. Jennifer was fixated on him, his resemblance to last night's fantasy was scary.

'Shall I get us a drink?' Jennifer asked, reaching for the drinks card.

'Great idea, a beer, my dear,' Keith replied.

Jennifer strolled the length of the pool deck to the bar, trying to avoid the staring eyes and wishing she'd put her top back on. This public display of her topless body was a bold step and making her rather nervous.

I can do this. I have a nice body, she reassured herself.

She stepped up to the bar, a naked male customer was also standing there waiting to order. This was pushing Jennifer to her absolute limit. She told herself again that she could 'do this.'

She did start to relax as she waited. She turned to look at man waiting to be served next to her. He stepped closer, extended his hand, and casually said, 'Hi, I'm Greg.'

The thunderbolt happened in that split second. She'd turned instinctively toward the voice to offer a cursory polite greeting. His penetrating eyes captivated her. It was such an unexpected and powerful response that she froze, her mouth falling slightly open. She quickly wiped her mouth to see if she had dribbled.

Rendered near speechless, she thought to herself, *if there was such a thing as 'love at first sight,' this was it.*

'I'm... err... I'm Jennifer,' she managed to stammer out in her light Texan accent. She slowly held out her hand to accept his greeting, desperately wanting to cover herself in case her stiffening nipples were obvious.

The barman arrived back with the cocktail for Kara.

'It was so nice to meet you, Jennifer, I really hope I see you again, and… You have beautiful eyes, by the way.'

'Thank you,' she said with a shy smile and slowly turned back to the barman who was now waiting for her order.

She muttered, 'A beer and a champagne, please.' As soon as that was out, she turned to watch Greg as he walked away with his drinks, noting his firm butt and muscular legs. She looked back to the barman, who gave her an acknowledging smile. She blushed and looked down, now consumed with embarrassment and shyness. *He must see this all the time!* She looked up again. *My, my, that made me tingle alright!* she thought to herself.

She tried to imagine telling her Texan high society friends how she'd flirted with a naked man at a bar while topless, on a ship where everyone fucks each other.

The barman didn't flinch or react more than to simply say, 'My assistant is here now, so if you like, I'll bring your drinks to your table, madam.'

'Thank you' she said, turning back towards her lounge. Her eyes searching for another look at Greg.

'You want to go to the pool, don't you?' Tom said giving her a cheeky look.

'Well, yeah… Just for a look.'

'Are you prepared to get your gear off, girl?'

'You bet I will!'

'Alright, but let's not sit with Greg and Kara. Maybe we can catch up with them tomorrow in Kingston for lunch, and not smother them, hey? Remember, there are 3000 other people on this crate. Deal?'

'Deal.'

Tom and Mel arrived at the pool, easily spotting the standout Texan's Stetson and the gorgeous topless Jennifer straight away. Mel rushed over.

'Hi there! How are you going you two?' she said, giving Jennifer a kiss on the cheek. 'You look amazing,' she whispered in Jennifer's ear.

Tom had already fully appreciated Jennifer's breasts and it took all his effort not to stare or stiffen at the sight of her.

Tom moved to sit on one of the empty lounges next to them, purposely not moving them closer until invited.

'I'm feeling a little overdressed,' Mel said, as she slipped off her top and reached behind to remove her bra. She wasn't really a barbie figure, but for a middle-aged woman she looked pretty good. Her breasts were a lovely shape, tear drops with large dark nipples. Not like the perky enhancements adorning Jennifer's chest, but they were a beautiful natural shape, and she felt comfortable with them being on show. More importantly in Mel's thoughts, they were now on show for Greg.

So, where is he sitting? her mind and eyes searched earnestly.

Keith suggested it was time to go and have a look around more of the ship. Jennifer reached for her bra and top and slipped on her shoes. Tom watched her refit every garment almost like a reverse strip. It so turned him on.

Keith turned to Tom and said, 'Y'all make sure we catch up soon, ya hear? I want to hear some more about the company you work for, Tom.' He leant over and kissed Mel on the cheek.

Mel offered a cheery goodbye, but she was still largely distracted in her search for Greg. However, this time, sadly, he was nowhere to be found.

Kara finished the cocktail in about three slurps, it was hot in the sun now. 'Thank you, Greg, that was yummy. I'll be having another one of those later. Hey, what shall we do now? I'll get burnt if we stay too long out here,' she said.

'Let's go to the waterslides, have a late lunch, maybe an afternoon siesta, and then get ready for the playroom tonight?'

'Sounds absolutely perfect,' Kara replied as she slipped her knickers back on.

They dressed and headed for the other end of the ship.

The water slides were fantastic; probably suited for much younger and flexible people, but on this occasion, there weren't many of those around, allowing them to enjoy doing their own 'wet and wild' as they slid down every turn and tube.

It was well after 2.00 p.m. when they ordered some lunch at the Slide pool restaurant, and after a couple more drinks were blissfully exhausted, fully ready to put their heads down.

They headed toward their cabin for a nap. As they passed by the arcade entrance, Kara remembered Greg had suggested they buy a few nibbles to keep in their room for hosting or snacks. 'I might duck in and grab some room supplies; I won't be long.'

'Great idea. Do you want me to come, too?'

'No—it's fine, I'll meet you back at the cabin. I'll only be a few minutes.' Kara gave him a quick kiss, before entering the passageway leading to the little shopping precinct.

As Greg continued on at a casual pace, he glanced ahead, noticing a couple walking toward him. A grey headed gentleman, with a large Texan hat, and his obviously much younger 'pride bride' by his side. As they drew closer, both Greg and Jennifer recognised each other; their eyes locked and followed each other for the next few seconds. As they passed, Jennifer looked and smiled at him, something Keith didn't see.

It was really a magical moment. So much was said in that gaze, without a pause or a sound.

Back in the cabin, Greg stripped off, closed the curtains, and hopped on the bed; his thoughts coming back to that little, yet significant, eye exchange with the beautiful lady from the pool bar.

Greg lay there thinking. Jennifer was an absolute masterpiece. He would really like to see her again.

Kara soon joined him in bed, and within moments they'd snuggled together and drifted off, letting their daytime fun fade into a catalogue of dreams.

It was close to 7.00 p.m. when they awoke, almost simultaneously.

'Are you looking forward to the playroom, Kara?'

'Absolutely, I imagine it's going to be a high-class swing club, quite a bit different to the ones we've been to back home.'

'Just remember, No pressure. Just do what you're happy to do or want to do.'

'You know me, right? Despite how we might have fun on our own, I'm the cautious one— remember?' Kara said, her head now turned towards him, offering a small grin.

'You're right. Let's get going then. You have first shower; it'll take you longer to get ready.'

'On my way!' she said as she jumped up and disappeared through the bathroom door. Greg's mind slipped back to Jennifer. *Will I see her again? Is that her father or uncle that she's with? Of course, it isn't, it's just money.*

Tom and Mel had quickly established that the three bars had different levels of eroticism, and of course, there was the playroom which was a no brainer; you wouldn't be leaving there without having sex with someone. Tom decided on the middle bar, and if that didn't work, they would move up a level to the Tsunami bar. Mel looked lovely in a maroon pencil skirt and white blouse unbuttoned enough to see plenty of her white lacy bra. Tom ordered a drink for them both. They sat at a raised black table with four stools. They'd only had one sip when a tall, handsome man in his early thirties approached them. 'Hi there,' he said, 'I'm David or Dave, whatever you like. Would you be interested in a threesome? I'm happy to pleasure you both.'

'Oh, no thanks, we are all good,' responded Tom without a hesitation. 'We're after a couple.'

'All good. I'll be here if you change your mind.'

'Thanks David,' Mel said, raising her eyebrows.

'Have you ever thought about another man touching you?' Mel asked Tom.

'Nah, I don't think I could do it; as you know I've been naked with other men, but we don't touch.'

'It might not be all that bad,' Mel suggested 'Or you could both share me? It's our third day of five tomorrow, and you realise we haven't been with anyone yet!'

'Would you like to fuck him, my love?' Tom said, putting his hand on her arm.

'Who wouldn't? Let's be honest, he's pretty bloody hot!'

Tom looked over at David, who was now leaning back on the bar talking to the attendant. Tom already knew Mel was keen but asked, 'So, what are you thinking, Mel?'

'Well, we could invite him back and you could watch him do me, wank if you want, or join in?' suggested Mel.

'But didn't we agree that we'd find one couple that we really like, play games, and make love to them?'

'We could have a little entrée before main course, you know!'

Tom turned back to look at David with a scrutinising gaze. 'Okay, go and ask him,' Tom conceded, as he reached for his glass and took a huge gulp of beer, signifying that no more discussion was needed.

Mel also took a sip of her drink, stood, straightened her skirt, and headed towards the tall, slim, younger man.

When Greg and Kara opened the door to the playroom, they were flabbergasted.

'My God, this is amazing!'

They were greeted at the door by a crisply dressed attendant who quickly explained the rules, escorted them to the change rooms, and showed them how the lockers worked. The middle of the room featured a huge spa bath that could easily accommodate thirty people or more. This centrepiece was surrounded by at least twenty rooms, some with doors open and some closed. Only subtle LEDs provided enough light to move around. The music was a perfect volume, carefully sensitive to most guests' tastes. They noticed that one wall was adorned by a bar that was completely lined with naked clientele. After the tour, Kara and Greg headed back to the change rooms. They removed their clothes alongside the other couple who had taken the familiarisation tour with them. They both thought it weird stripping off in front of complete strangers, but somehow, here it all seemed normal.

The four of them smiled at each other, as they discreetly checked each other out. The lady was slim, with long, bouncing blonde hair which she was in the process of tying up with a hair tie. Her breasts were small but suited her petite figure. Her face was similarly pretty, with twinkling blue eyes. He was also slim, probably a bike rider, with a slim bum and tightly pencilled, muscly legs.

'We're Steve and Judy,' the now naked man said, as he held his hand out to Greg.

With a reply as strong as their handshake, he responded, 'I'm Greg and this is Kara. Nice to meet you both. Are you enjoying the trip so far?'

'Yes, it's amazing!' Judy said, while flicking the last twist of the band around the grasp of hair. She stepped up to Kara and Greg, giving each a welcome kiss on the cheek. 'Hello there! Sorry, my hair has a mind of its own and needs some control before the spa!'

'The spa is like an Olympic pool!' Kara said. 'Have you tried it before?'

'Yes, first night. Couldn't resist.' Steve offered. 'We figured it was the best place to meet and talk to the others, and if we got lucky, we'd head to a room, and do whatever.'

Would you like to join us?' Judy asked.

'Why not!' Greg said, as he grabbed two towels and took Kara's hand. They followed the other two toward the main arena spa. The boys waited as the girls hopped into the bubbling suds and sat next to each other, as Greg and Steve followed suit, sitting either side of their partners. Steve and Judy chatted freely about their previous cruises and experiences, including a couple they'd enjoyed last night. The explicit sharing soon had the four of them aroused. It was clear that Steve and Judy had their hands in each other's laps, and although Greg was quite aroused himself, he resisted starting anything yet. 'Hey, maybe you and I could swap seats, Steve?' Greg suggested.

'Sure,' he said. He stood, fully erect from the caressing Judy had been performing below the surface, and moved to sit next to Kara. Almost immediately he took Kara's hand and placed it on his erection. She obliged, and he leant forward and kissed her. Both Judy and Greg watched them before Judy turned to Greg, pressing a distracting kiss against his lips while her hand took a decisive hold of him.

The foreplay between the four was accelerating, prompting Steve to mutter, 'Let's get a room, shall we?' They all agreed, climbed out, dried themselves, and walked to the nearest free room. Their every glance and movement signalling willing consent and desire for more. Steve gently guided Kara to lay on the bed, then found her firm bud with his tongue. *My God, he's good at that!* she thought.

Greg began kissing Judy, allowing his fingers to find her sweet wetness. Steve had almost brought Kara to an ecstatic brink, but just before she came, he climbed over her and entered her. She came quickly as he pumped her fast and hard.

Greg had also soon found himself inside Judy, in contrast filling her with slow, deep, firm strokes. Judy wrapped her legs around him and rocked her hips to match his thrusts. Kara turned to watch Greg and Judy. She loved watching him clench those butt cheeks when he was giving himself to another woman.

The four of them swapped a few times before they were all completely spent. Eventually, the four of them lay naked and exhausted. It's hard to explain the feeling you have as you lay with people intimately that only an hour ago you didn't know existed. There is a bond, only small, but a bond all the same. They all dressed together back in the change room and thanked each other for the fun night. It was simple, fun, and thoroughly sexy. It gave each of them the rush and compersious connection that seeing their partner pleasured by another always provided.

Mel walked up to Dave and tapped him on the shoulder, 'We may have reconsidered.'

'Great!' he said.

'Now, my husband may not want to be involved, he'll probably just watch. Is that okay?'

'Of course, whatever you want.'

'Hey, tell me, do you normally get a couple to say yes?' she asked.

'Every night,' Dave said with a smile.

'Really?' Mel said, taking his hand and leading him back to where Tom sat.

Tom swallowed the rest of his beer and stood. He looked at Dave and said, 'Alright then, let's go have some fun.'

Kara was fast asleep when she felt the ship bump against the wharf at Kingston Harbour the next morning.

'Hey Greg, wake up, we're here!' she said, jumping out of bed. 'The tour starts in half an hour!'

The engine on the bus was running as Greg and Kara reached the door to clamber aboard. The bus was almost full, with only two seats at the back still free. Greg caught Mel's eye as they passed, and she mouthed, 'Hello'.

'Did you see Mel and Tom halfway down the bus?' Greg asked Kara, still with a hint of their last-minute race in his throat.

'No, I didn't—I was still worrying about the driver being annoyed and not wanting to hold anyone up any longer! Why's that?'

'I think she must've had a big night last night,' he replied.

'Really? What makes you say that?'

'I'm not sure. She wasn't quite bouncing out of her seat when she saw us.'

'Let's just wait and see. She might not be a morning person?' Kara said. She could tell Greg had already moved on from those thoughts.

Greg was quietly scanning the bus, hoping Jennifer might be aboard, the look they had shared still in his mind. He was very keen to see her again. There were at least ten buses all going to different attractions, although most would overlap at some places. *Perhaps we'll see each other in passing somewhere,* he thought.

The first stop was the Bob Marley Museum. Greg and Kara were the last two off the bus, figuring that was only fair, given their late arrival. Tom and Mel were waiting for them as they finally alighted. This was the first time Kara had taken any real notice of Tom. Was it the way he looked at her this morning? Did the fact she had her hair down today make Tom see her differently? Something had definitely changed in him since they'd last met.

'Good morning, you two,' Tom said, shaking Greg's hand. Kara and Mel shared hugs and greeting kisses all around.

'I'm really keen to see this,' Tom said. 'This is the music from my day!' They strolled through the friendly, colourful garden that led to a red-shuttered, rattling-style house which was humming a welcome of familiar songs. It beckoned them inside. It was a befitting tribute to the iconic musician.

Tom turned to Mel, exclaiming, 'This couldn't be a better song to play for guests from a swing cruise!' They all stopped and listened and started to laugh together on hearing *'Let's get together, and feel alright.'*

They stayed for over an hour, before the bus departed for Fort Charles and then onto Hellshire Bay for lunch. The four of them stayed as a team for the rest of the day, sharing a delicious lunch of succulent fish, followed by a walk along the glorious, aqua-coloured bay surrounded by the blue peak mountain that could be seen out across the sea. Tom had started to pay more attention to Kara, maybe since Mel's insistence that she and Greg were the couple she wanted them to enjoy. He'd really taken a liking to Kara, that grew even more throughout the day. He'd caught her unique charm, wrapped up in understated intelligence and a lively sense of humour. They'd all been discussing the history associated with Port Royal; its Spanish heritage, the earthquake, and the remaining Giddy House from their tour at Fort Charles. The bus didn't leave for another half an hour, so Kara suggested they take a walk along the beach.

Tom now took the opportunity to chat more privately with Kara and started walking by her side.

Mel's desperation for Greg appeared to have subsided slightly, which made it all a little more comfortable for Greg to engage in light conversation as they followed behind Kara and Tom along the beach.

'So, Greg, did you and Kara get up to anything last night?' Mel asked.

'We did, we went to the playroom and met a nice couple.'

'I see. Was it fun?'

'Yes, really simple, they were a nice couple; we shared a room and we all enjoyed ourselves.'

'Did you swap?'

'Yes, we started and finished with the other person, with a couple of swaps in between.'

'Are you sure Kara doesn't mind sharing you with another woman?'

'Not at all, we both love it. I'm not sure if you and Tom have experienced it, but we really get pleasure watching each other's erotic enjoyment. What about you, Mel? What did you get up to last night?'

'Let's just say, I had a "very big" night—I'm struggling to walk today, to be honest!'

'I did notice that you weren't quite your usual bright self!' Greg said, smiling as he pictured that.

'Kara, can I tell you something,' Tom said as they strolled further away from Mel and Greg.

'Sure, Tom.'

'I, err... I mean, Mel and I are keen for you and Greg to be the ones we make love to on this cruise. You must know how infatuated Mel is with Greg, and I think you're just gorgeous, you just ooze sex appeal. Would you two like to join us, maybe, and play some sex games before the cruise is over, and see how it goes?'

'That's lovely of you to say. I'll talk to Greg but I don't think that'd be a problem, it sounds like fun. Thanks for asking. Hey—perhaps we should head back? I don't want another sprint to the bus again!' Tom laughed and they started a quicker pace to join the others.

The buses arrived back to the port in time for everybody to get aboard and freshen up before dinner.

Kara told Greg all about the conversation with Tom. Greg agreed it would be fun to play some games. 'We only have two nights left, you know. If we do our singles night and then a night with Tom and Mel, that's pretty well it.'

'That's okay, isn't it?' Kara said.

'Absolutely. What order shall we do it? Singles tonight or couples sex games?'

'Let's do singles tonight and then Tom and Mel tomorrow night,' Kara said, as a message came through on her phone.

Keith and Jennifer arrived back to the ship from their trip to Somerset Falls. Keith hadn't realised the amount of walking required and was exhausted from his day out. They both showered and dressed for dinner.

While Jennifer was doing her makeup, she said, 'Keith darling, we haven't really done any naughty stuff yet, we only have two more nights.'

'We've been pretty busy,' Keith said, busy texting a message to Texas.

'Yes, we have darling, but we don't want to go home without at least sharing in something exciting… other than seeing the two young ones in the pool.'

'What are you suggesting?' he said, looking up from his phone for the first time.

'Well, like Mel said, we could maybe watch a couple… having sex… in the playroom?' her voice trailed into a whisper, as she cringed awaited his reply.

'The playroom! I don't think we're ready for that, are we?'

'Well, I've been topless at a pool, and I never thought I'd ever do that!' She replied in a near defiant tone.

Her mind already pacing. *And I met a hunk at the bar, who I really want to see again*, she thought to herself. Her memory drifted once more back to last night, when she lay in bed touching herself while Keith slept. How that naked man she'd locked eyes with at pool bar had taken her back to his room, kissed her passionately, undressed her, and looked deep into her eyes, as he moved slowly in and out of her body. She came so easily, his piercing eyes watching her intensely as he pulsed inside her, her juices of passion mixing with his at that heightened orgasmic precipice.

'Let's see how we go after dinner, maybe we can havva quick look,' Keith replied, still focused on his phone. He didn't want to disappoint his wife, but his bed and his book on the bedside table were beckoning him loudly.

'I spoke to Kara about her and Greg coming back to our cabin for some games,' Tom said as he stepped out of the shower.

'I was wondering what you two were talking about! What did she say?'

'Yes, sort of, she was going to talk to Greg about it.'

'When were you thinking of inviting them?' Mel asked.

'We didn't talk about exactly when.'

'We only have two nights left, so where's her card? Let's send her a message'

Tom knew exactly where it was and picked up his phone.

> Hey gorgeous, have you talked to Greg about us maybe catching up and playing a few games?

> Yes, we are keen for tomorrow night, is that okay for you two? How about 9 p.m. in our cabin, 525. You bring the games! K & G x

'They're good for tomorrow night, love. They've offered to host in their cabin around nine o'clock,' Tom said, reading the message again.

'Thank God, it will take until then for my vagina to recover!' Mel said, relieved.

'Well, it sure had a pounding all right—he was a big fella! Two hours if I remember rightly.'

'Yeah, something like that!' she smiled.

The singles night could go either way, Greg thought, *I could end up sitting on my own all night*. Greg kissed Kara and said, 'I'll see you sometime, call me if you need, I'll come running.'

'Thank you, Superman. I will. You go have fun, but please don't break any hearts!' she called out after him as the cabin door closed.

They'd both decided they weren't really all that hungry yet, and each would just get some nibbles through the night. It was soon dark, and the restaurants emptied while the bars filled.

Keith and Jennifer arrived at the restaurant at the same time as Mel and Tom and happily decided to have dinner together. They chatted about their day out in Kingston, with Keith saying he wished he'd done the same tour as Mel and Tom. He was not into all the climbing to get to waterfalls—you seen one, you've seen them all. They talked about their time at the pool and how they'd seen the young ones having sex in the water.

'We were thinking about maybe watching some couples have sex tonight,' Jennifer admitted, though with difficulty.

'That great,' said Mel. 'It's a great place to start.'

Mel noticed that Keith wasn't all that excited and was clearly exhausted from his day out. His eyes would close for long moments before he jolted himself back to catch the conversation.

'Would you suggest the playroom as the best place to watch?' asked Jennifer.

'For sure, have a seat at the bar and when a couple or couples or threesome go off to a room and leave the door open, it means they're happy for people to watch them.'

Jennifer looked at Keith, 'What do you think darling?'

'Okay, but I really don't need a late night.'

'Me too, I'm ready for an early one,' Tom said, 'but what's say we come along with you for a start? I'm up for a little look.'

'That would be great, Tom, thank you,' Jennifer said, now sensing her body tingling at the thought of watching others.

Kara had decided to start at the more sedate bar, Swell, and work her way from there, whereas Greg opted for the Tsunami bar, one step before the playroom. The room was dark, the same as the last time they were there. The couches were full of couples kissing and groping, girls' pashing each other while their husbands sat back watching with beers in hand. Greg really didn't know what he wanted, but he at least wanted a story to tell Kara in the morning. He was happy just to watch for a while, realising it was going to be much easier for Kara to make up a threesome than for him to have someone's wife to himself. He started thinking about what Kara might be doing and wondering who she might be with. Suddenly, it didn't seem like such a great idea to have a singles night.

Meanwhile, Kara sat at the bar and chatted to the young barman in between him serving customers, when a pair of bouncing breasts barely held in a little black dress were leading a short, middle-aged, dark-haired woman over to her. 'Excuse me. I'm just wondering if you might like to join me and my husband for a drink and maybe some playtime?'

Kara looked over the woman's shoulder to see a man, his barrelled stomach bursting through the buttons on his shirt, complete with tattoos, hovering a few metres behind her. Kara swallowed the gulp of her first reaction. *My God, the two things I can't stand.* She looked back at the lady and said softly, 'That sounds like fun, but I am actually waiting for someone.' It was true, she just didn't know who that was yet. The barman stood back, but heard the whole conversation.

'Oh, that's all cool. Just thought I'd ask, babe.' And the couple went back to their seats.

'I couldn't think of anything worse!' she whispered to the barman, and he smiled back with a knowing nod.

'What time do you finish, Mark?' Kara asked, noting his name tag.

'Oh, sorry ma'am, we are not allowed to get involved with the passengers.'

Kara laughed, 'Now Mark, there's over a thousand men on this ship that I am sure I could have, and you're almost half my age! I was just wondering how hard they work you.'

'I'm so sorry madam, it's just...' Mark paused, realising it was better if he just didn't say anything. 'Err, I finish at midnight, and another team will go through till 4.00 a.m.'

It wasn't long before another gentleman sat down next to her and offered her a drink.

The playroom had been open for nearly an hour or so when the four of them walked in. The attendant explained the rules and the amenities.

Keith started to say they were only there for a look when Jennifer signalled to him to keep quiet with a glare. They thanked the attendant and headed for the bar, collected a drink each, and sat at a small four-person table. They sat in silence for a while as they watched the six naked bodies in the spa, other couples strolling naked to rooms, and couples on couches, sucking, and licking to their heart's desire. Most of the private room doors were open with combinations of two, three, and four people, all in different positions.

Mel took Jennifer's hand. 'Let's go and watch that four in there.' Mel stood, almost lifting Jennifer from her seat. As they strolled away, Jennifer turned her head toward Keith, with a hesitant beseeching look. He just looked uninterested. Keith lifted his hat, slicked his hair back with his other hand, and refitted the hat with the precision of an engineer. Keith wasn't very comfortable in here at all.

As the two girls approached the doorway, they were greeted by the unmistakable sound of slapping flesh and moans from the four bodies on the bed, before one of the women let out a shrill orgasmic cry.

Mel could sense Jennifer's body shifting, as if using Mel as a shield. She shot her a glance. Jennifer's head was half bowed, her eyes peeking coyly over Mel's shoulder.

'Hey Jennifer, it's okay. The door is open, so they want us to watch. Besides—you wanted to! So have a good look!'

Jennifer raised her head a little more and stepped to stand next to Mel. She looked beyond the door to the bed. All she could see were four naked bodies, resting on the bed.

'I hope they haven't finished,' Jennifer whispered.

'I think they're just warming up. Look,' Mel said, seeing the two guys move to swap partners. Within moments, one woman was being taken from behind doggie style, the other with her legs raised high over the man's shoulders as he thrust into her rhythmically. Each were again moaning with pleasure.

'That is so hot!' Jennifer said, without looking away. Having quickly shed any embarrassment, she was now engrossed.

'I'm so wet!' Mel said, in return. 'God, after last night, I didn't think I would want it again for another week.'

Jennifer turned and looked at Mel with a smile. 'What happened last night, Mel?'

'I had this young lad who pounded me for two hours—I'm lucky I could walk this morning!'

'Wow, where was Tom?'

'He got naked and sat on the couch, tossing off as he watched me being done from every angle. After about thirty minutes, he blew and then fell asleep; we then screwed our hearts out for the next hour and a half. Tom came to bed, just as the guy left.'

'My goodness, I'm speechless. And Tom was alright with that?'

'Yeah, blew all over himself.'

They'd moved away from the door when Mel said, 'What about you, Jennifer, what did you get up to?'

'Nothing really, especially compared to your night,' Jennifer replied.

Mel gave her a look that said, 'You have to tell me something.'

'Well alright, I touched myself thinking about a man I met at the pool bar yesterday, while Keith slept.'

'So, this guy was hot?'

'He was very attractive, but you'll think this sounds silly… It really was much more intimate than that.' She stopped and drew in a breath.

Mel was intrigued. 'So, what happened?'

'His eyes pierced my soul, in an instant,' she said, letting out a breath of submission. 'It wasn't even because he was naked and I was topless! We were just standing at the bar, side by side, and we both turned and just looked at each other. It was love at first sight. I know it was. I wanted him then and there. So last night I did get to have him—in my imagination, anyway.'

'Have you seen him again?' Mel asked.

'Just briefly, and he did it again with his eyes.' Jennifer put her head in her hands and said, 'I'm such a bad person, aren't I? I'm married, for goodness' sake!'

'Don't be silly, you can't help that feeling. Besides, look where you are! You will probably be the only person on this whole ship to leave not having fucked a stranger.'

'Not fucked anyone, more like it!'

'You must be kidding?' Mel said, lowering her voice.

'Keith is a generous man, but in the bedroom he just reads his book or checks the price of beef, and then goes to sleep.'

Mel didn't say anything for a moment.

'Right, you and I are definitely going out tonight! You need to find this guy or someone and have some fun!'

'What about you, Mel, have you met someone really special that you're desperate to be with yet?'

'Actually, I have. There's something special about one man I've met.' Mel's eyes glazed over as she pictured him, before looking back at Jennifer. 'And I plan on having him tomorrow night. What's more, Tom's done all the work arranging it.'

'Oh wow, that sounds perfect,' Jennifer said.

'Let's get back to the boys,' Mel said, still smiling from the thought of Greg between her legs.

Kara looked over at the man next to her, now finding it hard to focus and read his expression. *You've only had three drinks so far, woman. When did I change from champagne to wine? Or was that three champagnes?* Her thoughts and body seemed to have faded into slow motion, her eyes only just keeping up with her head movement. Kara gripped the bar, sitting up straighter on the bar stool, steadied her gaze, and turned slightly toward him.

He looked at her and asked, 'You come here often?'

Kara burst out laughing, much louder than what she should have. 'That's so funny. About once in a lifetime to be exact,' she rolled out in reply.

'Aussie, are you?'

'Yes, from little old Adelaide.'

'Is that near Sydney?' he replied with his west coast American accent.

'Yep, right next door,' she said, taking another mouthful of wine.

'Are you here on your own, a lovely thing like you?'

'Sort of. Well, at least I am tonight.' Kara stopped to listen to herself and thought, *maybe I have had a few more than three drinks?*

She turned to him and said, 'I'm sorry, I'm Kara,' and held out her hand.

'Daniel,' he replied.

'Well, I'm on this cruise with a man who I love more than anything in this world; we aren't married, we aren't even boyfriend and girlfriend, just friends with benefits, I guess. I actually don't know what the fuck we are! And tonight, *I* had a great idea to send him out to find a fuck on his own. So there! That's my story.'

Kara turned her head to Daniel. 'So, what about you, Daniel, why are you here on your own?'

'Well, there are a lot of single women. Most are looking for threesomes but some are just after a good time—it's easy pickings to be true.' Daniel relaxed now, realising he was more of an intrusion for this lady, who, while beguilingly attractive, was barely treading water in her sorrows. It was almost midnight, and he decided if he was going to score tonight, he needed to move on to the next bar.

Daniel rose and stepped closer to her. 'Kara, it's been nice chatting. I truly hope it all turns out okay for you.' He bent down and kissed her on the cheek. He hesitated for a second at the smell of her perfume, her hair combined with her natural odour… it was paralysingly alluring. For a split second he imagined closing his eyes and rendering himself spellbound in her seductive fragrance. He paused again for one more second as Kara looked up, now starting to wonder what was happening.

'My God, you smell delicious. A hint of naughty and seduction. You really are an attractive mixture… Goodnight Kara.'

He turned and walked away before Kara could consider her options. At the doorway he stopped and looked back, giving her a last chance to pursue him but she didn't see it.

'Have you girls seen enough?' Keith asked. 'It's been a long day.'

Mel tapped Jennifer on the arm gently and threw her a little wink. 'Hey, how about you fellas go and have a beer or head to bed—us girls might head to a bar for a night cap.'

'That suits me,' Keith said, 'I'm as buggered as a bucking quarter horse in the last round of the Cheyenne rodeo.'

'Yeah, that's cool with me too,' said Tom. 'Don't be too late, girls!'

'Well, you know we'll be onboard somewhere,' giggled Mel.

They kissed their men goodbye and headed for the wildest bar, Tsunami.

'There will be sex on tap at this bar, my girl. Hey, grab a seat and a drink if you can and I'll just have a pee,' said Mel.

'Hey Mel?'

'Yes, dear?'

'I don't really want sex.'

'Why not?'

'My husband would kill me—and him.'

Mel, still busting to pee, could see she was deadly serious. 'You're not kidding, are you?'

Jennifer just shook her head, her eyes burning with sincerity.

'Okay then, get me a drink, I want to discuss this more.'

'Sure,' Jennifer replied. 'A red wine again?'

'Yes, thanks,' Mel called out as she raced off to the bathroom.

Greg was about to leave when he saw Jennifer walk into the bar, like a super model, she seemed to be walking in slow motion. His heart nearly missed a beat. His head lifted slowly, as he stood taller and straighter, to focus on this sight. He had to be sure this wasn't a dream.

That's her. Warm tingles burst from his chest and throughout his body. It was as if he'd been injected with a serious dose of lust. He watched her walk up to the bar and order two drinks. His excitement dipped slightly. *Her husband must be with her.* He decided to stay a little longer, at least just to watch her. She hadn't seen him yet. *Should I leave it that way? She has such a sense of class about her, but so sexy at the same time.* He recalled the look she gave him at the bar—it meant something, he knew it did. *God, what was her name? Jan, Jane? No, it was longer. Janine? No—Jennifer. That was it!* Greg kept stealing glances as she walked to a nearby table, then sat perched, with the two glasses of red wine in front of her while she took in the surroundings, sex on the couches all at different stages.

Jennifer looked around the bar, feeling somewhat intimidated and conspicuous being there on her own, surrounded by flirting, kissing, and sex happening at every table. Then she caught sight of him, looking straight at her. It was him. *My God!* He was alone, watching her from the far end of the bar. Their eyes locked for what seemed an eternity. They were too far away to fully read their expressions, but what she could see told her that he'd remembered her; she'd left an impression, as he had on her. Greg quickly ordered another drink from the bar. He desperately wanted to learn more about this gorgeous woman.

'Hey there, Mel!'

She'd spun around on hearing her name to see David, the man who brought her to six orgasms the night before.

'Hey Dave, how are you going? Thank you for last night, it was fucking amazing,' she said in a flirty voice.

'Where's Hubby?'

'Gone to bed.'

'Look, would you like a quick top up from last night? I'm really horny,' he said.

'I'd love to, but I'm sort of here with someone.'

'Can you bail and come back to my cabin? It's just here, really close by. Come on, just a quickie.'

He stepped forward, reached under her skirt, and rubbed his finger between her legs. An overwhelming burst of heat exploded through her body as a pulsing desperation swept over her. She instantly recalled how his young, fit body had filled her deep, to the essence of her soul, only twenty-four hours ago.

'Stay here, let me see what I can do,' she said, the taste of lust drying her mouth.

'I'm cabin 318, four more down this passage. I'll be naked and waiting for you.'

'Jesus, alright. I'll see you soon.'

Mel arrived back at the bar, desperately scanning for her friend. She spotted Jennifer at a little table, a wine already waiting for her. She walked up, gave her a peck on the cheek, and quickly sat beside her.

'Hey, thanks for the wine, Jen. Can I call you that?' But without waiting for an answer, she continued, 'I've just had an offer I can't refuse. Will you hate me if I bail on you? He's so fucking hot!' Mel was rambling now, only focusing on the young naked body down the passage in room 318.

'I hope it's that man you've wanted. Of course, I don't mind—about you calling me Jen, that is. Go on, have some fun! I'm ready for bed anyway,' she said, knowing this could work out perfectly with the stranger from the pool bar.

'You are a darling, Jen,' Mel said, as she picked up the glass of red wine and drained it in one mouthful. Blowing Jennifer a kiss, Mel turned and rushed out the door.

Greg collected his drink, and himself, and turned to look at Jennifer once more. She was still seated there by herself. He then noticed the second drink on the table was now empty. *How did that happen? It doesn't make any sense. Maybe it was empty all along, and she really is on her own?* He stood, resisting the temptation to rush, and headed towards her table.

By the time Mark's shift ended, he'd watched Kara succumb to a sad place. He'd rarely witnessed a guest quite like this before. Sure, she was lamenting over someone she loved. He'd clearly heard her mention someone named 'Greg' at least four times to the last poor guy who tried to talk to her. But somehow, she didn't really sound upset with him, just herself.

'Kara—excuse me, may I call you that?' Mark asked. 'I'm about to finish my shift and I'm happy to walk you back to your cabin,' he said as he handed her a glass of water.

'Sure, thanks.' She hesitated, then looked up at him. 'There will be no hanky panky, young man.'

'No ma'am, of course not.'

'Okay then, let's go,' she said, reaching for her bag on the floor and nearly falling flat on her face.

'Whoa! This boat is pitching a *lot*,' she cried, as her body reeled. She grabbed the edge of the bar to steady herself. It was only now she realised how drunk she really was. She put her arm around Mark, letting him take the lead, as she willingly followed toward the door.

'What cabin are you in, ma'am, er, Kara?

'525 or 529—I think?'

'Okay, we'll try them all,' Mark said, still secretly questioning his generosity, unsure that if in his position he should really be escorting her. But somehow, leaving her to find her own way didn't seem right. *She is a lovely woman, who at least deserves to have a man escort her to her door to end the night*, was his sweet chivalrous thought.

They reached the elevator and once inside, Mark pushed the level 5 button. Kara closed her eyes as she leant back against the cool mirrored lift wall. Mark stood tall, inwardly appreciative that they didn't have to take the stairs.

Kara suddenly opened her eyes and stared hard at him. 'Do you think I'm attractive, Mark?'

'Yes ma'am, you are very attractive.'

'Why is it then that no one in that bar wanted to have me tonight? It's a sex ship, isn't it?'

'If I may say, ma'am, many people wanted you. You did just shrug them off.'

'Oh. Did I? Well, maybe I did.'

'No one was good enough for you, ma'am.'

'Thank you. You're a sweetheart. I just didn't get into the swing of it tonight, did I?'

The lift landed with a jolting ping on the fifth floor, and the doors opened to signal the end of a long night. Mark stepped close to her, lifted her arm over his shoulder and placed his arm around her waist. *She did smell nice*, he thought.

As Mark reached the suite, he asked, 'Is this your room, ma'am?'

'If the key fits, it is,' she said. 'Careful though, young man. Greg, my partner, or friend, or whatever the fuck he is, could be in there. He could be fucking someone in the bed. So, please, shhhhh,' she said, wobbling a finger across her lips.

The door opened; the room was dark, only the moonlight shone in though the balcony doors. The bed was empty.

'Would you like the light on, Kara?'

He spoke her name, for only the second time.

Kara kicked her shoes off and sat on the bed.

'No, leave it off, thanks.'

'Can I do anything else for you, Kara?'

There was something sobering about having returned to the cabin, and all Kara now wanted was calm and sleep.

Kara rallied enough to stand up again, step toward him awkwardly to place both her hands on his cheeks, and then kissed him firmly on the lips.

She slowly pulled away and said, 'Thank you, Mark, for everything. You're a real gentleman. My humble apologies for you needing to escort me home and putting up with my pitiful company this evening. Now please, head off, before someone sees you in here.'

'Yes ma'am' he said, as he turned and left the cabin.

Greg, now sure she was there on her own, took no time to approach her table. 'Hello Jennifer, nice to see you again. May I sit with you?'

'Please do,' Jennifer replied, delighted he'd remembered her name. *He remembered me.* Her heart released a little flutter.

Greg looked around and asked, 'Would you like to go for a walk, get some fresh air away from… this?' he said, gesturing at the debauchery happening in every booth.

'I would love to. I came here with a friend for just a quick drink who suddenly got a better offer and bailed on me. I was starting to feel a little intimidated, to be honest.'

'May I say, you don't seem the type that I would expect to find on a cruise like this,' Greg said as they headed out of the bar.

'You're right. No, I don't really feel at home,' she grinned, remembering he had seen her with her top off. 'Mind you, dare I say, it was little exciting and naughty being topless at the pool— I've never done that before!' she said.

Greg offered only a knowing smile in return, knowing any comment about her breasts would be inappropriate.

Jennifer could barely look at him. It was nearly too much to be so close to this man, hear his voice, and look into those seductive eyes.

The deck was almost deserted; the sky was clear with a billion twinkling stars looking down, the warm breeze just enough to tease Jennifer's hair and soft skin.

'I see you're married,' Greg said, taking her left hand and holding it in front of them. They both looked at the huge diamond that sat next to a shiny wedding band.

'Yes.'

'The rings don't look very old.'

'No, they aren't,' Jennifer replied softly.

Jennifer told Greg briefly about her first marriage, which was a disaster, and how with her new husband she had comfort, security and extravagance. He'd been her boss for a few years, and she explained how his power and confidence had become very alluring.

'But there's something missing, isn't there, Jennifer?'

'Yes,' she replied softly, her vision narrowing to a couple of steps in front of her.

Jennifer looked at Greg; she felt she could tell him anything and he would not judge her. She asked him about his life and if he was on the cruise with anyone. Greg explained his relationship with Kara and how they were best friends, always would be, and how she was his first kiss at school all those years ago.

'That's so romantic,' Jennifer offered.

'It was, but we have something better than a love affair.'

'Really?' Jennifer asked. 'What's that?'

'We really like each other and truly want the best for each other, without selfishness or jealousy. Most of all we will always be there for each other.'

'That is very special,'

'May I hold your hand?' Greg asked.

Jennifer looked at him with a smile, 'Of course you can.' She knew there was no way Keith would be out of their room, he was buggered.

Her hand felt small in his; her skin soft, her long fingers, her perfect nails. It felt like a part of her was being transferred through the connection, or was that just his imagination? He decided the latter was probably the case.

'Have you enjoyed the cruise?' Greg asked.

'Not really,' she replied. 'Not until now,' she added, looking at him with a smile.

He smiled back without a reply. He was starting to feel something for this lady that he hadn't felt in a long time. He just wanted to take her in his arms and kiss her for the rest of his life. She was just so delicious, he could eat her.

He looked out over the ocean, just water and stars. *Could this night possibly be any better?* he thought.

Reaching the rear-guard rail at the most aft of the deck, they watched the wake of the twin screws that propelled this massive ship. They were silent for a time till Greg turned to her and asked, 'May I kiss you, Jennifer?'

The butterflies that had been fluttering inside her all seemed to stop as her heart rose into her throat. She desperately wanted to kiss him, but where will that lead? She was already heading quickly down a path into an abyss.

She looked at him. 'Greg, I do want to kiss you; my heart is pounding. I have never felt like this before, I'm really scared…'

He placed his hands on her cheeks and looked into those exquisite eyes. Time stopped for her until his lips pressed softly against hers. He saw her eyes close as his tongue touched her lip. He moved his left hand and placed it firmly on her back, pressing her close. He could feel her bra strap through her thin shirt. He was unsure why this was such a turn on, but it was. His right hand found its way under the loose-fitting shirt, the touch of his hand on her bare skin making her gasp.

He brought his lips to her ear. 'I want to make love to you, Jennifer.'

She didn't answer, but pressed her face to the side of his neck and squeezed him tight with both arms. The only thought in her mind now was how badly she wanted that too. Her body was burning at the thought and her heart was thumping in her chest. She tried to say no, she wanted to say no…

Greg was starting to regret saying it, but it was what he felt. He had never been so desperate for someone.

'Would you like to feel me inside you, Jennifer?'

There was a pause before she replied. 'Yes. I want you inside me,' she whispered in his ear.

He gently took her hand, carefully trying not to break the spell and led her back inside. They reached the playroom, which was almost empty now.

Greg asked the attendant, 'May we please have a fresh room?'

'Yes, certainly, sir. Please follow me.'

Greg tipped the attendant, and quickly guided Jennifer in and closed the door. He dimmed the lights to low and took her again in his arms. He drew her lips to his; he wanted to pick up from where they had left off, to reignite the magic. Her kisses were hard and desperate now—there was no outside, no other people, no husbands, no girlfriends, just them. Their hearts pounded. They pulled apart just long enough to look at each other before their lips clashed again with a passion neither had ever known before. He needed more of this woman.

He lifted her top over her head and removed her bra. He reached for her skirt and within seconds she was fully naked. He shed his own clothes and lay her down softly on the bed, like he was placing a precious artifact onto its velvet case. This was not about having sex with someone for the first time, making sure you ticked all the boxes with just the right amount of foreplay and touching.

This moment was about uniting himself with a goddess, being connected to her—body, mind, and soul. He stood at the end of the bed, and in the low light took a second to admire the beautiful creature now holding his throbbing heart in her hands. He moved to place himself above her; her legs, slightly bent, fell apart for him.

He poised above her just as his knob touched her. He was on his elbows, his mouth an inch from hers.

'Are you sure you want this?' he asked in a soft husky voice.

'More than anything,' she begged. There was no doubt in her mind as she stared deep into his eyes.

His lips met hers and he entered her with a slow, deep stroke. The feeling as he pushed her swollen flesh apart and became a part of her was not sex, it was a moment of two hearts melding. This was a spiritual experience; he was making love to an angel. It wasn't long before it became too much for her. Greg felt her tense and arch her back in response to his penetrating force. He broke the kiss as the euphoric moans surfacing from deep inside her escaped. He increased his thrusts, feeling her orgasm arrive hard and fast, feeling her clamp tight around him, as each wave shuddered through her body. One last exhale and she slowly fell limp, now only her pounding heart against him and her breath in his ear told him she was still alive. He was still hard inside her, saving himself so these divine hours of intimacy could last for ever.

He heard her first sob, and then paused, waiting for the uncontrollable tears. He'd heard it before, recognising the cocktail of pleasure and shame, and he comforted her by holding her tight.

'I'm a married woman,' she managed to say through her sobs. 'How is it that I've fallen so deeply for you?' She broke down again. 'I have never felt like this. Is this what love feels like?'

The tears poured freely. Greg was desperate to tell her that he'd also fallen for her, but thought it was better left unsaid for now. He knew he would probably never see her again, but he would never forget her, this angel in paradise.

Greg wiped away her tears and kissed her again. He knew he shouldn't say anything, but before he could stop himself, he said, 'I love you, Jennifer,' and again she burst into tears.

Greg never did come that night, though he would have loved to have left something physical in that beautiful body and know she would leave with a part of him inside her. He delivered her back to her suite around 4.00 a.m., where she snuck into bed next to her snoring husband. She never slept a wink—tears filled the next three hours.

Kara opened her eyes and groaned as the first thump pelted inside her head.

She looked over to see Greg still fast asleep. *At least he came home*, she thought.

He'd obviously put a blanket over her.

Kara clambered slowly out of bed, still fully dressed and headed for the bathroom with lumpy steps, desperately needing to pee. She sat there long after she'd finished, her head in her hands.

'How much did I drink last night?'

A sight of the young barman in her room and her kissing him flashed through her mind. She then recalled him leaving. She found some Panadol in the cupboard and swallowed two down, cupping the water from the tap in her hands. She undressed and turned on the shower. Water inside and out was what she needed to flush the whole debacle of last night out of her system. She barely dried herself before returning to bed. She was asleep again in seconds.

Mel woke with a smile on her face, as she quickly recalled the previous night—how David had fucked her against his cabin wall, the couch, the bed, and then finished her off on the floor. She had come four times before he finally removed himself from her, putting his cock into her mouth and filling it. It was the first time she had swallowed cum, and was surprised at how hard he blew and the amount. She had nearly gagged. Somehow, it was still her first 'morning after' memory, a sensation and taste she now wanted more of. He had become her highlight of this trip.

If everything went to plan, she would have Greg tonight, and could consider it a very successful trip. Feeling very satisfied, she turned over and went back to sleep.

Jennifer was staring at the ceiling when Keith woke and looked over at her.

'Good morning, my dear,' he said, a little confused as to why she was awake. 'Are you okay?' he said sitting up, with a slight concerned look across his brow.

'Yes, my love, I just couldn't sleep for some reason,' She replied, looking at him with a gentle smile.

'Have you been crying?' he asked.

'No, don't be silly, just sore eyes from not sleeping'.

'Mel didn't lead you astray, did she?' Keith asked as he got up to head to the bathroom.

'No, we just had one drink.'

A pang of guilt, then a stab of sadness shuddered through her body. She felt a tear run down her cheek. She replayed in her mind the lust, the passion, the love. Yes, the love, and the man who had made love to her, invading her body physically and mentally to the depth of her inner being. The pain she was feeling was tumultuous. Was it just passionate lust, or was it true love? Her heart told her it had to be the latter. She had never felt like this before and believed she would probably never feel it again. Her eyes were streaming now as she rolled over to hide her face from Keith's return as she heard the toilet flush.

'I will get us coffee,' Keith said, pulling on a pair of shorts and a white Texas Rangers t-shirt.

'Okay,' she said, as controlled as possible. She knew her life had changed forever.

The ship was quiet what morning as it sailed gracefully into the Gulf of Mexico. Tom was waiting for coffee in the breakfast bistro when Keith arrived to order his.

'Top of the morning to you!' Keith said to Tom with a hearty laugh.

'Good morning, Keith,' he replied, somewhat subdued. 'The girls were late getting home last night,' Tom said as he watched the barista making another coffee.

'Were they?' questioned Keith. 'Jennifer was awake before me this morning.'

'Well, Mel didn't get in till after 3.00 a.m.'

'Really? I must ask Jennifer what happened. She said they only had one drink. Well, no harm done, I guess. At least no one fell overboard!' he offered lamely, as he turned to order his coffee.

Jennifer was asleep when Keith returned, so he quietly picked up his phone and went to the balcony and called Jerry to confirm that a particular job had been completed.

When Kara awoke the second time, she was feeling much better; in fact, she felt surprisingly spritely. By this time, Greg was awake and quietly leaning back against the bedhead reading next to her, but his mind was elsewhere.

'Big night, sexy?' he asked, putting his left hand on her bare chest.

'Are you talking about drinking or sex? Well on a scale of 10, drinking was a 9.5 as far as sex goes it was a 1.'

'A one? Can I ask, what's a one? A kiss?'

'Yep, I kissed the barman!'

'At the bar?'

'No in here, in this cabin, right over there somewhere,' she gestured her hand vaguely toward the door with a wobbly finger.

Greg turned to face her.

'Are you telling me you brought the barman back to your cabin, kissed him, and nothing happened?'

'That's pretty well it… And what about you, Mr Sheppard?'

Greg's heart nearly exploded out of his mouth. *How can I tell Kara that I made love to an angel and have fallen madly in love with her?* But he had to tell her something.

'Do you remember that woman at the naked pool bar?'

'Oh, I don't think so. No, not really,' replied Kara.

'Well, I met her at the Tsunami bar...'

'Of course, you did!'

'It—rather, she—wasn't like that. She'd gone there with a friend who'd run off with someone, and she was actually about to leave.'

'Don't tell me, then came along Superman to rescue her and saved her with his charming powers, orgasmic pleasure, and big cock.'

'Hey, hey, Kara...' He stopped at her tone, more than the words. He waited a second, seeing her head turn away and drop.

His next words were hushed and soft. 'What's this? Are you a little jealous?' he said as he leant over, gently turned her to face him, and started to wipe her hair away from her face.

'I don't know, maybe a little.' She sniffed, holding back tears. 'Actually yes, I'm jealous, mostly about you having fun, not of another woman. I'm sorry, it's so silly, we'd both agreed to have a singles night, it's just that mine was shit. Somehow, just after you left, it felt like a really bad idea. It's probably a crazy thing to say, but I suddenly realised it wasn't going to be exciting without you being there. I'm feeling even sillier that I suggested having a singles night in the first place. I really *do* hope you had fun though.'

'Did you meet anyone to chat to, at least?' he asked.

'I had plenty of opportunities, I just wasn't interested. Someone did say I smelt nice, maybe I should have fucked him?' Kara said.

Greg felt a pang. He knew just what she was feeling. He'd felt the same at first. But he also felt a twinge of guilt. In contrast, he'd found a goddess, who was now embedded in his heart.

'I really do understand, Kara. I'm so sorry you had a rough night. We're seeing Tom and Mel tonight, and you know he's dead keen on you.'

'Yeah, well, he'd better watch out! I will need two nights worth out of him,' she smiled and looked up at Greg.

'Poor chap, he has no idea what he's in for!' Greg said with a soft smile, as he spooned himself in behind her.

Jennifer woke just before lunch time; it took all her energy to not start crying again. Her heart pounded with love for a man she didn't even know. Greg had unleashed her innermost need for intimacy, with such tenderness and passion. She closed the bathroom door behind her and leant her back against the wall, with her hands hiding her face. *I must see him again, I can't leave it like this, I will die. Just one more time.* She raised her head, looking up to the ceiling. 'Please God, I must see him,' she whispered to herself.

That day Jennifer did many laps around the ship, trying desperately to find the man that last night she'd given her heart to.

Tom didn't question Mel too hard on her activities last night, as he himself still wasn't sure if it was a turn on or not, that his wife may have been out fucking other men. *Well, she will be tonight anyway, so what's the difference really*, he thought. His mind had already moved on. He was already distracted by the fact that tonight, the enigmatic Kara would be his, to have and make love to. He had now really developed some strong lustful feelings for her. Last night when he was in bed alone, while his wife was out doing who knows what, he'd wanked, imagining Kara was there with him. He went through all possible scenarios about how Kara would give herself to him. Eventually, he exploded and fell asleep knowing she would be his for real the next night.

Greg and Kara decided to have a quiet day; a late lunch delivered to their room, which they ate on the balcony in the balmy breeze. Greg found himself constantly thinking about the beautiful angel he'd made love to last night, wondering what she was doing, and if in a few days she would even remember him. There was something about her that he couldn't get out of his mind. He had never felt such a deep connection with someone before. He kept wanting to tell Kara about how this woman made him feel, but decided against it. He'd always been able to tell Kara everything, neither of them ever holding any secrets, but he was sure this wasn't the time—not yet.

'Do we have a time to meet Tom and Mel, sexy?' Greg asked.

'Tom sent me a message. I thought our cabin might be a bit bigger, so I invited them here at about 9.00 p.m. tonight. Is that okay?'

'Sounds perfect, and besides, you could do him here on the balcony!' Greg smiled at her.

'Sure, but only for your viewing pleasure,' she said with a cheeky grin.

Keith could see something had changed in his wife, but had no idea what. What could have happened in just twenty-four hours? Maybe she was just homesick for her family and friends back in Dallas? He tried to convince himself of that, but deep down he feared it was something far more serious.

Keith's thoughts didn't dare step anywhere beyond those markers.

Mel and Tom had agreed to come to Greg and Kara's cabin and were five minutes early when they knocked on their door. 'Welcome,' Kara said, opening the door.

Mel stepped in and Tom stopped to kiss Kara on the cheek, not without a meaningful look. She'd carefully chosen her slim-fitting, blue, halter neck dress to match her sparkling eyes. Tom had a bottle of wine he'd convinced the bar staff to sell him, and two glasses. Greg had placed the two chairs from the balcony inside next to the couch, giving each of them a seat. Greg poured the wine as they chatted about the cruise experience so far. Mel told them about a couple they had met who were clearly out of their depth, the lady telling her just last night that she hadn't had sex with anyone—including her husband—the whole time.

'Well, I hope they're enjoying the food!' Greg said, holding up his glass with a 'cheers'.

'So, Tom, care to tell us more about these sex games you and Mel play?' Kara said.

'There are many, especially online—all different levels for all different preferences.'

'Did you bring one?' Kara asked.

'We only brought a truth or dare card game. It's pretty simple but it always seems to get the party going.'

'Let's get started?' offered Mel, looking over at Greg.

'Lets!' Greg said, looking straight back at her.

'There are two packs; the mild cards, and the wild cards. We change over when the time is right,' Tom explained as he started to shuffle the deck. 'We play as singles unless the cards ask for a couple's answer. You shuffle and ask someone from the other pair, "Truth or Dare." They nominate first. The person selects a card and must answer the question or fulfill the dare.'

'Sounds simple, let's go, Greg said.

As Tom tapped the deck on the table and cupped the cards into his hands in readiness. 'Rules for couples are that the last woman to have had sex goes first.'

They all looked at each other before Kara said, 'This morning?'

'Well, you win, sister!' Mel said.

Kara picked up the cards with a small grin. 'Are they shuffled enough?' she asked.

'It doesn't really matter, babe, it's not poker' Greg said with a smile.

'Yeah, I guess not, so here we go.'

Kara turned to Greg, she fanned the cards, and extended the deck toward him. 'Pick a card, don't peek, and hand it to me.' As she read the card in hand, a devilish grin spread across her face. 'Truth or dare, sir?' She'd already guessed what his reply would be.

'Dare.'

'Dare you to get naked enough for all to see and start touching yourself while we watch.'

Greg stood, unbuttoned, unzipped, and lowered both jeans and jocks to the floor. Reaching one hand for his wine glass, he took a sip, sat back down, and leant back to casually take hold of himself. He looked over to see Tom and Mel's reaction. Tom's look and grin said 'well done, mate,' while Mel's eyes were swallowing him in. She was already so wet, even before he ever so naturally started sliding his grip up and down his shaft.

With the three pairs of eyes watching, Greg was quickly aroused. He barely had to stroke, before being filled, erect, and sitting proudly.

'Reckon it's my turn,' Greg said nonchalantly, reaching for the cards from Kara's hands.

'For sure, I think you've risen to the challenge brilliantly!' Kara said, as they all grinned. Mel's eyes were now owl-like, not able to avert away from Greg's hard flesh. *God, I want to feel that.*

Greg sat his glass down, but, rather than shuffle, he flipped through the cards, quickly scanning the questions.

'I've found one! It's for a couple. Like to try?' Greg said, looking directly at Tom and Mel.

Before Tom could barely even blink, Mel said, 'Yes! We say dare!'

Tom flashed a small frown at Mel, as if to say, 'settle down.' He turned back to Greg and replied, 'Sure. So, this will be something we both have to either answer or do?'

'Yep! So, are you two taking the dare?'

Both nodded back at Greg... waiting.

'Get naked and show us the position you were in when you last had sex,' Greg read.

'That's a great card to choose, mate. Dare accepted!' Tom said. As Mel shed her clothes, her eyes were fixed on Greg, turning it into a strip tease for him.

The two of them landed on the bed, Mel straddling Tom as he lay back, saying, 'You two had better come closer—to be sure we aren't cheating!'

It was only a minute before Kara and Greg were right there alongside them, naked, kissing, sucking, thrusting, and fucking. The fever of the four, each partner watching the other, saw them erupt, landing in a frenzied tangle over the bed. Once the pulsing and panting had subsided, they tempered down enough to stop to catch a breath and regroup.

Greg climbed off the bed, helped Kara to rise, and gave her a hug, before they both turned to look at Tom and Mel. They were laying side by side on the bed, Tom still panting heavily.

Kara winked at Greg. 'Well, that really was a great game, Tom!' Kara said with a smirk.

'Thanks, err... yes. Mel and I definitely enjoy it!' came Tom's rasping reply.

The room fell silent for only a mere second, but long enough for all of them to wonder if their time might end right there, or who would break the ice.

Kara had not forgotten Greg's utterance about imagining her having a balcony experience. *This is the time*, she thought. Now or never. She stood up with a deft determination, and reached for

Tom's hand leading him outside onto the balcony. She turned to him and gave him a *'one time only'* look. He responded, offering her a soft kiss to her cheek, before trailing down to her neck and across her left shoulder. She didn't resist; she was now starting to respond to his hands as they scrolled and glided down her sculptured flesh.

Greg and Mel watched the pair as Tom's fingers traced her form, starting a slow massage that wandered to the desired destination—between Kara's legs. Kara looked at him for a split second, then over his shoulder, searching for Greg's eyes.

Only after her eyes had locked with the shine of Greg's affirmative look did she smile, before turning her attention back to Tom. She turned and leant forward, holding the railing, as he entered from behind. Bending over her he took both her breasts in his hands. He whispered to her as the breeze tussled her hair, 'I've been waiting for this moment all week.'

Tom was strong and Kara felt his thrusts push deep and hard. Without warning he insisted his desire upon her, until she came resoundingly, in full sail, out on the balcony.

Greg and Mel lay side by side on the bed, their hands casually teasing across each other's bodies as they watched their partners screwing on the balcony in front of them. They watched as Kara came for a second time; *she was certainly making up for last night, alright,* Greg thought.

'He can go all night,' Mel said, 'he has a stash of blue pills.'

'So can she,' Greg offered. 'It might be a long night, then!'

He and Mel had both had a big week and a big night last night, so there wasn't the fervour that the two on the balcony showed. Greg's mind drifted to picturing Jennifer beneath him with tears running down her face, telling him how much she loved him. His attention was brought back to the cabin by Mel taking him in her mouth. He really didn't have his heart in it, but felt he owed it to Mel to satisfy her. He took Mel and lay her on the bed, then kissed her gently as he lowered himself between her legs.

Tom returned to lay on the bed beside Mel and Greg. Kara crawled from the base of the bed to straddle Tom. 'Watch us,' was all that escaped Kara's lips, as she started a delicate rise and fall on Tom's still rock-hard erection, which glistened from the juices of Kara's three orgasms. She held poised, keeping his knob just inside her all the time, while moving her body to slide and press down hard, to allow him to feel her juicy heat, and reach the hilt, before gliding back, in a continuous temptation. Kara fought her own desire, in order to keep the slow deliberate pace of her squat as she slid over him.

Greg found himself inside Mel, and with the gentle rhythm of a rippling pond, he made love to her. She came with a feeling of intense pleasure, which had slowly built up inside her in waves of heat that rose to a slow boil. It was nothing like she had felt before; it was flowing, soft, and gradual. With the sex so delicate, she could feel the pulse of Greg as he released inside her. Greg looked down at her pretty face and smiled; he kissed her and moved to lay next to her. She turned her back to the frenetic sex happening next to her and whispered to Greg, 'That was amazing, so soft and gentle, an orgasm like I've never felt before. Thank you.'

Tom could barely hold on any longer. He gripped Kara by the hips and started to pump up and into her with a fevered pace, now unable to control his need to blow inside her. Kara could feel his orgasm rising and glanced over in search of Greg's eyes, knowing how much he enjoyed witnessing these moments. She couldn't find them. She'd been poised on her own release, but she felt her pleasure drain from her body, like a deflating balloon. At that point Tom's cum burst inside her, and with a loud groan his body shuddered. Kara held there for a second, as her rocking drained ever drop from him. She stayed there a while as Tom recovered and then gently climbed off him and the bed.

Mel enjoyed just lying there and playing with Greg's hair as his fingers slowly caressed her nakedness. Kara could see him staring at the ceiling. He wasn't looking at her, or anyone. She sensed he wasn't really in the room at all. His mind was somewhere else.

Kara had soon found a dressing gown and Tom was tugging on his jeans when Greg eventually drew himself away from Mel and rose from the bed. He found his jocks and pulled them on, before taking a sip of wine and walking over to Kara. He gave her a little kiss on the cheek and settled back into the couch. Tom helped Mel stand, handing her the clothes she had discarded in a hurry. Once dressed, they sat together briefly, finished their drinks, and without saying much more than the usual goodnight and thanks, Mel and Tom left for their cabin.

After their guests departed, Kara felt a wave of exhaustion and confusion flood over her.

'Well, you had a good old time, sexy,' Greg said, genuinely pleased that she had made up for her miserable night the previous evening.

'Yeah, for the most part I did. Boy, he really pounded me!'

'Yeah, he certainly did. I'm sure you came at least five times,' Greg said with a smile as he headed for the bathroom.

She held back from saying more. No matter how much she'd enjoyed the sex with Tom, it was bittersweet. Greg hadn't been there with her. She was sure she hadn't imagined it.

With a tender kiss goodnight, they climbed into bed. With Kara soon asleep, huddled close to him, Greg lay back, thinking about their evening and the memory of their first day on board when they met Mel and Tom. *She said she wanted to find a couple to make love to. Mel did make love to me tonight. I think Kara and I were the couple they chose, and they satisfied their wish.* His thoughts drifted to Jennifer, their passionate lovemaking, the tears, and the love. *She told me she loved me, but how could she?* She didn't even know him. Yet he knew her feelings were real. He'd said that he loved her too. It had been a long time since his heart had beaten like this for a woman. *This one is special, very special,* he thought. Her beautiful face was the last thing he saw as he drifted to sleep.

Jennifer woke with a pain in her chest much like chronic anxiety, but she knew what it was—her heart was breaking. She couldn't breathe. She'd fallen head over heels for a man she barely knew, and most likely would never see again. *How do people do this?* she thought.

Jennifer convinced Keith that it was just anxiety; she was homesick and just needed to get off the ship and back to Texas. Keith had now convinced himself she was speaking the truth.

The ship was bustling with the sound of packing and farewells as it arrived back at Port Miami, Florida. Most people filled the railing and watched the captain bring the massive ship up to the wharf. It signalled the end of an amazing trip.

Jennifer's eyes were desperately searching for the man that stole her heart. She wasn't sure what she would do if she did see him, and a part of her decided it might be better if she didn't.

The lower levels were first off, so Keith and Jennifer could see Tom and Mel already ashore as they descended the gangplank.

'Hey there partner, are you waiting for someone?' Keith asked.

'Yes, we met up with a couple last night, we just wanted to say goodbye,' Mel replied, giving Jennifer a wink.

It was just before dawn when Greg woke. He blinked into the realisation this was not a welcome morning. In just a few hours he and Kara would disembark the floating paradise of fun, and he and Jennifer would depart for opposite sides of the world. At the mere thought of this, he felt an unexpected pain in his chest.

He sensed Kara stirring and he rolled to his side and slid up closer behind her. He looked at her and instinctively started to stroke her hair as his thoughts swelled. Every emotion swirled like a rising king tide. He was torn again. He hadn't felt like this since all those years ago, when he first encountered Kara while he was still in love with Teresa, the woman he'd nearly married.

Kara wriggled and snuggled back into his warmth. 'Good morning, gorgeous,' she murmured. Her hand reached to naturally glide over his leg and arm now wrapped around her, as she did most every morning. 'Are you feeling alright this morning? I sensed you weren't yourself last night.'

'I'm fine. I think I just didn't want the cruise to end. It's been one of our most amazing adventures yet.'

'Yes, it has. Some parts better than others!' she giggled. 'You know, I never would've dreamt I'd be here. I will never stop believing that the best thing I ever did in my life was to kiss you back then! Thank you.'

'It was. You're right. I wouldn't be here or have enjoyed so many amazing encounters if it wasn't for you too, Kara.'

Neither said more, but there was something lingering beneath each of their words.

Greg smiled as his fingers ran over her body in a most delicate trace. They fell silent as their bodies melded lyrically together, intimately filled with the love and trust they'd always shared.

They roused again, just before 8.00 a.m. This time it was a hurried kiss to launch them into the day in earnest. There was little time to shower, dress, and pack before they docked. They were quickly packed and heading for the exit.

Jennifer saw Greg as he appeared at the top of the gangplank; her heart pounded and her legs started to buckle.

'Oh look—here they come!' Mel said, almost bouncing out of her skin. As Jennifer heard Mel, she realised then that Mel had fucked her man, just last night, the man that owned her heart, who had made passionate love to her just two nights ago.

Jennifer could see the dark-haired woman closely followed by Greg, as they descended the gangway. She was sure she was going to faint—her heart pounded louder than the ship's engines at full power. Everything was going white.

'Jennifer, Keith, I'd like you to meet Greg and Kara,' said Mel with a gleeful tone.

Greg looked up to see the woman who just two nights ago held his heart in her bare hands. His heart missed a beat. He thought he would never see that beautiful face again. He saw her eyes, at first filled with pain before starting to roll back in her head. He recognised it instantly, dropped his bags, and dived to grab her. He wrapped his arms around her, pulling her tight to his chest. Her legs buckled and head fell limp against his shoulder, his left hand quickly moving to support it. He just wanted to kiss her again, just one more time, but he lowered her to the wooden wharf instead, as Mel placed her handbag under her head.

Keith called out her name, trying to bring her to, the medics already running from the terminal. Greg held her hand as she lay there, while Keith rushed off to direct the medics to where she lay.

Greg reached forward to touch her face, as she slowly started to blink and move.

'She's coming round,' Mel said.

Kara touched Greg on the shoulder. 'Hey, I think we need to go, it looks like she will be okay. There's only one bus before our plane leaves,' Kara said softy.

'I can't leave her!' He cried out quickly, before realising how loud his feelings might have been heard. He checked himself quickly, 'Oh, yes, okay. Hang on one sec, medics are nearly here.'

His eyes were the first thing Jennifer saw as she came too. Only love was exchanged in that moment. Utterly compelled, he leant forward and whispered in her ear, 'Goodbye Jennifer, I love you.' He kissed her cheek, before standing slowly, the paramedics almost pushing him out of the way. He picked up his bags and turned to leave with Kara. He quickly looked back, she was now completely surrounded, he took a deep breath and headed off to the concourse and through the arrival gates.

Keith arrived back to see the man who had caught her whispering something in her ear. The second medic started moving people away, asking, 'Did she hit her head?'

'No, a stranger caught her,' Keith said, looking to see where he'd gone.

They hurried through immigration and toward the waiting airport bus; they had little time to talk about Jennifer's collapse at Greg's feet.

'I hope she's alright. I feel bad just running off,' Greg said.

'I'm sure she'll be fine, just a little overwhelmed. She was lucky you caught her, though!' Kara said.

'I could see her going, her eyes started to roll back,' he said.

After boarding the Qantas A380 to Sydney, they settled in for the fourteen-hour flight and the comfort of a glass of wine and a meal, which arrived in the first hours of their trip. Kara remained quiet and pensive. It had been a full-on adventure for sure, and both she and Greg welcomed the opportunity to re-charge during long flight home.

As Greg dozed beside her over the vast Pacific Ocean, Kara spent time retracing her cruise adventure, before her thoughts fixed on Jennifer's incident. She replayed the whole thing in her head; the way she looked at Greg, the fact she had fainted when he touched her, the whisper in her ear as they left. Then it came to her—she must be the woman he had been with on their singles night. It all made sense now, she'd fallen for him, head over heels. *My God, that wasn't just it. He's not landed back in sync with me completely since either.*

She wasn't upset with him—but herself. She'd remembered enough of her alcohol-induced disclosure to realise her true dilemma. *You let all those old insecurities in again, and you couldn't stand the idea of being with someone if Greg wasn't with you. In Greg's usual style, he wouldn't want to upset you by telling you that he'd fallen for someone on his 'date night.'*

She glanced over at him sleeping quietly next to her.

Her mind replayed their scene on the deck again. Then she caught it. Her thoughts landed on the moment when Mel introduced Jennifer to Greg. She'd glimpsed a tiny radiant flash in Greg's eyes. Like the first flicker of starlight that shone on a summer's night—it could make a wish come true. Kara recognised it. Greg's eyes had only ever sparkled in this way when he'd spoke of Tess, his fiancée, back when she was alive. *Maybe the ghost has finally been replaced by a living angel?*

As if her gaze shook him, he roused and sat up. 'Hey there, how are you going? Did you sleep?'

'No, but I dozed a bit,' Kara replied. 'Greg, can I ask you something?'

'Sure.'

She hesitated, then turning her head to face him asked calmly, 'Do you love her?'

'What the hell are you talking about?' he stammered, not fully awake.

'You know, Jennifer, the woman that fainted on the dock—are you in love with her?'

Greg's whole heart climbed into his throat at her words. Kara's ability to read his feelings was a shock. He'd always prided himself on being in control and keep his emotions in check. He wasn't ready for this.

Kara looked into his eyes. There it was again, at the mere mention of her name.

'You do remember what love feels like, don't you? You know—real love? Is that what it felt like when you were with her?' she asked calmly.

Greg took in a breath and exhaled slowly, surrendering to her question. 'Yes, it did.'

'Do you think she loves you?'

'Yes,' he replied, having turned away to fix his stare on the screen in the back of the seat in front of him.

'Well?' Kara asked softly.

'Well, what?'

'What are you going to do about it?'

'Nothing—she's happily married and lives in Texas. We were just ships in the night, so to speak.'

'It's not that simple. That woman has completely fallen for you, her life will never be the same. I can see you feel the same way too.'

'Yeah, she did say that... and maybe... I don't know, can we please drop it for now?'

'Yes, sure. But I want to help you. If you're troubled, I am too.'

With that, Kara squeezed his hand and then turned into her seat to find sleep. While their dreams were each more turbulent than the flight, they both managed to get some sleep under their belts before the plane touched down in Sydney.

Jennifer was never far from Greg's mind as he replayed the conversations they shared as they walked the decks of the ship. Her smile, the kiss against the rear rail, and of course the lovemaking. They made a love that was embedded into their hearts and touched every nerve. Somehow, since departing she pulsed even harder through his veins; after all, his heart was now hers.

Kara resonated with the kaleidoscope of intense memories of the times she shared with Greg. No two friends shared as much love, loss, fun, and pain with and through each other. While his eyes had never sparkled for her, his love for her was absolute, as was hers for him.

They disembarked and proceeded through customs and immigration. They both stood quietly at the baggage carousel. Kara looked over at Greg, who was staring at each panel as they rolled on by; he was somewhere else, she could see it. They collected their cases from the carousel and started the long walk through the terminal.

Kara was a couple of paces ahead when, suddenly, she sensed Greg wasn't behind her. She turned to see that Greg had stopped, motionless in the middle of the walkway, looking up at the international departures screen mounted on the gantry above.

Then she saw his left hand, every finger flexed and twitching. It was what he did when he was working through a problem or deep in thought.

Kara's heart started to tear. It would be heartbreaking if he left, but it would hurt her even more if he stayed, ignoring his heart's longing to be somewhere else. She needed to help him go. She had to remind him that she was only truly happy if he was. With or without her.

Kara turned and walked back, each step softening until she was next to him.

He neither heard nor sensed her approach. Standing just behind him, she placed her hand gently on his shoulder, fixing her gaze with his on the huge departures screen above.

'I see there's a flight to Dallas in two hours. I really think you should be on it,' she said softly.

His head turned to her, startled not by her presence, but by her words. He let his bag drop to the ground and turned to face her.

'Hey, there,' Kara said softly, 'Greg, it's alright. I understand.'

He looked directly into Kara's eyes for the first time since leaving the cruise dock. 'But, Kara, I can't just leave you here, like this...'

'Shh now. Of course you can—and you must. You need to know.'

'Are you sure?' Greg said in a whisper.

'Your happiness is mine. You should know that by now.'

'But, Kara, I...'

'Hey! That's enough. First and forever, remember?'

Greg reached out and drew her close, cradling her face in his hands. He kissed her deeply. As their bodies parted, their eyes held fixed, filling with tears and a myriad of mixed emotions.

There was nothing else that needed to be said. They held a bond that would never be broken. He turned and headed for the international ticket counter.

The story of Greg and Jennifer continues in *BEN, Designated Marksman* by the same author.

About the Author

Gary Baxter is a highly regarded South Australian, renowned for his lifetime professional career in motorsport, and more recently as a major contributor to film production. Since the 1980s he holds a long list of achievements as a car and motorcycle racer, pilot, movie action vehicle coordinator, and stunt driver/rider, and more, with much of this work continuing today.

Gary has been an articulate, entertaining wordsmith since his youth, with a love for action novels and writing. His long-held desire to write an Australian-based action story to captivate readers has been suspended for years. He produced his first novel, *Ben Designated Marksman*, published in 2022.

Having advised fellow authors in the creation of adult romantic fiction, Gary decided to venture into this genre.

Gary continues to entertain crowds with his V8s and perform stunts and precision driving for the film industry across the country—while catching every spare moment to write.